MINDSCAPE

ALSO BY M. M. VAUGHAN

The Ability

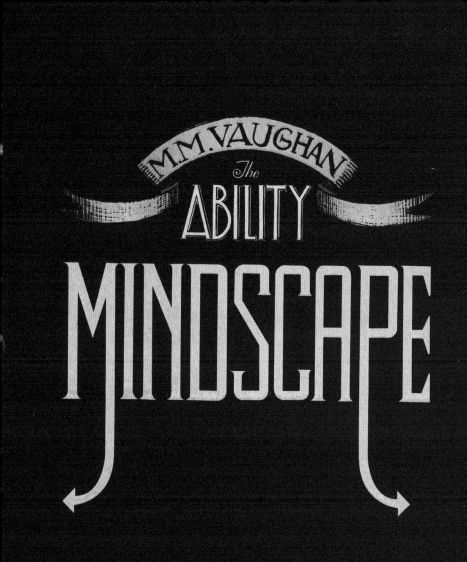

M.M. VAUGHAN

The

ABILITY

MINDSCAPE

Margaret K. McElderry Books

NEW YORK   LONDON   TORONTO   SYDNEY   NEW DELHI

Thank you to all my amazing friends and family and the incredible team at Simon & Schuster. And a special mention to: Rūta Rimas (editor extraordinaire), Tina Wexler and Stephanie Thwaites (my wonderful agents), Paul Crichton & Siena Koncsol, Federico & Kathy Meira, Mary Jane Vaughan & Peter O'Regan, Jessie O'Regan, Andres Meira & Cinthya Chavez, Margaret Rosenheck, Candy Seagraves, Amanda Nixon, Laura McCuaig, Alex O'Brien and Joanna McCracken. Also: Lily & Chloe Reneau; Lucia Meira; Eli Seagraves; Lila, Elsie, Willoughby & Rufus Metternich; Oliver & Alexander Lawson; Katie, Aurora, Maya, Abby, Robin & Rosemary Lesinski; Sophie and Elliot Wright; Toby Johnson; Ben—who came to see me at Blue Willow Books in Houston on his 12th birthday—and Felix & Anya Donald. Finally, Mark and Emilia Johnson—my two favorite people in the world.

MARGARET K. McELDERRY BOOKS
An imprint of Simon & Schuster Children's Publishing Division
1230 Avenue of the Americas, New York, New York 10020
For information about special discounts for bulk purchases, please contact Simon & Schuster Special Sales at 1-866-506-1949 or business@simonandschuster.com.
The Simon & Schuster Speakers Bureau can bring authors to your live event. For more information or to book an event, contact the Simon & Schuster Speakers Bureau at 1-866-248-3049 or visit our website at www.simonspeakers.com.
The text for this book is set in Garamond MT.
Manufactured in the United States of America
0214 FFG
2 4 6 8 10 9 7 5 3 1
CIP data is available from the Library of Congress.
ISBN 978-1-4424-5203-9
ISBN 978-1-4424-5206-0 (eBook)

FIRST
EDITION

For the boy who once told me
he wished he had special powers.

· PROLOGUE ·

A storm was brewing over Darkwhisper Manor. The skies were a deep, dark gray, and the wind, increasingly angry, tore through the grounds of the estate, surrounding the imposing building with a low howling sound that shook the windows as if trying to find a way in.

It was only four o'clock in the afternoon, but already lights were being switched on in homes across the country as families took shelter indoors from the bitter cold. And yet, although the house wasn't empty, Darkwhisper Manor showed no signs of life from the outside—not a single light or flickering reflection of a roaring fire. Nobody would have guessed, had they managed to somehow overcome the practically impenetrable security of the manor, that inside, a pale twelve-year-old boy was living alone, grieving for his dead twin brother and his traitorous mother.

Unlike his identical twin, Ernest Genever had always been a sensitive boy. He had cared for injured animals, cried when his mother punished his brother (more so than when he was punished himself), and always sought to please the only two people he had ever really known, no matter how little he received in return. It was all the more surprising, therefore, that he had not shed a single tear since the moment he had finished digging his brother's grave. In fact, in spite of only ten days having passed since his brother's death and his mother's arrest, Ernest was now barely recognizable, as if another being had entered his body. And, in a sense, that is exactly what had happened. The day Mortimer Genever was killed and Dulcia Genever had unknowingly revealed that her sons meant nothing to her was also the day the sweet and gentle Ernest Genever died.

Ernest sat at one end of the long, antique dining room table and looked down at the blank piece of paper in front of him. The howling from outside filled the large, dark-paneled room, but Ernest paid no attention. Instead, he slowly placed his hands palms down on either side of the page and turned his head toward the worn-down pencil lying next to it. In his mind, he focused on a single image, an image that had been burned deeply in his mind, and then, using his Ability—the mind powers that he had acquired only four months earlier—he watched as the pencil shook gently and then slowly lifted itself up vertically into the air. Ernest kept his mind focused as the pencil moved across and then lowered itself down on the paper. Keeping his hands facedown in front of him, he watched as his mind began to move the pencil across the page, gently, almost hesitantly at first, scratching faint lines across the white paper. Ernest furrowed his brow, and the pencil pressed down harder and began to move faster and faster until it was furiously filling the paper with deep black lines. Then, all of a sudden, it stopped. The pencil rose off the page, hovered for a moment, and collapsed onto the table, lifeless once more. Ernest pushed his chair back and stood up slowly. It was only then that he looked down at the picture that his mind had created: a picture of his brother's killer, a boy named Christopher Lane.

Ernest leaned over, picked up the paper and a brass tack lying on the table, and walked over to the wall behind him. Holding the picture up against the only piece of the dark wood paneling still visible, he pushed the pin in and then stepped back. He turned slowly around, the anger rising up inside him as he stared at the drawings that now wallpapered the room, the drawings of the boy who had murdered his brother, and he realized he was ready: It was time for revenge.

. CHAPTER ONE .

Wednesday, January 2

Christopher Lane stood on the sidewalk outside his house, his bags at his feet, and waited for the car that would take him back to school. He was half an hour early but was eager to get away, exhausted by the silence and tension in his house. It had been a difficult few days. His mother had not once celebrated Christmas with him in the seven years that had passed since his father's death, and so, as usual, there had been no gifts exchanged, his efforts for their Christmas meal had gone unmentioned, and he had watched the New Year's celebrations on the television by himself while his mother slept upstairs. This year, however, he had had even more to contend with—not the least of which was that he had barely slept the entire time, his mind plagued by the memory of the boy he had killed. Chris had always managed to cope on his own, but for the first time in years, he had needed his mother. And she had let him down.

So much had changed since his twelfth birthday: His scholarship at Myers Holt Academy, the exclusive government school that he had enrolled at only a few months earlier, had included the payment of bills and renovations to his house. Everything possible had been offered to his mother to help her, and Chris had expected that for his mother, as much as for himself, this marked a new beginning. Instead, she had ignored it all, choosing to remain locked in self-pity. It was a decision that Chris could not begin to understand. He missed his father every day, but if he, at twelve years old, could understand that life had to go on, then surely so should his mother.

He had watched her over the last few days, staring blankly at the television, looking up only to bark orders in his direction, and any sympathy that he had previously felt completely disappeared. That morning, he had packed his bags with the clothes that his new school had bought for him and a photograph of his father and left without bothering to wake his mother up. He doubted that, even if she noticed he had left, she would care. Chris resolved to think no more of it until he returned home—which, assuming he was allowed to remain at school on their free weekends, would not be until the Easter holidays in three months' time.

"Oi—you, Twist!"

Chris jerked his head round at the sound of the familiar

voice. Kevin Blunt, his old nemesis, who had made his life a living nightmare at his old school, was walking quickly toward him, his gang following behind. For a split second, Chris felt himself tense up, before suddenly remembering what he was now capable of. He stood straight and watched the boys approach.

"Whatcha doing?" asked Kevin, looking down at the bags by Chris's feet. "Your mum thrown you out?"

Arch, Kevin's gormless sidekick, and the other boys laughed.

"I'm going back to school," said Chris.

"Oh, yeah, didn't you get into that special school?" asked Kevin.

"That's right," said Chris.

"What is it, a school for poor thieves who can't take a beating?"

"Something like that," said Chris, refusing to let Kevin rile him.

Kevin, on the other hand, grew increasingly agitated by Chris's calmness.

"Hope you've learned something, then, 'cause I reckon I owe you a beating," said Kevin. He walked up to Chris and looked him square in the eyes.

"I don't think you want to do that, Kevin," said Chris, looking around to make sure the coast was clear.

"Oh, yeah, and why's that?"

"Because last time you threatened me with a beating, you ended up sitting in a tray of custard."

Arch and the other boys laughed. Kevin's face turned red.

"What's so funny?" he asked.

The boys all stopped laughing immediately. "Uh, nothing," they all mumbled, looking down at their shoes.

"Good. You got lucky last time, Twist," said Kevin, turning back to face Chris.

"I can do it again, Kevin, so back off," said Chris, surprised at the confidence he had now that he knew about his Ability, the powers that all twelve-year-olds had for one year only. Lucky for Chris, this was a well-kept secret—one that Kevin, although twelve himself, was completely in the dark about.

Kevin frowned but didn't respond. His eyes went down to the bag at Chris's feet. Chris could tell Kevin was unnerved by his confidence.

"What's in there?"

"Just clothes."

Kevin bent down.

"Don't touch it," said Chris, but it was too late. Kevin had already unzipped the bag.

"What?! Where did you get these from?" asked Kevin, pulling out a pair of designer sneakers that had been bought for him by the teachers at his new school after he had run away from home carrying nothing.

"They were a present," said Chris, grabbing them out of Kevin's hands.

"Yeah, right. Still robbing, then," said Kevin, pulling out some more clothes from Chris's bag.

Chris looked down at Kevin, and he clenched his jaw in anger. He breathed in deeply, reminding himself that the use of the Ability without the permission of his school was strictly banned.

Kevin, taking advantage of Chris's silence, continued to rummage through the bag.

"Get your hands off my stuff!" said Chris.

"What's this?" asked Kevin, pulling out the photograph of Chris's father in his military uniform. Kevin smiled. If there was one thing he knew, it was that the surest way to rile Chris was to mention his family.

"Don't touch that!" said Chris.

"If he was anything like you," said Kevin, looking at the picture with a smirk, "he probably died trying to run away. The world's a better place with one less coward from the Lane family."

"He was a hero—not that you'd know anything about what that means," said Chris, leaning forward to grab the picture.

Kevin snatched it away and held it up over his head. For a moment, Chris and Kevin stared at each other, and then, before Chris had a chance to react, Kevin opened his hand and the picture fell to the ground, the glass shattering all around their feet.

In that instant, Chris forgot all about the rules of Myers Holt and the consequences of using his Ability out in the open. He looked up at Kevin, and his mind went blank.

Arch and the rest of the gang, who had been laughing up until that point, turned silent as they watched Kevin begin to shake.

"Uh . . . what's happening?" asked Kevin, suddenly looking very frightened. "Why am I—"

Before Kevin had a chance to finish the sentence, he flew straight up into the air, as if he were a rocket launched full throttle into space.

"*Help me!*" he screamed, but his friends didn't react—they stayed rooted to the spot in shock as they watched Kevin flying up past the lampposts.

"Nobody insults my dad," said Chris, never taking his eyes off Kevin, who was now a small figure way up past the rooftops.

And then, when he'd reached the point where he was barely visible anymore, Kevin stopped rising. For a moment, there was total silence as everybody watched Kevin, too high to be heard, flail about uselessly.

Chris furrowed his brow and placed the image of Kevin being thrown about in the air into his mind. As soon as he had done so, Kevin immediately began to move again, this time looping the loop over and over again.

"*AaaaAAARRGHHaaaaargh . . .*" Kevin's screams increased in volume as he neared the ground, upside down, and faded out again as he was lifted up into the skies once more. Chris was about to throw Kevin into another loop when a booming shout interrupted him.

"*Christopher!*"

Chris jerked his head round, and immediately his focus was broken. There, to his horror, he saw the two figures of John and Ron, the security guards from Myers Holt Academy, standing by a long black car with darkened windows. The car doors were still open from where they had jumped out.

Chris hesitated and then opened his mouth to try to explain what had happened, but a loud screeching sound interrupted him.

"mmmmmUUUUUMMMMYYYY!"

Chris looked up and saw Kevin freefalling back to

Earth, his voice now loud and clear. John took three enormous strides forward, put his bulging arms out, and caught a whimpering Kevin with a soft thud. John leaned forward, then placed Kevin gently on his feet, his legs still trembling so hard that he fell backward into Arch, who put his arms out to hold him steady.

"What did you do?" blubbered Kevin, tears pouring down his face. "What was that?"

Chris was about to respond when Ron, wearing his trademark sunglasses and black suit, stepped forward and grabbed Kevin by the scruff of his neck. Although half the size of the gigantic John, Ron nevertheless cut a very intimidating figure when angry.

"Now you listen here, and the rest of you too. You saw nothing. You heard nothing. In fact, if anybody asks, you're going to tell them you had a nice day at the park. Do you understand?"

"Yes," whispered Kevin.

"Good. Now tell me, what did you do today?"

"We went to the park," said Kevin, his bottom lip wobbling.

"And what did you do there?"

"We . . . um . . . played soccer?"

"Good," said Ron. "Now, before you boys run home crying, I think there's something you need to know. Unfortunately for you all, you are looking at two of the government's top agents, which basically means we know everything. Isn't that right, John?"

"That's right, Ron," said John, his arms folded across his enormous frame.

"You can't so much as sneeze without us finding out about it," continued Ron, "so, if we hear that one of you has breathed a word of what happened today, there will be consequences, and believe me, with the connections we have, the police won't be coming to your rescue. Do you understand?"

"Yes," said Kevin, nodding his head vigorously, still sniffling.

"Yes, what?"

"Yes, sir."

"Good. Now get out of here."

The boys all looked up at Ron—their eyes wide and teary, their bodies shaking with fear.

"*Scram!*" shouted Ron, and without giving Chris another look, Kevin turned and ran off, the other boys following quickly behind him.

"Come on, Christopher, let's get this mess sorted out," said John, stooping to pick up Chris's bag.

Chris knelt down and started to pick up the clothes and shoes scattered about the pavement. "I'm going to be in so much trouble, aren't I?"

"Only if your teachers find out about it. We're not planning on telling anybody, are we, Ron?"

"I didn't see anything at all, John, did you?" said Ron, picking up the shards of glass and placing them in a nearby bin.

"Not a thing, Ron," said John, picking up the photograph of Chris's father. "Bit of an accident here, though, but it's nothing that Maura won't be able to sort out. I'm sure she has a spare frame you could put this into."

"Thank you," said Chris. "I didn't think . . . It's just that . . ."

"You don't have to explain anything, son. We saw what that boy did as we drove up. I'd have done exactly the same if I'd been in your position."

Chris smiled, grateful to be back around people who genuinely cared for him. He put the last of his clothes back in the bag and zipped it up.

"Right, then, let's forget all of this and get you to school. Your friends are waiting for you."

CHAPTER TWO

Without the usual morning school traffic, the streets of London were quiet and the journey to Myers Holt Academy took only ten minutes. Chris had been away for only a few days, but it had felt like a lifetime, and though he knew he shouldn't be, he was surprised to see that his school looked just as it had at the end of last term. The building was just as tall and imposing as all the other buildings on Montague Street, and nothing about it suggested the secrets it held within. As Chris stepped out of the car he thanked John and Ron. Then, his bag slung over his shoulder, he made his way to the top of the steps.

The door began to open before he had a chance to ring the doorbell.

"Well, well, if it isn't Christopher Lane!" Maura, the

school's housekeeper, opened the door wide, and before Chris had a chance to say hello, he was swept up in a big, warm hug.

"Ah, look at you, pet, you must have grown a foot since I last saw you."

"It's only been a few days, Maura," said Chris, smiling and slightly embarrassed as Maura ruffled his hair.

"A few days is long enough—I've missed you all. Philip is downstairs—the rest will be along in just a moment, I'm sure. Now tell me, did you have a nice Christmas? Did you eat enough?"

Chris opened his mouth to answer, but Maura was already walking ahead of him down the bare corridor, jabbering away.

"There's a late breakfast waiting for you downstairs, and fresh sheets on the beds. Do you need me to do any laundry for you?"

"No, thanks, I washed everything yesterday," said Chris, stepping into the small kitchen behind Maura. He closed the door and looked over at the dirty, cluttered counter.

"Can I?" asked Chris, nodding his head in the direction of the kettle.

"May I," said Maura, correcting him. "And yes, course you may, love." She squeezed herself against the wall to let Chris through.

Chris reached over and pressed his thumb onto the kettle's switch.

Maura smiled back at Chris as the room began to shake. Chris put an arm out to steady himself as the room dropped, beginning a thirty-second descent.

"Welcome back," said Maura, opening the door, the familiar sound of classical music filling the air.

Chris didn't speak for a moment as he looked about, his heart in his throat. It was just an entrance hall, but, for him, it was so much more. It was a place where he was valued, where he could be himself, and where there were people who actually wanted him around. It was, he realized, his home—much more so than the house he had shared with his mother. For a split second, the thought entered his mind that he would have to leave here in a few months' time, but he pushed it away—for now, he just wanted to see his friends.

"Where's Philip?" asked Chris.

"In the Map Room, I expect, waiting for you. Why don't you run along—I'm sure you have lots to catch up on. Sir Bentley wants you all in the classroom for a briefing at ten, so you have an hour to yourselves."

"Thanks," said Chris, running off in the direction of the student quarters.

Chris walked into the spectacular Map Room, covered floor to ceiling in maps as its name suggested, and found Philip curled up on an armchair reading a book. He was dressed in a three-piece suit and a red bow tie, and his hair was slicked down in a side parting. Chris smiled at his best friend, who always looked as if he had time-traveled forward a hundred years.

"Haven't you read every book by now?" asked Chris, smiling.

"Not even close," said Philip as he threw the book

down and jumped up to greet Chris. "I'm so glad you're here—wait till you see this!" he said, grabbing Chris by the arm. "Apparently, there were two phases of renovations— Maura said they didn't have enough time to finish it all before we started last term. Honestly, you won't believe it. They left the best till last."

Chris, intrigued, dropped his bag on the floor and followed Philip over to the back of the Map Room, where a map of Oxford taller and wider than either of the boys hung next to the row of pool cues.

"This was here last term," said Chris, confused.

"I know, but look closely. Do you see anything strange?"

"Um, no," said Chris, scanning the names of the roads that he had memorized early on in his time at Myers Holt. As far as he could see, nothing had changed.

"The Bodleian Library," said Philip.

Chris's eyes ran back across the map to the library.

"Oh! What's that?" said Chris, peering in at the small black button protruding from the center of the circle.

"Press it."

"Press what?" said a voice that made both of them jump. They turned to see Lexi at the doorway, her mass of frizzy curls even more wild and unruly than they had been last time the boys had seen her, her smile in contrast to the stern sound of her voice.

"Lexi! Come here. Look at this," said Philip.

Lexi, having grown up with three older and mercilessly teasing brothers, looked over at them, and her eyes narrowed.

"Yeah, I'm not falling for that one," she said, arms folded.

"Suit yourself," said Philip, turning back to the map. Chris waved Lexi over and turned back himself, eager to press the button.

"Go on," said Philip, excited.

Chris pressed the button and jumped away as the map suddenly swung backward, revealing a large black, door-shaped hole.

"What's in there?" asked Lexi, her curiosity having led her over to them.

Chris stepped in first and a light came on automatically, revealing a secret room that was, it turned out, a library—but a library unlike any that Chris had ever seen.

Chris found himself standing on a wrought-iron balcony that ran along the perimeter of the relatively small room, giving access to the books on the dark wood shelves. He stepped forward and leaned over the railing.

"Wow!" said Chris, surprised to be looking down at bookcases that continued below them for three stories at least, making the sofas and large, ornate rug lying at the bottom of the room seem tiny.

"How do you get the books down there?" asked Lexi.

"That's the best bit," said Philip, walking out on the balcony to a gate. He lifted the latch, stepped onto what looked like just another section of balcony, and closed the gate behind him. He leaned over, lifted a hatch that Chris hadn't noticed, and climbed down.

Chris walked over, followed by Lexi, and saw that Philip was standing on what looked like a window-cleaner's platform, suspended by ropes.

"There are ropes to winch you round and down if you feel

like making things difficult. Or, if you're twelve and have the Ability, like us, you could just do this," said Philip, grinning as he looked up at them. Suddenly, he disappeared from view.

Chris and Lexi ran over to the railing and looked down to see the platform zooming around to the other side before coming to a sudden stop.

"Chinese-language books over here," shouted Philip, pulling one out with a wild, excited look on his face. He looked back up at the ropes, and the platform suddenly sprang to life again, dropping toward the ground.

"Or advanced mathematics, if that's your thing," he said, taking out a couple more books and placing them by his feet.

Chris watched as Philip zoomed round and up and down collecting a mountain of books. Finally, the platform whizzed back up to where he had started.

"That's amazing," said Chris, taking and setting down the books that Philip passed up to him.

"I want a go!" said Lexi. "Come on, Chris."

Chris waited for Philip to climb up through the hatch and then let Lexi down first before following her.

"Any spy novels? I finished all the ones I got for Christmas already," said Lexi as Chris looked at the map framed on the railing of the platform.

"Yep," said Chris, pointing to a section of the map. He turned to the far wall and pointed across from where they were hanging.

"They're over there. Hold on." Chris turned his attention to the ropes above him and let his mind go blank except for the image of the rope moving in the direction of the shelf.

Chris, who had expected to be moving to the left gently,

fell forward onto Lexi as the platform started spinning around the room uncontrolled.

"*Chris!*" shouted Lexi, pushing Chris off her as she looked up at the rope. She willed the platform to stop dead, and it did. Chris looked over at Lexi apologetically.

"Sorry, I didn't realize it would go that fast."

"Someone hasn't been practicing the Ability over the holidays," said Lexi, sounding amused. She looked up at the rope again, and the platform began to move gently.

"No . . . well, not much. I thought we weren't allowed to," said Chris. "Why, have you?"

"Maybe once or twice," said Lexi as they came to a smooth stop. "I didn't tell anyone, though," she said, seeing Chris's look of surprise. "It's just that sometimes you need a bit of help when you've got three brothers picking on you."

Chris thought back to that morning and the incident with Kevin, and he nodded.

"Yeah, I understand. Now I'm wishing that—"

"*Ooh!* They've got the entire Ian Fleming collection," Lexi said as she grabbed an armful of books. "One day, they're going to write books about me, you know," she said, placing the pile down by her feet.

"What kind of books?"

"Books like these," replied Lexi. "I was thinking about it over the holidays, and I've decided I'm going to be the next James Bond—but better."

"James Bond is a man."

"So?" said Lexi.

Chris thought about it for a moment. "Okay, well, good luck with that. Where to next?" asked Chris.

"Don't we have our Latin A level soon?"

Chris nodded. "I'll do it," he said, looking up from the map toward the ropes.

"Okay, but try not to throw us off this thing this time," said Lexi as she grabbed on to the railing.

Chris focused once again on moving, and the platform went into a sudden drop, making Lexi gasp.

"Only joking," said Chris as he slowed the platform. They glided smoothly across to the Latin section at the bottom of the room, where they both collected some books before making their way back to Philip.

"Best thing ever, right?" said Philip, grinning as they reentered the Map Room.

"Yep," agreed Chris. He closed the door behind him just as another door across the room opened.

"Tidings to you all," said Sebastian with a small bow.

For a moment, nobody spoke as they stared at Sebastian in his new outfit.

"What are you wearing, Sebastian?" asked Lexi with a small laugh.

Sebastian, who normally wore T-shirts and jeans, ran his hands over his canary-yellow suit.

"Do you like it? I have been investing much thought in Philip's sayings—dress to impress, isn't this correct?" said Sebastian, his Spanish accent thick.

"Very nice," said Chris, still in shock. "Where did you get the pink shirt from?"

"Savile Row," said Sebastian, clearly very pleased with himself. "I asked for a new wardrobe for Christmas."

"You have more of this?" asked Philip.

"Yes, a different color shirt, suit, and tie for every day of the week. Do you approve of my new attire, Philip? I took my lessons from you."

"It's all right. A bit showy," said Philip flatly, walking off.

Chris turned and saw Philip by the pool table looking down at his own clothes with a miserable look on his face. Chris was surprised—Philip had always seemed so self-assured.

"You look fine," Chris whispered as he approached Philip, leaving Lexi and Sebastian to catch up.

"I look like a middle-aged professor next to that," said Philip.

"You always look like a middle-aged professor," said Chris smiling. "It worked for Einstein, though, didn't it?"

"I suppose so," said Philip, shrugging his shoulders.

"Come on, you should be flattered: He just wants to be more like you. Don't let it bother you," said Chris as he dragged a reluctant Philip back to the others.

Twenty minutes later and Philip had cheered up after Sebastian convinced him to teach him how to tie his tie in a Windsor knot.

"Maybe it's not so bad," said Philip to Chris as they sat down in front of the television. "Nothing wrong with all of us making an effort, I suppose. You could borrow some stuff from me if you want. I have a monocle that would look good."

Chris imagined himself wearing a bow tie and monocle and winced. "Thanks, but I'll stick to my own clothes for the moment."

"Fair enough," said Philip, "but the offer's there if you change your mind."

The sound of the door opening once more saved Chris from continuing the conversation. They both turned to see Daisy standing in the doorway in a new pink dress, a sad smile on her face.

"Has she been crying?" whispered Philip.

"She just doesn't like to say good-bye to her family," said Chris, remembering how inconsolable Daisy had been on their first day at Myers Holt. He stood up to go and say hello but was beaten to it by Sebastian, who grabbed Daisy's hand and got down on bended knee.

"So doth thy beauty make my lips to fail, and all my sweetest singing out of tune," he said.

"Er, thanks," said Daisy as she pulled her hand away. Chris noticed that she was blushing.

"Daisy!" said Lexi as she ran over to give Daisy a hug. "I'm so glad you're here. These boys get weirder every day."

Daisy giggled and she hugged Lexi back, her homesickness quickly disappearing. "I know. Well, not Chris—you're still normal, right?"

Chris shrugged. "I guess."

"Nah, he's just as weird as the others, he just hides it better," said Lexi. She gave Chris a playful punch, then grabbed Daisy by the arm and dragged her over to the other side of the room.

"Game of pool?" asked Philip as the girls disappeared into the library. Chris and Sebastian nodded.

"You two play first. I'll play the winner," said Chris. He sat down in an armchair next to the pool table.

"Where is Rex, anyway?" asked Philip. "Then we could play doubles."

"Did I hear my name?"

Chris turned as he saw Rex walking into the room looking just as he had before Christmas: round faced and freckled, wearing his favorite orange T-shirt.

"Hi! Game of pool?" asked Philip.

Rex nodded and had begun to walk over to them when he suddenly saw Sebastian and stopped dead. He glanced over at Philip and then back again at Sebastian's suit.

"Nobody sent me the memo," he said finally.

"What memo?" asked Philip.

Rex broke out into a wide grin. "The one about Halloween moving to January."

Philip shook his head, half-smiling, half-exasperated. "Same old Rex."

"Missed you, too, Einstein," said Rex. He walked up to Sebastian and leaned down to examine his perfectly knotted tie. "Purple tie with lime-green stripes? Interesting choice, Pedro."

"Dress to impress," said Sebastian.

Rex stood up and looked over at Philip in mock horror. "Oh, no, it's contagious. What next? Chris wearing a top hat?"

"Yeah, I left it in the bedroom," said Chris.

Rex's eyes widened in shock. "Seriously?!"

Chris laughed. "No, of course not."

"Great, I leave you guys for not even a couple of weeks and everything's changed; Sebastian's raided Bozo the Clown's wardrobe, and Chris has gone and got himself a sense of humor."

"Nothing's changed with you though, Rex—still as charming as ever," said Philip.

"Thank you, thank you," said Rex as he picked up a cue. "Now, who wants to lose to me at pool?"

The game of pool, which had soon become a Mind Pool tournament—where they used their Ability instead of cues to move the white ball—was interrupted by Maura, who came to remind them that they were expected in the classroom in five minutes.

"We'll just say I won," said Rex.

"Only if winning means potting the least number of balls," said Philip.

"Fine by me," said Rex. "Better luck next time, losers."

"Please, let us be friends," said Sebastian, exasperated, as he led the way out. Chris and the others followed him through the door, down the corridor, and into the Dome.

"Oh, it's always lovely in here. I'm so glad to be back," said Daisy as they stepped into the warmth of the artificial sunlight. Chris, nodding his head in agreement, stopped for a moment to look up at the Dome's panels, screens that replicated sunlight as well as projecting a landscape of a summer's day. The panels were so real that it was hard to remember they were, in fact, standing deep underground in the middle of winter. Chris decided to take the long route to the classroom. He climbed up to the top of the hill and, standing under the blossoming tree, looked around at the swimming pool, the soccer field, and the vast expanse of manicured lawn surrounding him.

"It's amazing, isn't it?"

Chris turned to see Daisy walking up toward him. He nodded.

The two stood side by side in silence for a moment, taking in the view.

"How was your Christmas?" asked Daisy finally.

"It was really good," said Chris automatically but then, remembering that Daisy was the only one of his friends who knew the truth about his home life, corrected himself. "Actually, it wasn't good at all. My mum hardly talked to me, and I was feeling pretty bad about, you know, the stuff that happened at the ball. What about you?"

"It was good. Dad and Mum worrying about money the whole time as always," said Daisy, "but we had a good time. I got a new dress."

"It's, uh, nice," said Chris, not sure what else to say about it.

"Thanks. And sorry about your mum, Chris. I'm sure she'll get better soon."

"I don't think that's going to happen," said Chris, but, realizing how miserable he sounded, he pulled himself together and smiled. "Still, I don't have to worry about it now—it's good to be back here."

Daisy smiled back. "We're going to be late. Race you?"

Chris didn't have a chance to answer before Daisy ran off down the hill.

"That's cheating!" he shouted after her. He chased her down the hill, laughing. It felt good to be back.

CHAPTER THREE

Chris and Daisy walked into the classroom to find everybody else already seated, waiting for them. Behind the teacher's desk stood Sir Bentley, the headmaster of Myers Holt and director general of MI5, standing tall and imposing in his dark tailored suit, his arms folded. Chris imagined that there might be a lot of people who found him intimidating—he was a man of great power, after all—but Chris was not one of them: Sir Bentley had only ever been both kind and fair with him.

"Ah, Daisy and Christopher, thank you for joining us," said Sir Bentley, smiling. "Quick, sit down and we'll get started."

Chris took his seat, a tall blue chair in front of a single desk, and looked up at Sir Bentley, eager to get started.

"Well, first, welcome back. I hope you all enjoyed your well-deserved break and that you're feeling full of energy for the new term, yes?"

"Yes, sir," said Chris and the others in unison.

"Wonderful. I have a few bits of housekeeping first, and then we'll get on to discussing this term's work. First, as some of you may have already seen, there has been a bit of renovating done on the building while you've been away—namely, the library. . . ."

Everybody nodded their approval enthusiastically.

"Very good—I'm glad you liked it. Now, on to our lessons. As I explained at the end of last term, you'll go back to your normal studies with Miss Sonata—you have a lot to catch up on after missing so much during your training for the Antarctic Ball."

Chris's stomach sank at the mention of the ball.

"Mr. Green will continue to keep you fit and active, and Ms. Lamb"—there was an audible groan across the room at the mention of Ms. Lamb's name, but Sir Bentley pretended not to have heard it—"will be taking you for further work on your Ability. Professor Ingleby has been working on improving the experience in the think tanks for you, and he really has outdone himself."

Chris, remembering sitting in his think tank using his Ability during car chases around London and treasure hunts in medieval times, wondered how something so incredible could be improved.

"Now," continued Sir Bentley, "about the work for the government that you'll be undertaking whilst continuing with your studies. In the past, Myers Holt pupils did not

begin any work for us until their second term. However, in your case, our hand was forced with the matter of Dulcia Genever, which you all handled incredibly well, especially given that it was so early on in your training."

Chris pursed his lips. He wondered how Sir Bentley could say that, considering he had killed a boy.

"You saved a lot of lives that night," said Sir Bentley, and when Chris looked up, he saw that Sir Bentley was talking directly to him.

"Yes, sir," said Chris quietly.

"This term, with the exception of a couple of loose ends that need to be tied up, we'll go back to doing what Myers Holt pupils did so well back in the old days, and that's helping the police to solve crimes."

"Yes!" said Rex.

Sir Bentley gave a small chuckle. "Good to see you so enthusiastic, Rex. Now, to explain. You will not be helping us with anything that would involve you seeing any violence."

"Oh," said Rex. Daisy, however, breathed a sigh of relief.

"I'll explain more in our briefing which is on"—Sir Bentley walked behind the desk and opened up his planner—"Friday. We'll talk more about that then."

Sir Bentley closed the planner and looked up. For a moment, there was silence.

"I know that the end of last term was difficult," said Sir Bentley finally. "I am torn between being glad that you were all there to save the lives of so many, myself included, and being horrified that we put you in the center of such

distressing events. I think you all must be very affected, and that's completely normal. I have therefore decided to bring a new member of staff on board. His name is Hugh Valedictoriat. He has worked as an army psychologist for many years and comes highly recommended. I have arranged for him to be here every day during the week. Your new timetables are in your bedrooms, and you'll see that you've all been assigned slots with him. You can speak to him about anything on your mind in the strictest confidence. It's completely up to you if you want to use these slots—it's not a requirement—but I do urge you to at least meet him once and see how you get on. Yes?"

They all nodded.

"Excellent. And finally, I want to talk to you about the loose ends that I mentioned earlier. As you are all aware, Dulcia Genever was arrested on the night of the Antarctic Ball, thanks to all your good work. We have been unable to get any information from her whatsoever. Of course, we know now that she harbored considerable resentment for the events that took place back when she was a child and had decided to seek her revenge. I'm not going to excuse what happened all those years ago—I am still in disbelief that she survived that fall and went on to suffer so horribly—but, nevertheless, what she did was wrong, and she must be held accountable for the lives of the people she has destroyed. More of a concern, however, is the boy. We are guessing that it was her son and that the boy who didn't make it was his twin brother."

Chris closed his eyes, and suddenly all he could see was the image of the dead boy at his feet. He shook himself

to try to get rid of the picture in his mind, then sat up straight, doing his best to focus all his attention on what Sir Bentley was saying.

"Whatever the brother who survived did," continued Sir Bentley, "I am certain that it was on the orders of Dulcia Genever, and we need to find him—not because of the crimes he was trying to commit but because he is a young boy and we need to make sure he is being taken care of. We also need to know that Dulcia Genever was not working with anybody else, so that we can be absolutely certain this matter is settled once and for all. Tomorrow we are going to take one of you to use your Ability to read her mind to find out where the boy is and to ensure that this whole plan for revenge is over."

Sir Bentley turned to Chris. "Christopher, you have been through enough. I know last term was difficult for you, and we wouldn't expect you to have anything more to do with this matter. The rest of you, I leave it up to you to volunteer yourselves if you think this is something you would be comfortable doing. Yes, Lexi?"

"I was just wondering, what would you need us to do?"

"Well, it should be fairly simple. We will be going to the prison where she is currently being held—it's not far from here. She's in a cell with a two-way mirror on one wall, so she'll have no way of knowing who might be watching her. You'll just have to do a quick runaround to a couple of places in her mind in order to find the information we would need, and that's it. The whole process should take no longer than a few minutes, and then we'll be done."

"Oh, that's not too bad," said Daisy.

"Well, don't make up your mind just yet. Have a think about it, and we can decide in the morning."

Chris followed the others out of the classroom and up to the top of the hill in the Dome to wait out the fifteen minutes until the start of Mr. Green's swimming lesson. He took a seat next to Philip and listened as the others chatted about putting themselves forward for the prison visit. Chris, however, did not join in. He thought he had been getting better at pushing out the bad memories, but right now all he could think of was the night of the ball—the fight with the boy, the moment he realized he had killed him, the brother crying, and the look he gave Chris before he carried his brother away—it was as if a horror film had turned on in his mind and he couldn't find the switch to turn it off.

By the time their break was over and they needed to get changed into their swimsuits for Mr. Green's lesson, Chris had made a decision. He excused himself quietly and headed out of the Dome to Sir Bentley's office, where he found the headmaster talking on the phone.

"Come in. I'll be just a moment," whispered Sir Bentley, his hand over the mouthpiece.

Chris took a seat and waited, tapping his knee. Finally, Sir Bentley put the phone down and clicked open the locks of the briefcase lying on his desk.

"How can I help you, Christopher?" he asked as he began to gather up the papers around him.

"I want to go with you to access Dulcia Genever's mind tomorrow," said Chris.

Sir Bentley stopped and looked up at Chris. He raised

his eyebrows in surprise. "I see. I was going to decide tomorrow morning."

"I know, sir, but I really want to go."

Sir Bentley shook his head, as if he couldn't believe what Chris was saying. "I would have thought you'd want nothing more to do with any of this."

Chris took a deep breath. He knew he was going to have to be completely honest if Sir Bentley was going to understand how important this was to him. Sir Bentley waited as Chris tried to work out how to say what he was thinking. In the end, he decided it was best just to come straight out with it.

"I killed that boy's brother."

Sir Bentley opened his mouth to speak, but Chris interrupted him. "I know you're going to say that it was an accident, sir, but that doesn't change anything—I was the one who did it, and it would make me feel better if I could help find him and make sure that he's okay."

Sir Bentley considered this for a moment. "Christopher, you know that I admire your integrity very much. You have a sense of responsibility that is far beyond your twelve years. However"—Chris's heart sank—"although there are many people who should feel guilty for the death of that boy, myself included—and I'm not sure how to convince you of this—you are not one of them. You did what you had to do. You saved a lot of lives that night, and that, I believe, is enough."

"But, sir, I lost control. He didn't need to die."

Sir Bentley frowned. "That, Christopher, is not your fault. Yes, your Ability is incredibly powerful, and controlling it takes a lot of training, but I put you in a difficult situation knowing that, and so the blame for what happened falls squarely on my shoulders, not yours."

Chris could see the opportunity slipping through his fingers. He wasn't sure why this was as important as it was to him, but from the moment Sir Bentley had told them about the visit, Chris had known he was the one who had to do it. Before he could stop himself, his eyes began to fill with tears. "I need to do this, sir. Please let me go. I just want to know that the boy is found—it would make me feel better."

Sir Bentley looked at Chris for a moment and then sighed. "You do like to make things difficult for yourself, don't you?"

Chris wiped his eyes with the back of his sleeve and nodded.

"Very well," said Sir Bentley finally, "if you really feel that this is what you need to do, then you can go. However—and this is nonnegotiable—I need to know that you'll meet with the psychologist when he arrives. I think he'll do a better job of helping you to understand that you are not to blame. Is that fair?"

"Yes," said Chris, only because he didn't feel he could say otherwise. He had never spoken to a psychologist before, and he wasn't sure he wanted to, but he knew he had no choice.

"Good, when is your first appointment?"

"Erm, I don't know. I haven't been to my room yet."

Sir Bentley slid a pile of papers on his desk over and rifled through them until he found what he was looking for.

"Your first meeting is scheduled for tomorrow. Hmm . . . Let me see. . . ." Sir Bentley picked up the phone.

"Allegra, could you call Hugh and find out what his schedule is for today—tell him I'd like him to meet with Christopher this afternoon if possible . . . Yes . . . Good. Thank you." He hung up and turned to Chris. "I'm sure that will be fine. I'll get somebody to let you know when he arrives. Have a chat with him, and if you decide to change your mind, I will get one of the others to come instead."

"Yes, sir."

"And, Christopher, I hope you remember that there is nothing wrong with saying you'd rather not do this—I know how stubborn you can be about doing the right thing."

Chris reddened, remembering his badly planned escape from Myers Holt to keep his promise to a shopkeeper.

"Yes, sir," he said.

"Very well. Meet me here tomorrow morning at nine. If you wish to come, I'll brief you on our way, and if you don't, it won't be any problem at all to take one of the others instead."

"Thank you, sir."

"You're welcome, Christopher. I have to rush off to a meeting now, so will you let the others know?"

"Yes, sir."

"Thank you. Now off you go to your lesson, and I'll see you in the morning."

Chris came out of the locker room, having quickly changed into his swimsuit, and ran over to the pool. There he found Mr. Green, the phys-ed teacher, wearing a red tracksuit and waving his arms around as he attempted to motivate Chris's classmates in the water.

"Suffer the pain of discipline or suffer the pain of regret! Clear your mind of 'can't'!" he shouted.

He stopped and turned when he saw Christopher, and the others, seeing an opportunity, immediately came to a standstill. Before they had a chance to react, though, Mr. Green had swung his head round and caught them resting.

"I did not tell you to stop! Get back to it: forty more laps to go! Fifty more for you, Rex! Go! Go!"

"What? *Why?*" shouted Rex, bright red and looking like he was about to explode with anger.

"Because I can see your feet on the floor. You will not stroll your way to peak fitness."

"I don't want peak fitness. I want lunch."

"In that case, you'd best get moving."

Rex practically growled as he pulled his goggles back down over his eyes. He had only just begun his painfully slow doggy paddle when Sebastian swam up to his side and gave him a thumbs-up.

"You are never a loser until you quit trying!" said Sebastian cheerfully.

"Don't you start," said Rex. Sebastian shrugged and glided off into the clear blue water.

Mr. Green tutted and turned to Chris. "Christopher, ten minutes and . . . thirty-five seconds late. Can you explain?"

"I had a meeting with Sir Bentley."

Mr. Green considered this for a moment, then nodded and motioned for Chris to jump in.

. . .

"That man is a sadist," mumbled Rex as they all walked back with damp hair toward the Map Room.

"Aw, don't be mean, Rex. I think he just wants us to get fit," said Daisy.

"No—he wants us all dead." Rex suddenly remembered something and turned to Chris.

"How did you manage to miss the beginning, anyway? You didn't even get told off. You know what? I'm sick of you—always the teacher's pet."

"Calm down, Rex," said Lexi. "It's not Chris's fault that you're so unfit."

Rex ignored Lexi. "So, what did you do? Slip him an apple?"

"Back off, Rex," said Chris. He opened the door of the Map Room and walked quickly over to the pool table, hoping to end the conversation.

"I haven't finished yet!" called Rex. "What were you doing?"

Chris had wanted to bring up his conversation with Sir Bentley over lunch on his own terms, so that he could explain properly, but he could tell that Rex was in one of those moods. If Chris didn't say something, Rex would just go on and on about it.

"I went to see Sir Bentley."

Chris said this as casually as possible. He picked up a cue from the rack on the wall and was about to start shooting balls when he noticed nobody was talking. He looked up and saw that they were all staring at him.

"Why?" asked Rex, his arms folded. It was a loaded

question. Chris could tell by the dark tone in his voice that he knew exactly why.

Chris sighed. He leaned the pool cue against the table and walked over to the group. "Look, I was going to tell you all at lunch. I . . . well . . . I went to ask if I could be the one to see Dulcia Genever tomorrow."

Lexi's eyes narrowed. "And?" she asked.

Chris hesitated. "He said yes."

Rex exploded. "What? Why didn't you talk to us first? I wanted to do that!"

"Myself also," said Sebastian, who looked more disappointed than angry. Chris looked at Philip, Lexi, and Daisy, but not one of them looked him in the eye.

"I'm really sorry," said Chris. "I know you all wanted to go, but I just thought that it should be me—you know, because . . ."

"What? Because you shouldn't have killed that boy?" said Rex with a snarl.

There was a sharp intake of breath from the others as Chris stared back at Rex. For a brief moment, Chris felt a surge of anger rise up inside him, and then, just like that, it was gone. Rex was only speaking the truth.

"Yeah, that's right," said Chris quietly. He walked out, leaving the others standing in silence.

· CHAPTER FOUR ·

Chris spent the mid-morning break in his bedroom to avoid the others. The only person who came to see him was Maura, who had noticed he was missing and brought him his snack. Chris was grateful that she didn't ask any questions. He ate in silence, his mind replaying the conversation with Rex, and all he could think about was how stupid he had been—he should have spoken to the others first, but it just hadn't occurred to him. He had spent his whole life making decisions on his own. He realized glumly that it was probably going to continue that way—he had been back at school for only one day, and he had already managed to ruin the only true friendships he had ever had. Finally, knowing that he couldn't hide away any longer, Chris made his way to the classroom, grateful to find that he was the first one there.

He took a seat at his desk and waited. After a few minutes, he heard the voices of the others coming up the corridor, and he quickly looked down as they entered the room. When they saw Chris, they stopped. From the corner of his eye, Chris saw Philip whispering something to Rex before pushing him in Chris's direction.

Rex gave a nervous cough. "I'm, er, really . . ."

"You don't have to apologize," said Chris, glancing up.

Rex sighed with relief. "Good. I hate all that apology stuff. So, no hard feelings?"

Chris shook his head.

"It's just, you should have talked to us first. We all know you're a bit, you know, messed up after . . ."

"Rex . . . stop talking," warned Philip.

"It's okay, Philip," said Chris. "He's right. I should've checked with you all."

"We would have said yes," said Daisy. Chris could hear the hurt in her voice, and he put his head in his hands.

"That is sufficient," said Sebastian, slapping Chris on the shoulder. "We can all proceed with our friendship, yes?"

Chris gave a small smile and nodded, and Philip, looking relieved that the awkward situation was over, sat down next to him and started chatting about a robot he was designing that would be able to clean the windows of skyscrapers. Chris did his best to pay attention, but all he could think about was how he didn't deserve such good friends. He was trying to work out a way to make it up to them when Ms. Lamb, their Mind Access teacher, walked in.

Ms. Lamb was, if possible, even more hideous and angry looking than she had been the last time they had seen her before Christmas. Her leg was now fully healed from the rather unfortunate but, in hindsight, quite amusing, incident with a dog, and the bandages had been replaced with fluorescent-green tights that matched her new green-leather stiletto boots, tightly strapped to the knee with pink laces around her short, thick legs. Her much-too-small purple suit, made of a shiny material that Chris couldn't identify, squeaked as she stomped around the room placing booklets on each desk. Chris took his seat and looked down as she approached him and placed the booklet on his table.

"I suggest you keep your mouth shut this term. I don't want any of your nonsense."

Chris kept his head down and said nothing, but his jaw hardened and he gripped the sides of his chair in anger. Although she was despicable to everybody in the class, she had singled Chris out in particular from the very first lesson, and she had not eased up on him for one moment since. Clearly, this term was not going to be any different.

"You, in pink," barked Ms. Lamb, pointing a short, stubby finger toward Daisy. Chris couldn't work out if she had still not managed to learn any of their names or if she was just refusing to use them.

"Yes, Ms. Lamb?" asked Daisy, sounding as terrified as she always did when called on in class.

"Stop your pathetic whimpering and stand up."

Daisy, her bottom lip beginning to wobble, stood up slowly.

"Tell me all the buildings you will pass from the Reception of a mind to the end of Calendar Street, taking the route through Emotions Street."

Daisy who, like all of them, normally had no problem memorizing anything after a few seconds, struggled to find the answer as panic clouded her mind. She turned to the mind map painted on the white wall of the classroom.

"Don't you dare cheat!" said Ms. Lamb. "Look at me!"

Daisy's face turned red as she desperately searched her mind for the answer.

"Um . . . uh . . . Reception. Then, um . . . I don't know, I can't think."

"You'd better start thinking now, or you can have detention every day for the rest of the week. *Get on with it.*"

Chris could see that Daisy was shaking with fear as she tried desperately to focus, and he willed her to pull herself together.

"You are a pathetic little girl," continued Ms. Lamb. "Spoilt rotten—I can tell from a mile off. Well, let me tell you something, princess, the world is not made of rainbows and fluffy marshmallows—it's tough. So you'd better start talking, or you're going to see me lose my temper. *Start!*"

Daisy looked up at Ms. Lamb, and then, just as Chris thought she might start reciting the street names, she burst into tears.

It didn't take Chris more than a few seconds to figure out that this was his opportunity to make up for what had happened earlier, even if it got him into trouble. Keeping his head down, he closed his eyes and let his mind go blank.

Within a couple of seconds, Chris found himself looking around at the swirling thick fog consuming the Reception of Daisy's mind. Chris focused on pushing the fog away with his Ability, and within seconds, as if he had turned on a fan, the gray cloud began to disappear. Almost immediately, Daisy began to think clearly, and Chris watched as the colored blocks of the mind began to appear, then the streets and, finally, the streets names, which landed on top of the city now floating in the middle of Daisy's mind. And then he blinked and, just like that, he was back in the room—only to find that Ms. Lamb was staring directly at him.

"Oh! I know it now," said Daisy, trying to distract Ms. Lamb. "Sorry. Family building, Brief Encounters, Famous People, Strangers, turn right onto . . ."

Daisy trailed off as she saw that Ms. Lamb was paying no attention to her, she was too busy glaring at Chris.

"Stand up," hissed Ms. Lamb.

Chris pushed his chair back and stood up slowly.

Ms. Lamb walked over to him and leaned in so that her face was within inches of his. "I may not have the Ability myself, but I know exactly when somebody is using it. How dare you help somebody to cheat in my class?"

"I was just . . ."

"You were just what, exactly?" asked Ms. Lamb, her hands on her hips.

"I was just helping her to think clearly. You were making her upset."

Chris looked around, but nobody spoke up in his defense, not that he would have expected them to considering everything that had happened that morning.

"You are nothing but a troublemaker," said Ms. Lamb, walking over to her desk. "I tell you, if it were my decision, you would have been expelled months ago." She reached down to a drawer and took out a blank piece of paper and a thick black pen. She scribbled something on it and walked over to the corner of the classroom.

"This, boy, is where you will be sitting from now on. On the floor, facing the wall. Go on, sit."

Chris hesitated and then began to walk.

"Not so pleased with yourself now, are you?" she said.

Chris stared down at the corner and then over at Ms. Lamb to see if she was serious, but her face said it all: This was no joke. He sat down cross-legged, and looked up to see Ms. Lamb pinning the sign she had made to the wall: DUNCE CORNER.

Daisy gasped, and Chris turned to see his classmates looking at the sign in horror as Ms. Lamb walked away. Even Rex, who normally saw the funny side of everything, looked aghast.

Chris heard the clip of Ms. Lamb's heels coming back toward him.

"This should keep you out of trouble," she said, tipping out onto the floor the contents of the large drawer in her hands.

Chris looked down at the hundreds of colored pencils and knew exactly what was coming. A sharpener landed at his feet.

"Well, best get to work, and not one word out of you. I have a class to teach."

Chris stared at Ms. Lamb's smug face and he closed his eyes. If only, he thought, he could use his Ability right now, he would throw Ms. Lamb six feet into the air and . . .

Chris stopped and pushed the thought away. If there was one thing he had learned since finding out about his Ability, it was that often the things he imagined had a way of actually happening. Chris had come close enough to being expelled the term before, and he had a feeling that throwing Ms. Lamb across the room with the power of his mind might just be a step too far. He looked back down at his feet and picked up the sharpener.

"I can't believe how awful she's being," said Daisy, trying to comfort Chris as they all walked out of the classroom.

Chris rubbed his raw hands and scowled. "She's like a cross between a witch and Godzilla."

"Only uglier," said Rex, slapping his hand on Chris's back. "Sorry about not saying anything. Didn't think there was any point in all of us sitting in the corner sharpening pencils."

"It's all right," said Chris. "I don't blame you."

"There's got to be a law against that," said Philip as they entered the dining room. "In fact, when we finish lunch, I'm going to go and look it up. I'll bet there's something."

"She's not going to care," said Lexi.

"She will if I go and tell Sir Bentley," said Philip.

Chris stopped and turned to Philip. "*No!* Don't say anything to him or any of the other teachers. I'm just going to get on with it. If Sir Bentley finds out I've been getting into trouble again, he'll expel me—I've had too many chances. Just don't do it, okay. *Okay?*"

Philip's eyes widened, and he stepped back. "All right, all right. Don't worry, I won't say anything."

"Good—thanks. Let's have lunch," said Chris, changing the subject.

"Hands-free?" asked Sebastian as he gave Chris a friendly slap on the shoulder.

They all grinned. Even Chris managed a smile. There was no question in his mind that choosing his friends over not getting into trouble had been the right decision.

Chris sat down at the table and placed his hands behind the chair as the others did the same. A few minutes later, the room was filled with food flying up and into their wide-open mouths when Maura walked in.

"Honestly, children, you are terrors."

They all laughed.

"Just don't spill any on the floor. I've got enough to get on with." Maura placed a jug on the table and walked out, shaking her head as the food continued to rise from the table behind her.

Chris lined up grapes along the ceiling and let them drop into his mouth one by one. As the lunch went on and everybody carried on around him as normal, he felt himself relax until, eventually, the dark and depressing thoughts that had been following him around all day left his mind.

CHAPTER FIVE

Miss Sonata was waiting for them in the classroom after lunch. As always, she was immaculately dressed in a fitted suit jacket and skirt, her blond hair cut into a perfectly symmetrical bob.

"Welcome back. It's so lovely to see you all!" said Miss Sonata as they walked into the room.

Chris smiled. Miss Sonata was about as opposite to Ms. Lamb as it was possible to be.

He took his seat as Miss Sonata picked up a booklet on her desk. "I hope you're all rested and ready to get some serious examinations under your belt."

There was a time, not so long ago, when that sentence would have sent shivers down his spine. Now, with his Ability, Chris was not only able to memorize entire books within minutes, he also had no problem understanding exactly what the books were saying. It was the same for all of them. Only Philip, who had always been a straight-A student, had enjoyed constant success at school. The others, Chris and Rex in particular, had struggled their way through. Now, with the Ability, they had all discovered exactly how much fun could be had from learning. Who would have imagined, thought Chris, that he might one day be at the top of his class. Maybe even at the top of the school. It was the first time since he had arrived at Myers Holt that the thought of starting a new school in September didn't make him feel physically sick.

"Chris? Open your folder, please. Page two."

"Oh," said Chris. "Sorry." He opened up the green file and turned the page to a timetable.

"The following is a list of examinations you will be sitting over the next few months. When your Ability ends, on your thirteenth birthdays, you will, as you know, keep all the knowledge that you've acquired here. Your understanding of it will also remain exactly the same, but anything new you learn will take as much time to learn as it did before. Well, less actually, because you'll have so much extra knowledge to help you understand new ideas. Does that make sense?"

They all nodded.

"Good. Right, we'll start with Latin today. Chris, I spoke with Mr. Valedictoriat. He's ready to see you now."

"Thank you," said Chris, a bit embarrassed that the others now knew he had to meet with the psychologist, until he remembered that they were all going to be meeting with him too.

"The reading list is in your folder," continued Miss Sonata, "and under the folder are the first three books on the Latin syllabus. The rest of the term's books are in the library. Make sure you get through them at some point this evening."

"Yes, Miss Sonata. Where do I go?"

"Ah, yes. One of the new rooms down this corridor. Mr. Valedictoriat's name is on the door. I'll see you tomorrow."

Chris stood up, picked up his folder and books, and left the classroom.

"Come i-in," sang a voice from inside Mr. Valedictoriat's room.

Chris opened the door and found Mr. Valedictoriat, a large, friendly looking man with dark brown skin and white hair wearing a bright red jacket and matching red-frame glasses, sitting in an armchair.

"I think I have an appointment with you, Mr., er, Vale . . . dictor . . ." said Chris, standing in the doorway.

"Call me Hugh. That's spelled 'hug' with an *h*!" he said, holding two thumbs up and grinning. "Mr. Valedictoriat's a bit of a mouthful. Now come, take a seat, and make yourself comfy cozy."

Chris walked over to the armchair opposite Hugh and looked around at the small room filled with shelves of what looked like trinkets and toys—toy soldiers, marbles, cars, dolls, little figurines, amongst other items. Next to the armchair, Chris saw a sand table.

"Do you like playing with sand?" asked Hugh.

"I haven't really played with sand since nursery school," replied Chris.

"That's a shame indeed. I think the world would be a better place if we all played a little bit more, even when we're as old as I am. Don't you think so, Christopher?"

"I guess so," said Chris slowly.

There was a pause. Chris wondered whether Hugh was expecting him to play with the sand now, but Hugh didn't say anything, so Chris, who just wanted to get on with whatever it was that they were supposed to be doing, sat down.

Hugh gave a wide smile and sat back in his chair.

"Let's start. Why don't I tell you a little bit about myself first to break the ice. I'm a psychologist. That's a big word. I prefer 'friend.' Do you know why I'm here?"

"To talk to us?"

"Exactly. To talk, to share. Think of me as an imaginary friend that you can tell all your worries to. My job is to listen to you—really listen. You can tell me anything, and I promise you it won't surprise or shock me and it won't go beyond these four walls. Now, let's sing."

"Excuse me?" asked Chris, hoping he had misheard.

"Let's sing together. It'll break the ice."

"Oh, um, I don't know. I'm not a very good singer."

"Now, now, I don't believe that for one minute. If you can speak, you can sing. Just copy me. La, la, la, la, la, la, la, la, LAHHHHHH. Your turn."

Chris shifted uncomfortably in his chair and looked at the door. He wondered if it would be rude to run out.

No sooner had he thought that than the door swung open.

Hugh looked round, surprised. He stood up and walked over to it, then peered out into the corridor.

"Nobody here," he said, confused.

"Sorry . . . that was me. It was my Ability."

Hugh's eyes widened in exaggerated amazement, and then he started laughing.

"Oooh! My first time seeing it. Very i-m-p-r-e-s-s-i-v-e," said Hugh, closing the door and going back to his seat.

"That spells 'impressive,'" he said, sitting back.

"Er, yes," said Chris, feeling increasingly irritated.

"Okay, I guess the door thing was your way of telling me you're not comfortable. Let's try something different."

Chris sighed in relief as Hugh leaned over the side of his chair and pulled out . . . a teddy bear.

Chris winced.

"Say hello to Boo Boo."

Chris tensed as he looked at Hugh. "Really?"

"It seems strange, I know," said Hugh, smiling broadly, "but just try it. Come on, free your mind." Then he held the teddy bear up and started talking in a high-pitched voice. "I'm your friend, Christopher. Talk to me!"

Chris looked at the teddy bear and, as he watched it dance from side to side in front of him, a furious heat began to take over his body. His fists clenched and he tried to calm himself, but it was no use—all the frustration and anger that had been building up inside him over the last two weeks exploded. Before he could think about what he was doing, his mind went blank and his Ability took over. Hugh's mouth dropped open as the teddy bear was ripped out of his hands and started spinning across the room, then slammed into the wall.

"I AM NOT TALKING TO A TEDDY BEAR!" shouted Chris.

Hugh stayed completely still and said nothing as Chris turned his attention to the shelves and, immediately, the room filled with an explosion of toy soldiers and trinkets.

"I AM NOT IN THE MOOD FOR PLAYING GAMES," he continued. "I KILLED A BOY—DID YOU KNOW THAT?"

Hugh shook his head. "I didn't know that . . ."

"WELL I DID!" Chris looked down at a toy truck lying on the floor, and it flew up in the air and across the room. "I killed him and he didn't have to die. I watched his brother—his twin brother—realize that he was dead. CAN YOU IMAGINE HOW THAT FELT FOR HIM? HE LOOKED ME IN THE EYE AND HE WANTED TO KILL ME. AND YOU KNOW WHAT? I DON'T BLAME HIM! I DON'T BLAME HIM ONE LITTLE BIT!"

Chris could see Hugh wanted to say something, but he wasn't finished. "And now you want me to talk to a bear? A TEDDY BEAR! I am not five years old, and I don't need to talk to it or you or anyone else about what happened, because *nothing* will change what I did. *Do you understand that?*"

Hugh motioned for Chris to sit down. "I understand, Chris. Why don't you come . . ."

"NO! I am not doing this anymore. I don't need a psychiatrist. . . ."

"Psychologist—"

"*Whatever.* I don't care if I get into trouble about this. I don't care about anything. I've looked after myself all my life, and I can keep doing it."

Before Hugh could say anything, Chris ran over to the armchair, grabbed his bag, and made his way to the door.

"Christopher, stop. Let's talk."

But Chris didn't stop. Instead, he rushed out and slammed the door behind him, tears running down his cheeks as he ran back to his bedroom.

CHAPTER SIX

Chris woke in a cold sweat. He sat straight up in his bed and looked around, disorientated. It had seemed so real—the pale boy (The twin who was still alive or the one he had killed? He wasn't sure) chasing him through cobbled alleyways, Chris falling over, the boy walking up to him calmly. Then, as happened every night, the boy lifted a knife—the same one that Dulcia had tried to kill Sir Bentley and John with—while Chris pleaded for forgiveness and for his life. Then, just as he was about to bring it down, Chris had woken up. But the image of the boy's face remained, etched into his mind. It never left him. It seemed as if his own mind was intent on tormenting him, tricking him into seeing the boy everywhere he turned—in the streets, on the television, even in his own reflection. And, of course, in his nightmares.

Chris looked around at his computer-generated bedroom walls, alive with the gentle swaying of green trees, and tried to calm himself. It was just a dream, he told himself over and over again as he tried to push away the image of the boy's face looking down over him, only to find it replaced by the very real memory of his session with Hugh. He closed his eyes and breathed in deeply. As the possible cost of his outburst dawned on him, he wondered what on earth he had been thinking.

"Are you nervous?" asked Philip from his bed on the other side of the room. Chris hadn't told him about his meeting with Hugh. In fact, he hadn't said much at all the night before and had excused himself to go to bed straight after dinner.

"I don't think I'll be going," said Chris.

"Why?" asked Philip, sitting up.

The picture of the teddy bear slamming into the wall flashed across Chris's mind.

"I sort of lost my temper with the psychologist. I don't think Sir Bentley's going to be pleased when he hears about it."

Philip shook his head, dismissing Chris's concerns. "Don't worry about that—Sir Bentley won't know anything."

"What do you mean?"

"They're not allowed to say anything about your session to anyone."

Chris wrinkled his nose, unconvinced. "Really?"

"Yes. My mum teaches psychology, and she used to *be* a psychologist. I promise you—unless you said you were going to kill someone or something like that, he can't say a word."

Chris frowned as he tried to remember everything that had happened.

"Chris . . . ," said Philip slowly, "you didn't say you were going to kill anyone, did you?"

Finally, Chris shook his head. "I said a lot of things, but I didn't say that."

Philip breathed a sigh of relief and smiled. "Well, then, it's fine. What time do you have to meet Sir Bentley?"

Chris looked over at the clock above the door and threw the covers back. "Oh, no! I've got fifteen minutes!"

He clambered quickly down the ladder, rushed into the bathroom, grabbed one of the freshly laundered towels that Maura had left for them in the walk-in wardrobe, and jumped into the shower, the water splashing onto the glass wall of the aquarium filled with gently pulsating jellyfish.

"See you later. Good luck!" shouted Philip as Chris rushed out of the room, his hair still wet.

Chris ran into the dining room, took a large swig of orange juice, and grabbed a couple of pieces of toast, then rushed out.

"Nice suit," he said, passing Sebastian, who wore a bright-blue suit, black-and-white leather shoes, and a clumsily knotted yellow tie.

"Gracias," called Sebastian, tipping an imaginary hat as Chris ran off toward Sir Bentley's office with his mouth stuffed full of toast.

Chris brushed the crumbs from his sweater and knocked on Sir Bentley's door.

"Come in," said Sir Bentley.

Chris opened the door. "Good morning, sir. Sorry I'm late."

"No problem, Christopher. How are you?"

"Good, thank you," said Chris quietly as he took his seat.

"Did you meet with Mr. Valedictoriat yesterday?"

He could tell by the sound of Sir Bentley's voice that Philip had been right. Hugh hadn't said anything, and while he wasn't going to lie, he didn't think it was necessary to offer more information than needed.

Chris nodded. "Yes, sir, I did."

"Pleased to hear that. And how are you feeling about today?"

"I still want to do it. I think it's my responsibility, sir."

Sir Bentley opened up the briefcase and pulled out some papers. "Very well, as long as you're sure. A car will be here in half an hour to take us to Holloway Prison. It's not too far from here, about twenty minutes with traffic. First, though, let me explain a little more about what we know of Dulcia Genever and what we're hoping to gain from our visit today."

Sir Bentley slid a photograph across the table, a mug shot of Dulcia Genever following her arrest before Christmas. Chris stared at it for a moment. Her pale face, completely devoid of any emotion, was framed by her jet black hair, and he was sure that even if he hadn't known what she was capable of, he would have been able to sense the evil in the cold, piercing stare of her emerald-green eyes. A shiver ran through him.

"You may remember some of this from last term, so excuse any repetition, but I want to be thorough. . . ."

Chris sat forward and listened carefully as Sir Bentley

ran through everything that he knew about Dulcia Genever—starting with how she had once been a pupil at Myers Holt, just like Chris.

"Then, one day, we began receiving anonymous letters to Myers Holt from people with knowledge about the Ability. We had no idea who they were—we still don't—but we did know what they wanted: money, in exchange for their silence."

"Did you give it to them?" asked Chris.

"The problem with blackmailers, Christopher, is that they tend never to be satisfied. They ask for a little bit, then a little bit more. It never stops. So our plan was to meet with the blackmailers, hand them the money, and then, in the process, the pupils from Myers Holt would wipe the minds of the blackmailers so that they had no memory of the Ability whatsoever."

"Using Inferno?" asked Chris.

"Precisely. Inferno was a very new technique at the time and had barely been tested. We knew that the person performing it had to be fairly close physically to the victim, and we knew how to do it, but there was no way to test it out until the actual moment. We trained as much as possible and took the pupils to the place where the blackmailers had asked to meet us."

Sir Bentley sighed and took a sip of water before continuing.

"I don't think I need to go into all the details. We were tricked. They didn't want money—they wanted one of the pupils. They could make a lot more than a briefcase of money using the Ability. In spite of what Dulcia might believe, we

didn't abandon her—everything was planned by her kidnappers to make us have no doubt that she had been killed."

Sir Bentley paused for a moment and cleared his throat. Chris could tell by the deep furrows in his brow and the way he was keeping his head down that this was far more difficult for Sir Bentley to talk about than Chris had imagined.

"Are you all right, sir?"

Sir Bentley looked up at Chris as if he had forgotten he was there.

"Yes, fine—there are some memories you just don't want to dwell on."

Chris understood exactly what he meant.

Sir Bentley shook himself and sat up straight. "Until the night of the ball," he continued, "everybody involved had thought that Dulcia, or Anna Willows as she was known at the time, had died. But, of course, she hadn't. She had been kidnapped, and although we have no information about the intervening years, one thing is certain: She spent a large part of that time planning her revenge."

"What about the boys?" asked Chris.

"Apart from their age, obviously, we don't know anything—not even their names. Dulcia has remained completely silent from the moment of her arrest. We need to make sure the boy is being cared for and that this matter is finished with. And although she tried to kill me, I don't blame her for her anger."

There was a brief moment of silence.

"So, what information do you need me to get from her?" asked Chris finally.

"It's quite simple. We have all the evidence we need to

proceed with charges of attempted murder—she tried to kill me in front of hundreds of witnesses, after all—so it's just a case of finding out whether she was working with anybody else, the name of the boy, and her home address—those three things. We'll take it from there."

"What will happen to the boy?"

"Nothing. We won't be pressing charges, if that's what you mean."

Chris nodded. "I don't think it's his fault."

"I agree. We will ensure that he is safe and get him the help he needs after everything that has happened." Sir Bentley looked down at his watch. "We'd better get going. Ron and John will be waiting with the car outside. I'll explain everything in detail on the way—but I'm sure it's nothing you haven't already practiced many times."

"Okay," said Chris, standing up. And then something occurred to him.

"What if she blocks me?" he asked.

Sir Bentley nodded. "Yes, of course. Well, she does know about the Ability, so the moment that she feels the ringing in the ears, she will know that somebody is trying to access her mind, and she may well try to block you. However, she won't know that you are there, so you'll have the element of surprise on your side. By the time she realizes what's happening, you should be well inside her mind, the ringing will have stopped, and it will be too late for her to push you out."

Sir Bentley grabbed his coat and hat from the wooden coat stand and, as Chris followed him over to the elevator and out of Myers Holt, something occurred to him for the first time, and he paled: In almost every one of the

few instances that he had used the Ability since killing the boy, he had let his emotions get the better of him. In fact, thinking about the incident with Hugh, the angrier he felt, the more out of control his Ability was. He climbed into the car behind Sir Bentley and buckled up in silence as the car pulled out into the street, his mind fighting the thought that maybe he shouldn't be trusted to use his Ability at all.

The gates of Holloway Prison opened slowly to let the car carrying Chris and Sir Bentley pass. Chris had only seen prisons as depicted in films and television and was half expecting to be greeted by chained inmates in striped uniforms shouting and rattling their chains, so he was relieved to see that the reality was quite different. In fact, Chris was escorted from the car by the prison warden, a serious-looking man in spectacles and a somber suit, to a surprisingly modern building without once seeing an inmate. Had it not been for the tall walls surrounding them, he might have thought he was entering a large office building.

"This way, please," said the warden. "You two can wait here," he said to Ron and John. Ron looked annoyed, but John nodded and sat down on a chair, pulling Ron down by the sleeve to join him.

"We won't be long," said Sir Bentley. "Come, Christopher."

Chris walked silently behind the warden as he explained how Dulcia Genever had been doing since her arrest.

"She hasn't said a word since she arrived. She's barely eaten, in fact. I'm not sure what you'll get out of your meeting."

"Thank you, but we're really just here to observe," said Sir Bentley.

"May I ask why?" asked the warden.

"Just a routine check," said Sir Bentley.

"And the boy?" asked the warden, opening a door.

"He's my grandson. Just here to see what his grandfather does."

The warden nodded, but Chris could tell by the way he pursed his lips that he was unconvinced. "Very well. I'll turn the light on for the two-way mirror. To remind you, you can see her but she cannot see you."

Chris turned to the dark wall that Sir Bentley was facing and waited.

Click.

The wall suddenly revealed itself as a window into the adjoining room.

The cell was empty except for a single seat in the corner and a bed that looked as if it hadn't been slept in. On the chair, with her back turned away from them, was Dulcia Genever, her black hair tied up, her hands on her lap.

"Could you leave us for a few minutes?" asked Sir Bentley.

The warden hesitated and then, finally, nodded. "Yes, of course. I'll be waiting outside if you need me."

Chris waited for the door to close and turned to Sir Bentley, who seemed lost in thought as he stared through the two-way mirror. "Can she hear us?" he whispered.

"No, not a thing," said Sir Bentley, still looking straight ahead. "She has no idea we're here—I promise. Do you need a minute, or do you want to get started?"

Chris knew that this would have been the right time to admit to Sir Bentley that he wasn't sure he was able to control his Ability anymore, but his desire to learn more about the boy won over. "No, I'll start now."

"You know what you need to do."

"Yes, sir," said Chris. He could feel Sir Bentley watching him as he looked at the back of Dulcia's head, only a few feet away from him, and let his mind go blank.

And then he waited.

Entering the mind of a person, he had found in the course of his time at Myers Holt, was so easy for him that he barely had to think about it before he was standing in the Reception of the mind, but nothing was happening.

Chris shook his head and blinked.

"Everything okay?" asked Sir Bentley.

"Yes, sorry. I think I need to start again."

Chris turned his attention back to Dulcia and let his eyes lose focus. And then he waited. And waited.

"Christopher?"

Chris looked up at Sir Bentley, confused. "I can't get in. I think she's blocking me."

Chris had blocked others, by filling his Reception with a familiar rhyme that filled his mind so entirely, nobody could enter, but it had never been done to him. People had tried, but Chris had always been too quick for them, and he had stopped them without any effort whatsoever.

"That doesn't make any sense," said Sir Bentley. "She has no idea that we're here. Try again. Make sure you focus on the back of her head and imagine standing in her Reception. By looking at the exact point where you want to go, it should make your Ability stronger."

Chris turned. Third time lucky, he thought, focusing once again on the back of Dulcia's head.

This time, Chris imagined that he was standing in her mind already, and as he focused more and more on the image a low haunting sound began to fill his head, softly at first.

"'Twinkle, twinkle, little star, how I wonder what you are. . . . Twinkle, twinkle, little star, how I wonder what you . . .'"

Chris tried to ignore Dulcia's singing and focused his mind even more. Slowly, his surroundings started to dim until they went black, and then, as if a button had been switched on, he was alone in a black room and the sound of the singing suddenly filled his head so loudly that his eyes began to stream and he raised his hands to the throbbing in his head.

"'TWINKLE, TWINKLE, LITTLE STAR, HOW I WONDER WHAT YOU ARE. . . . TWINKLE . . .'"

Chris felt the noise of the singing weighing him down, pressing in around him until he thought his ears were going to burst. He looked around desperately for the door to Dulcia's mind, but the singing continued to increase in volume and he felt himself spinning with pain. Spinning and spinning and . . .

"Christopher? *Christopher!*"

Chris felt two arms around him, and all of a sudden, he was back in the room, collapsed on the floor, with Sir Bentley trying to lift him.

"Everything okay?" asked the warden, opening the door. "My goodness! What happened?"

"Bring the boy a glass of water, please. Quickly."

The warden rushed out, and Sir Bentley gently lifted Chris to his feet and led him over to a seat on the back wall.

"She was blocking me. She was doing it before we even

started," said Chris, his head still spinning. "There was nothing I could do."

"Don't talk, Christopher."

"I'm sorry, sir, I really tried," whispered Chris.

"I know you did," said Sir Bentley. "You did everything you were supposed to do."

Standing by the window of the playroom in Darkwhisper Manor, Ernest watched Chris and Sir Bentley in his mind as they left the prison. Even though their mission had been unsuccessful, Ernest's heart was racing wildly and his hands remained clenched tightly—the whole incident having caught him unawares. He had, of course, known that Dulcia would be interviewed, he just hadn't expected the Ability to be used on her so soon. Ernest was furious with himself—he should have seen it coming. But he hadn't, and the sight of Christopher Lane arriving at the prison had hit him like a punch in the stomach.

As it turned out, luck had been on his side for once: For the time being, Dulcia had blocked Christopher. He didn't know how long he had until they tried again—although he had no doubt that they would—or what their intentions were once they entered her mind, though he could guess. He couldn't risk another surprise—he was going to have to put his plan into action immediately. Ernest ran to the dining room and started to rip down the drawings of Chris from the wall. All the while, he could think of only one thing— that Christopher Lane wiping Dulcia Genever's mind was not something he was ever going to allow to happen.

CHAPTER SEVEN

Chris returned to Myers Holt to a picnic that Maura had prepared for them in the Dome and an avalanche of questions from his friends. Despite feeling exhausted, and miserable about his failure to access Dulcia's mind, he didn't think they would forgive him if he didn't tell them everything.

"Do you think she's just been repeating the same song over and over since she was arrested?" asked Daisy once Chris had finished.

"I guess so," said Chris.

"She must have known that we would try to access her mind," said Lexi.

"That, or maybe she just heard 'Twinkle, Twinkle' on the radio and couldn't get it out of her head," said Rex.

"Seriously?" asked Philip, looking amazed at Rex's stupidity.

"No, of course not, Einstein," said Rex, "it was a joke. Doesn't anyone have a sense of humor anymore?"

"Yes," replied Lexi, "it's just that you're not very funny."

"Only compared with your face, Frizzo," said Rex.

"Will you two stop flirting for one moment, please," said Philip. "I want to hear what happened."

Rex turned bright red.

"Nothing else happened," said Chris. "They gave me a glass of water, and we left."

"Do you presume that Sir Bentley will require your services once more to attempt Mind Accessing?" asked Sebastian.

"English please, Pedro," said Rex.

"I speak more refined English than you will ever utter," replied Sebastian.

"Yes," said Chris, ignoring Rex, "Sir Bentley said that there's something else we can try. He didn't say what, just that he's going to talk to us about it after lunch."

"I think that means now," said Daisy, standing up. Chris turned and saw Sir Bentley standing at the entrance of the classroom corridor, waving them down.

Chris walked into the classroom to find that Sir Bentley was standing next to Professor Ingleby, the programmer for the Myers Holt computer training program.

"Pupils, I'm sure you all remember Professor Ingleby," said Sir Bentley.

The professor nodded enthusiastically at them all. "Welcome back, children. Lovely to see you all!"

"Professor Ingleby will be talking to you in a moment about one of the new programs he has developed for your think-tank training," said Sir Bentley, "but first I need to discuss with you what happened this morning. Christopher, did you explain about Dulcia blocking the Ability when we went to see her?"

"Yes, sir," said Chris.

"Good. As you all know, then, Dulcia Genever has obviously been anticipating our use of the Ability on her and has been keeping a constant block in her mind. So, we need to get around it. Any ideas? Yes, Philip?"

"What about trying when she's asleep?"

"That would be a very good idea, but unfortunately, it seems Dulcia is not doing much sleeping at the moment—or, at least, it's hard to tell. She's barely moved from her chair since she arrived at the prison. Now, assuming she's asleep on our return tonight, it shouldn't be too difficult to access her mind. If, however, she's awake and still using her block, then we need to try a technique that you'll be practicing in a moment in the think tanks. The technique is called a scramble block. I'll give you an example. Lexi, start counting to forty, out loud."

"One, two, three, four, five . . ."

Sir Bentley joined in loudly. "Six, seven, eight, nine, twenty-five, eighteen, seven, two, sixteen . . ."

Lexi tried to continue but was clearly getting distracted. "Thirteen, fourteen, fifteen, nineteen . . . oh!"

"And that," said Sir Bentley, "is basically what a scramble block is. You'll enter Dulcia's mind using the block she's using. Let's assume it's the same one all the time—'Twinkle, Twinkle, Little Star,' is that right, Christopher?"

Chris nodded.

"So, you'll start by accessing her mind using the same song. This will trick her mind into letting you in. Once inside, I believe you'll find that her Reception is completely blocking any further entry. So, to get rid of the block, you'll have to start changing it up. That should confuse her mind to the point that the block weakens, and then you can enter her mind properly."

"How do we change it? Do we sing a different song?" asked Philip.

"No, that would be too abrupt, and her mind will immediately resist. Instead, you'll just sing the song in the wrong order. I think the best way to explain is to let you try it out for yourselves in the think tanks. Professor Ingleby?"

"Thank you!" said the professor, jumping up from his seat. "I won't add much to that except to say that the main difference with your training is that you'll now be able to practice entering people's minds in the think tanks. I have spent the last few months programming thousands of different mind maps into the computer so that, hopefully, you'll be well prepared for any type of person you encounter. Unfortunately, I haven't had much time to develop the scenario for today—I've done my best with the information Sir Bentley has given me but I'm afraid it's going to be rather unsophisticated. However, I'm sure you'll enjoy that you're now able to link up to each other so that you can work together—lots of fun in store! I'll say no more. Your think-tank teachers can explain the rest. Let's go!"

Chris led the way out of the classroom and into the darkness of the think-tank room, where the cubicles hummed quietly, each glowing in a different color. He went over to his, the red one, and turned the handle. Inside, Chris saw the familiar built-in black armchair. He took a seat, fastened himself into his harness, and leaned back, ready for the lesson to begin.

After a few seconds, the walls of the cubicle started to brighten, and the soft sound of birds singing filled the space until the screens around him transformed themselves into the English countryside—so real it was hard to believe that if he reached out, he would be touching glass. He felt himself being gently lowered until he was sitting in the middle of a field of buttercups swaying gently in the breeze. Chris turned his head, and the chair moved smoothly round until he caught sight of Cassandra, his teacher, sitting on a rock by a slow-moving river. She looked up, smiled, and waved him over.

Chris leaned forward slightly, and his chair tilted in the same direction. He glided forward until he reached the river and leaned back. The image around him stilled.

"Welcome back, Chris," said Cassandra, her voice soothing, her smile warm. She stood up and straightened the red skirt of her dress. "How was your vacation?"

"It was okay," said Chris, "I'm glad to be back."

Cassandra nodded, as if she understood exactly what Chris meant. It was hard to believe that she was no more than a piece of programming, thought Chris as he turned his head to follow her along the riverbank.

"We have a lot of exciting new things for you to try this term," said Cassandra, picking up a pebble and tossing it sideways into the river. The pebble jumped three times across the water and sank.

"Your turn," said Cassandra.

It was so simple. Pick up a stone with his Ability. He knew he could do it, so finding himself frozen with nerves came as a complete surprise.

"What's the matter, Chris?"

Chris realized he was shaking. "I don't know. . . ."

But Chris did know—he just didn't want to admit to Cassandra how much his failure that morning had bothered him. Or how he was growing more nervous every day about the power of his own Ability since the death of the boy. Or how his anger had a way of taking over and making him lose control. He could think of many reasons for his nerves, but not one that he wanted to share with a computer that would almost certainly relay anything he said back to his teachers. For all his concerns, Chris was certain of one thing: He did not want to be thrown out of Myers Holt.

"Chris, are you okay. Do you want to stop?"

Chris shook his head, but he didn't say anything.

"If you don't feel you can talk to me," continued Cassandra, "maybe you could go and have a word with someone else, Sir Bentley per . . ."

Chris's head shot up. "No. I'll do it."

Chris looked down at the ground and found a small stone. He imagined it rising, and immediately, it did so, until it was hovering in front of him. Chris pushed it forward with his mind, and the pebble suddenly flicked over to the water, bouncing across the surface five times before disappearing. He breathed a sigh of relief.

"Very good!" said Cassandra. "You clearly haven't lost your touch. Now, today, we're going to work on a scramble block. Let's go meet up with the other students and try it together. How does that sound?"

"Okay," said Chris. Cassandra eyed him with a puzzled expression, so he forced himself to smile. "I mean that sounds great. Will the others be real, or are they programmed?"

"No, Lexi, Daisy, Philip, Sebastian, and Rex will all be here in person. The professor has created a network that links all your think tanks—you'll be seeing what they're seeing and vice versa."

"Cool," said Chris, and a part of him meant it. He had always loved the professor's think-tank tricks—he just wished he could shake off his unsettledness.

"Very," said Cassandra, laughing. "Let's get started. Sit back—you're going for a ride!"

Chris leaned back in his chair, which tilted all the way back until he was staring at the screen above him—a perfectly cloudless blue sky. The seat began to rumble gently, and then, suddenly, it felt as if he had been shot up into the air. Chris instinctively grabbed at the sides of his chair before remembering that he wasn't really flying. Suddenly, the chair tipped up straight, and Chris looked down at the fields below his feet, whooshing past him until houses began to appear, dotted far from each other at first and then gradually closer together until they were in the middle of a city. Chris's chair tipped forward and shot down to the ground, toward a large compound of buildings.

It was only when he landed and looked around that Chris saw he had been standing at the exact same spot that morning.

"We're at the prison?" asked Chris, surprised.

"Yes," said Cassandra, appearing next to him. "As you can imagine, the professor hasn't had very long to put this together, so the details may not be exact—they're based on Sir Bentley's description. However, we thought it best for you to practice in as similar a setting as possible. Let's go inside."

Chris followed Cassandra through the door. This time, there were no security guards, and the doors opened automatically to let them through into the stark corridor. Chris took the lead and went up to the door of the observation room he had sat in that morning.

"Ah, it looks like we're the first here," she said, stepping inside. She flicked a switch, and Dulcia's cell appeared.

Everything about the room was almost correct, but not quite. The doorway in the room was a little off center, the chair turned to face the wrong way, and the walls were painted a few shades darker than he remembered. Most jarring, however, was Dulcia herself. She was slightly shorter, her jumpsuit was orange rather than blue, and, strangest of all, she was pixelated. It was the first time Chris had seen anything in the think tank that was obviously a computer animation.

"Chris!" said Daisy, walking in. Although he knew that she, like him, was at this very moment sitting down in her think tank, in here Daisy was standing, and she was wearing a pink dress that Chris recognized as one she hadn't worn since the previous term.

"Hello, Chris," said a woman standing behind Daisy. "I'm Astra, Daisy's teacher." Chris smiled. She was just as he had imagined: like a fairy godmother, in a pale-pink dress that sparkled in the dark room.

"Greetings!" said Sebastian, walking in behind some-one who looked like a swashbuckler from a black-and-white Hollywood movie in a flowing white shirt, a large gold belt buckle, and tight black trousers.

"Buenos días. Me llamo Balthasar," said the man, run-ning his fingers through his long hair and leaning up against the wall.

"Sebastian, you're wearing your old clothes," said Daisy, laughing. Sure enough, Chris looked over at Sebastian and saw that the bright-blue suit he had been wearing that day had been replaced with a plain white T-shirt and jeans.

Sebastian looked down at his clothes and curled his lip. "This does not please me whatsoever," he said. "I will be having discussions with the professor."

The others joined them a few minutes later, and the room was soon filled with chatter between the six excited pupils standing next to the strange assortment of teach-ers. Chris looked around. Even if they hadn't walked in together, Chris would have had no trouble match-ing teacher to pupil. Lexi's teacher, Prometheus, was a tall, no-nonsense-looking man in a black suit. He didn't speak, instead choosing to survey the room with his arms folded. Rex's teacher was equally, if not more, intimidat-ing. Almost as wide as he was tall, his muscles stretching against his army uniform, Mars cut a terrifying figure. Rex, unusually, stood silently next to him, back straight, awaiting orders. And finally, all the way from ancient Greece with his long white beard and flowing robes, was Philip's teacher, Zeno, nodding quietly in conversation with Cassandra.

"Shall we get started?" asked Astra finally, clapping her hands. Chris, who was standing next to her, turned and waited, but most of the others, not having heard her, continued to talk.

Chris watched as Mars took a step forward, arms to his side, and shouted.

"STOP!"

Immediately, the whole room fell silent.

"You are all wasting time!" shouted Mars, despite having everybody's full attention.

Behind him, Rex rolled his eyes and shrugged his shoulders as if to apologize for his teacher. Unfortunately for him, he had forgotten that his teacher was computer generated and could see everything.

"Rex King, don't you dare disrespect me!"

"Sorry," said Rex.

"'Sorry' what?"

"Sorry, sir," said Rex and, despite themselves, they all grinned. Chris could see why Mars had been chosen as his teacher.

"Right, everybody," said Prometheus, stepping forward into the center of the room, which appeared to have expanded to accommodate them all. "Your teachers will explain what you have to do, and then we'll begin."

Cassandra turned to Chris as all the other teachers turned to their own pupils.

"You're all going to . . ."

Chris tried to lean in to hear the rest of what Cassandra was saying.

"I can't hear you," shouted Chris. Cassandra looked

around and then snapped her fingers. The noise around him completely disappeared.

"That's better," said Cassandra as everybody around them continued their conversations in silence.

"As the pupil with the strongest Ability, you are going to enter Dulcia's mind on your own to retrieve the information."

Chris tensed, and Cassandra, appearing to notice, put her hand on his shoulder. "However, the others will be in Reception should you need any help. If you do, you can go and get them at any time. That part will be fine, I'm sure—you already know what you're looking for. Yes?"

Chris nodded.

"Good. All that we need to practice today is the scramble block, which will allow you to get access to her mind in the first place. One of us will count you in, and then you'll all start simultaneously accessing her mind. You don't need to make too much of an effort—I believe you tried that already this morning and found out the consequences of fighting a strong block—"

Cassandra stopped, as if something had occurred to her.

"Is that what it was, Chris—what happened this morning?"

Chris wondered whether to say anything. In the end, he just nodded.

"You don't have to do it. We can choose somebody else. Sir Bentley will understand."

Chris shook his head. He knew, however difficult it might be, that accessing Dulcia's mind, and finding out if the boy was okay, was his responsibility. And the only way to lay his demons to rest. "No. I'm just a bit tired right now, but I'm fine—I want to do it."

Cassandra smiled. "Very well. Take it slowly and you'll do great. Once in, you should find yourself in her Reception with the others, and you'll all be singing the same song. The room will be foggy, but you should be able to see the others standing with you. At that point, having made sure everybody is there, you will give the signal—just a thumbs-up. That's when you'll begin singing the words in a different order. Don't do it too obviously, just quietly—otherwise you'll find yourself pushed out. Then, as you hear her singing start to falter or get quieter, you can start making it louder. Try to sing different words from the others: The more confused the song is, the quicker her block will disappear. After a few moments, the fog in the room should clear and you can run toward the door leading into the rest of her mind."

"Okay," said Chris, running through the steps in his head.

Cassandra clicked her fingers, and the noise of the room returned. They waited until, after a few minutes and some more shouting from Mars, everybody was quiet.

"Let's begin," said Cassandra, addressing everybody. "I'll count you in."

Cassandra looked over at Chris, gave him a thumbs-up, and disappeared. Immediately, the other teachers vanished also, leaving the six pupils in the room alone.

"This is weird," said Lexi, stepping up to the glass.

"It's even weirder when you've seen it for real," said Chris.

"We wouldn't know," said Rex, "seeing as you're always the one they choose to do everything."

Chris looked over at Rex to see if he was joking, but the frown on his face gave Chris his answer.

"That's not true," said Chris. "I don't always get—"

He was interrupted by the sound of Cassandra's voice. "Are you all ready?"

"Yes," they all replied.

"Good, everybody look at Dulcia."

Chris reminded himself that Rex always sulked when he wasn't chosen to do anything, turned his attention to the badly animated figure in the corner, and let his mind lose focus.

"And three, two, one, go. . . ."

Chris felt the room around him disappear as he placed all his focus on the back of Dulcia's head. And then, just as had happened that morning, Chris began to hear singing.

"'. . . what you are. Up above the world so high, like a diamond in the sky, twinkle, twinkle . . .'"

The voice was monotonous and dark, just as he had described, but it didn't feel as haunting as it had when he had heard it earlier, perhaps, he thought, because this time he knew it wasn't real.

Chris waited for the verse to end and then began to sing quietly. Seconds later, and much sooner than he had expected, he was transported into a room—a large, fog-filled chamber filled with the sound of the haunting voice. This time, however, there was no pain. He concentrated on keeping in time with the voice that filled the room until, a few moments later, the others joined him.

Chris looked around as they all began to line up next to him, the sounds of their voices muffled by Dulcia's singing. Rex was the last to appear, still pouting. Chris waited for him to take his place at the end of the line, and then he raised his hand to give the others the thumbs-up.

Chris began the verse just as Dulcia's voice was on the third line, but after a few moments, he found that he was singing in unison with her once more. He looked around and was relieved to see that he wasn't the only one finding it difficult. Only Lexi and Sebastian, staring straight ahead of them, seemed able to maintain the wrong verse—the others were all doing the same as Chris, once again singing in time with Dulcia, the fog still heavy around them.

Chris looked over, still singing, and motioned for them to put their fingers to their ears. He was surprised to find, when he did this himself, that it didn't help as much as he had thought it would—Dulcia's voice was still as loud as before—but at least the others were muted. He tried again.

"'Twinkle, twinkle, little star, how I wonder what you are. Up above . . .'"

Chris began to relax and, as he did so, his voice grew louder in his mind. The others were clearly having the same success as Chris began to notice Dulcia's voice falter slightly. He kept going as loudly as he could, forgetting his embarrassment at singing in front of others, and then, suddenly, Dulcia's singing stopped. The fog began to clear, but he kept singing, as did the others, loud enough that even when Dulcia's voice started up again, it was confused. The voice stopped again and started at the beginning of the verse once more.

"Go!" said Cassandra's voice from somewhere behind him.

Chris looked around and noticed that the room was now completely empty except for himself and the others and the sound of their singing. Turning, he found the door he was looking for, the entrance into the rest of Dulcia's mind, and he began to run.

"Quick—her block is getting stronger again," said Cassandra. Sure enough, Chris noticed a cloud begin to form on the ceiling of the room.

He raced up to the handle and opened the door. Usually, at this point, Chris would be looking at a large city filled with buildings, but in this instance, there was nothing, just a black void. He leaned forward, slowly moving past the doorway until, suddenly, the screens around him turned black.

"Excellent," said Cassandra, suddenly appearing in front of him. Chris looked around and saw that he was back in the room with the others, facing the window into Dulcia's cell.

"Let's try it again," she said.

CHAPTER EIGHT

That night, the pupils of Myers Holt were sent to bed early. Chris, although excited at trying out the new technique they had learned, fell asleep easily, only to be woken up what seemed like a few minutes later by Maura in her nightgown, carrying in a tray of tea and toast.

"What time is it?" asked Philip, bleary eyed.

"Three in the morning, not that you could tell in here," she said brightly.

Chris looked around at the bright blue skies and noticed that the sun was high, clearly a trick designed to wake them more easily.

"Urgh," he groaned, sitting himself up and taking the cup of tea from Maura.

"You've got fifteen minutes to get ready," she said.

Chris nodded and took a slow sip as Maura walked over to Philip's bed and shook him gently.

"Philip, love, no sleeping."

Chris turned to see that Philip had pulled the duvet over his head.

"Philip?" asked Maura, giving the lump a nudge.

"Okay, okay," said Philip, pulling the covers off himself. "I'm getting up."

Nobody said a word as Ron drove Chris, Sir Bentley, and Lexi to the prison. A second car, driven by John and carrying the rest of them, followed as they sped through the empty London streets.

"We're here," said Lexi, recognizing the building from their training that afternoon.

Chris nodded. In spite of their practice session in the think tanks, and that he now had his friends to support him, his heart began to race.

The warden, the same man who had escorted them that morning, was waiting for them.

"No explanation?" asked the warden.

Sir Bentley shook his head. "No, I'm sorry. I can't say anything."

"I see. So be it," said the warden. "Follow me."

Chris and the other pupils followed Sir Bentley into the building, where a guard was sitting behind a desk.

"Is she sleeping?" asked the warden.

"There is nothing to report," replied the guard without expression. "The prisoner remains seated and appears to be asleep. Nothing out of the ordinary has happened. Everything is just as it always is."

"Thank you, Russell."

"Yes, sir. Just doing my job, sir."

The warden looked at the guard for a moment and then shrugged his shoulders. "Okay, well, thank you." He walked over to the door and turned to face the pupils.

"The room you will be in is soundproofed, but the corridor is not. I believe you need the element of surprise—I have no idea why—but I therefore recommend that you remain silent until the door of the observation room is closed."

Everybody nodded, and the warden led them over to the door next to the guard.

"I'm nervous," whispered Daisy.

"Don't be," said Chris. "She won't even know we were here."

Daisy nodded but nevertheless clung onto Chris's sleeve as they walked down the hallway, as if she were expecting Dulcia to jump out at them any moment.

The warden unlocked the door and motioned for them all to enter. Sir Bentley stepped in first, followed by the children, who waited in darkness until the warden stepped in himself and turned on the switch.

The light from the adjoining room flooded the space as the wall turned into a window onto Dulcia's cell, lit harshly by a bank of fluorescent strip lights. Chris stared. It was exactly as it had been on his previous visit, with one notable exception.

"I'll leave you to it," said the warden, not having noticed the confused look on all the visitors' faces.

"Erm, Mr. Robinson?"

"Yes, Sir Bentley?"

"Where is she?"

It was the warden's turn to look confused. "What do you mean?" he asked, stepping back inside. "She's over . . . *What?*"

Chris stepped back as the warden rushed forward and pressed his face to the glass, frantically looking for Dulcia, though there was little to check: The small room, with its two pieces of furniture, offered no place for a person to hide.

"RUSSELL? RUSSELL! GET IN HERE!" shouted the warden. Then, changing his mind, he pushed past the children and ran off down the corridor.

Chris and the others followed behind Sir Bentley, who, although he hadn't said anything, was looking equally concerned.

"RUSSELL!"

"Yes, sir?" asked the guard calmly.

"Where is prisoner Genever?"

"In her cell, sir, of course. She's been there all night. Look."

The warden leaned over and stared at the screens on the guard's desk for a moment, his face slowly turning a deep red.

"Is this a joke? There is *nobody there!*"

The guard looked at his boss as if he were crazy. "What do you mean? She's right here," he said, jabbing his finger at the screen.

Chris craned his neck around the desk to have a look and saw that the guard was pointing at the clearly empty chair in the corner of the cell. His heart sank. He had been hoping for a rational explanation—that she'd been moved to another cell, perhaps. Chris could tell by the confused look on his face that the guard genuinely believed what he was saying, but there was no doubt: Dulcia Genever had escaped.

He turned to Philip to say something to him, only to find that he and the other pupils were all whispering excitedly among themselves.

"Magic—it's got to be magic," whispered Daisy.

"Yeah," agreed Lexi. "Maybe she's the Wicked Witch of the West."

"And somebody splashed her with water," added Philip.

"Argh," said Rex, in a hushed, high-pitched voice, "I'm melting. . . ."

Everybody giggled. Well, everybody except Chris, who stood staring at them in shock because it was only in that moment he realized that for them this was all a game—a real-life think-tank scenario they could just walk away from. They weren't woken up by nightmares through the night; they could never understand what he was going through or why he wouldn't make jokes at a time like this.

The warden, who had been leaning over the prison counter taking deep breaths, turned to Sir Bentley, his eyes about to pop out of his head. "The man's lost his mind," he said. "I don't know what to do. They're going to sack me for this." He turned back to the guard, *"What's wrong with you?"* he asked.

"Calm down, Mr. Robinson," said Mr. Bentley, interrupting with a hand on the agitated man's shoulders. "We need clear minds."

He turned to the guard. "Russell, can you rewind the tapes?"

The guard nodded and pressed a button. The group watched in silence as the clock on the tape clicked back in time—one hour, two hours, until, finally, there was a blur of movement.

"Stop there," said Sir Bentley. The guard paused the video, and simultaneously, the group gasped.

Chris looked at the screen in disbelief. There, standing up, was Dulcia, and next to her was the pale young boy he had seen at the Antarctic Ball. The twin brother of the boy he had killed. Chris felt his stomach turn. In guilt, perhaps, or fear, or maybe even relief—he couldn't be sure.

Chris turned his head and saw that his friends were no longer playing around. In fact, they had all frozen, looking almost as shocked at seeing the boy as he was. There were no longer any whispered jokes, only the sound of Sir Bentley, his face tight and somber, directing the guard.

"Rewind it, please . . . a little bit more. . . . Yes, stop. Play it from there."

Chris watched Dulcia sitting in her chair, not moving. The door opened, and the boy walked in calmly. He looked around, caught sight of his mother, and appeared to say something. Dulcia didn't move. The boy walked over to the chair, paused, and then reached out and shook Dulcia, who turned her head suddenly. There was a moment where the two stared at each other and then, slowly, a dark smile appeared across Dulcia's face. She stood up, placed her hand on the boy's shoulder, and they walked out, the boy following calmly behind her.

Chris looked over at the warden, whose face was now ashen.

"What . . . What is going on?" he whispered.

"I don't understand, sir," said the guard. "Everything looks normal to me."

Chris suddenly realized why the guard was acting so strangely.

"He used his Ability," said Chris quietly. Sir Bentley nodded.

"What are you talking about?" asked the warden, leaning over to the phones. "I'm calling the police. They could be anywhere by now."

Sir Bentley leaned over and took the receiver from the warden's hand.

"It's okay—we'll deal with it," said Sir Bentley in a calm but firm voice. He placed the phone back in its cradle, and the warden, too shocked to say anything, didn't resist.

Sir Bentley turned to Philip. "Suggestion, please. Immediately. Dulcia Genever has been transferred to another prison, and nothing out of the ordinary happened tonight. Repeat it clearly three times."

Philip nodded and turned to the warden, who was looking increasingly panicked at the strange reaction from his visitors. Chris watched as Philip's eyes glazed over and, after only a minute or so, the warden appeared to relax.

"I've done it," said Philip.

Sir Bentley nodded and turned to the warden. "Mr. Robinson, how are you feeling?"

The warden looked up at Sir Bentley and appeared slightly confused but calm. "Fine, thank you. Can I help you?"

"No, no," said Sir Bentley.

Chris felt Sir Bentley's hand on his shoulder pushing him toward the door.

"We seem to have made a mistake. We'll come back during visiting hours."

The warden nodded, as if a group of children coming for a visit to a prison in the middle of the night was a normal occurrence. "No problem at all. Have a good night," he said brightly.

"Thank you," said Sir Bentley. With a small wave of his hand, he signaled for the pupils to hurry out. Chris and the others walked as quickly as they could out the entrance and into the night, toward the waiting cars.

"Let's go," said Sir Bentley to John as he climbed into the car behind Chris and Lexi, "as quickly as possible."

"Yes, sir," said John as the engine fired up.

"What are we going to do now?" asked Chris as the car waited for the barrier to rise.

"There's nothing you can do. Go straight to bed when we get back to school, and I'll worry about this mess."

· CHAPTER NINE ·

Later that morning, whilst the pupils of Myers Holt were still fast asleep, Ernest was busy making breakfast for his mother at Darkwhisper Manor, an intense look of concentration on his face. Barely a word had passed between the two of them since they had left the prison the night before, though it was clear that she was pleased with him—she had sat next to him on their taxi ride home with her arm uncharacteristically wrapped around his shoulder. There was a time, not so long ago, when that small gesture would have meant the world to him.

"Good morning, Ernest."

Ernest looked up from the frying pan to see his mother standing in the kitchen doorway, looking very different from the night before. Her prison uniform had been replaced with one of her long black gowns, and her hair was washed and glossy, hanging down over her shoulders and framing her pale face. She had also, Ernest noticed, replaced her contact lenses so that her green eyes were once again pure black. Strangely, he found this comforting—it was clear that, as far as she was concerned, they were back to how they had been before everything had happened.

"Good morning, Mother. How are you?"

"Very well rested, thank you."

"There's tea for you on the table. I'm making pancakes, and I picked some strawberries this morning, if you're hungry."

"Yes, very much so. I barely ate while I was away."

Ernest said nothing. Instead, he piled the last of the pancakes onto the warm plate and placed it on the kitchen table, in front of his mother, who was now sitting down, sipping her cup of tea.

Ernest walked back over to the sink and started washing dishes in silence. A few moments later, he looked up to see his mother, though he preferred to think of her as Dulcia now, staring at him.

"Come and sit down, Ernest. We need to talk."

Ernest took a deep breath, put the tea towel down on the counter, and walked back over. He took a seat opposite Dulcia and waited for her to speak.

"How have you been?"

"Fine," said Ernest.

"I'm glad to see you've kept the house clean and tidy while I've been away."

"Yes."

There was an awkward silence. Ernest watched his mother fidget with her cutlery and realized that Dulcia was feeling uncomfortable about the talk that she clearly felt they had to have.

"I suppose it's been a difficult time for you," she said finally.

"Yes."

"But," said Dulcia, "there is good to have come out of your brother's death."

Ernest swallowed hard, trying to keep composed. "Why?"

"Because now you've seen for yourself how evil those people are. By leaving me to those kidnappers all those years ago, they caused this to happen."

Ernest was stunned. He opened his mouth to respond, to remind her that though she hadn't been the one who had killed him, Mortimer would still be alive if he hadn't been following his mother's instructions, but then he remembered that this was not the right time for a confrontation.

If Dulcia noticed the anger in Ernest, she didn't show it.

"Clearly you are stronger than I gave you credit for. Perhaps your brother's death will be the making of you."

"Perhaps it will," said Ernest as calmly as he could manage. Underneath the table, however, his hands were clenched tightly in fists. "And now?"

Dulcia calmly took a sip of her tea and then set it back on the table. "And now, my son, we continue with my plan, of course. Your brother's death won't make any difference—I still have you, and that is all I need. We'll begin training and planning immediately. I've decided that the attacks on the remaining traitors will begin in a month, once the storm has settled."

"What about the boy who killed Mortimer?"

"What do you mean?" asked Dulcia.

"Do you want revenge on him, too? He killed your son . . . my brother."

Dulcia thought about this for a moment and then shrugged her shoulders dismissively. "That boy is of no concern to me. What happened happened. If your brother had been as strong of mind as you are showing yourself to be, he would still be alive. Therefore, the original plan for my own revenge is your only concern. That is what I have spent my life planning, and I'm not going to be distracted by anything else. Understood?"

"Yes, Mother," said Ernest.

"Good," said Dulcia, standing up. "You have an hour of free time. Lessons will begin at eleven in the playroom."

Ernest didn't respond. Instead, he watched in silence as she walked out of the room, and then, once the door had closed, he raised his hands, still curled up in fists, to his face and shuddered with rage. Even after everything that had happened, part of him had still hoped for some explanation, maybe even an apology that would change how he felt. Instead, she had been even more cold and calculating than he had remembered. But, although he was angry with her, his so-called mother, the woman who had adopted him and Mortimer with the sole intention of exacting her own plans for revenge, he was even more furious with himself. If he had only opened his eyes to the true nature of Dulcia sooner, he could have done something. Then, perhaps, his brother would still be alive.

But it was too late, he thought, brushing off the tears that were beginning to form. He stood up and shook his head, as if trying to shake some sense back into himself, and picked up Dulcia's empty plate and mug. At least, he thought, this is the last day that he would ever have to set eyes on her.

Dulcia was waiting for Ernest when he entered the play-room. He checked the clock, and for a moment, before remembering that everything had changed, he felt himself tense up on seeing that he was five minutes late.

"You are lucky that I am in a forgiving mood," said Dulcia. "Take your seat so we can begin."

"No."

Ernest watched his mother's eyes widen in surprise. He felt his heart thumping against his chest and hoped that she wouldn't notice.

"Excuse me?" she asked.

"I said no. I'm not here to study."

Dulcia stared at Ernest, and her look of confusion gave him confidence. There was no turning back now, and for the first time in his life, he truly had nothing to lose.

"What are you here for, then?" asked Dulcia. "To play? I leave for a few days and you think you are in charge? Sit down this very second or else—"

"Or else what? I don't think you are in any position to threaten me."

"Of course I am," said Dulcia, folding her arms. "I am your mother, and—"

"No," said Ernest. "I thought you were. I thought you loved us, even though you didn't really show it, but I was wrong."

Dulcia said nothing, her face not displaying any emotion, as Ernest tried to stop himself from shaking and waited for a response.

Finally, Dulcia spoke. "Very well. I can see that you are angry. I understand—you've lost your brother, and it's made you emotional. So, tell me, Ernest, what do you want from me? Clearly you want something or else you could have left me in prison."

The coldness in his mother's response sent a wave of hatred through him—so forceful that all the fear he had been feeling about this moment disappeared. He stood up tall, and his face hardened.

"I want to enter your mind," he said.

Dulcia raised her eyebrows. "Really. And why would you want to do that?"

"I have some questions, and I don't trust you to answer them honestly."

"I see," said Dulcia. "What kind of questions?"

"About your time at the school—when they trained you to use your Ability. I want to see what it was like."

"Can I ask why?"

"No."

Dulcia thought about this for a moment. "And if I say no?"

"Then I don't help you. You need me more than I need you. I can manage on my own—the last two weeks have proved that—but you, you need me to carry out your plan."

Ernest stared at his mother in surprise as her lips slowly curled up into a smile.

"It seems I have underestimated you," she said finally.

Ernest nodded. For once, he was in complete agreement with her.

"Very well," said Dulcia, putting down the pen she had been holding in her hand. "When do you want to do this?"

"Right now."

"Can we go somewhere more comfortable?"

Ernest looked at the two child-sized desks that his brother and he had spent so many hours studying at. He nodded. "We'll do it in your study."

Dulcia said nothing. Instead, she walked past him and out the door. Ernest turned to follow her, amazed at how simply she had accepted his request. If only he'd known how easily the position of power could be reversed, he thought, he would have done it years ago.

Dulcia turned the handle of the door and stepped inside, and Ernest, his heart pounding harder than ever, his mouth dry, followed her. The room was one of the smaller ones of the house but just as soulless and impersonal, its shelves lined with leather-bound books that had never been read and gold-framed paintings of unknown aristocrats that had been chosen not for their beauty but for the air of importance and wealth they added.

"Let's get this over and done with," said Dulcia, taking a seat in an armchair by the unlit fireplace.

"Yes, Mother," said Ernest, who realized, as he was saying it, that this was the last time he would ever call her that. "Sit back and relax. This shouldn't take long."

Ernest sat in the armchair opposite Dulcia. For a brief moment, he felt an uneasy stirring in the pit of his stomach—guilt? uncertainty? Then he looked up, and there on the mantelpiece was a photograph of him and his brother, side by side two Christmases earlier, and immediately the anger that had been consuming him for the last two weeks came flooding back. Ernest looked away, his eyes cold and vengeful, and stared directly at his mother. The last thing he saw as he let his mind go blank was a brief look from Dulcia, one that he had never seen before—her eyes wide, her face even paler than usual. It was, he thought, as if she knew that this was the beginning of the end.

Ernest stood in the vast room that was the Reception of his mother's mind. It was no different from any other Reception he had visited; the darkness of her mind, he knew, was waiting for him behind the simple wooden door at the other side of where he was stood. Ernest walked over to it quickly, in case his mother decided to have a last-minute change of heart and began to block him. He placed his hand on the handle and took a deep breath, summoning up reserves of courage he hadn't expected to need.

The moment Ernest stepped into the mind of Dulcia Genever, he knew this was not a place he was welcome. Black clouds hung low in the sky, obscuring the tops of the decaying buildings, and a hostile wind whistled and howled around him, snapping at him as if it were a vicious dog protecting his master's home. Ernest knew, from his mother herself, that any thoughts beyond the conscious thoughts in a person's Reception could not be blocked, but that was little comfort—a block wasn't needed in a place so filled with anger. The anger was almost deterrent enough.

"I am doing this for Mortimer," said Ernest to himself as he took his first steps along the street, his eyes darting from left to right as if expecting someone or something to jump out at him from one of the dark alleys between the near-derelict buildings.

"I am doing this for Mortimer," repeated Ernest, louder this time, trying to block out the sound of the howling wind. But as he stepped out into the middle of the junction he had been heading toward he knew that something wasn't right.

This isn't Emotions Street, thought Ernest. To his left, where he would have expected to see a long row of buildings, each housing the memories relating to different emotions, there was nothing but a tall, single tower surrounded by wasteland.

"Where am I?" Ernest wondered as he stepped off the cobbled street and onto the rubble that filled the vast, flat space. Ernest leaned down and picked up a piece of shattered stone. He turned it in his hand, staring at it, his mind racing through all that he had learned about people's minds to find something of an explanation. It was then that he noticed, from the corner of his eye, a sliver of yellow sticking out from a nearby mound of rubble. Ernest dropped the stone in his hand and walked quickly over to the mound. At first, he wasn't sure what he was looking at, but as he began to kick away at the rubble beneath his feet a familiar shape began to appear.

Ernest stared at the door lying on the ground—its once-bright yellow paint faded and peeling and suddenly everything made sense. He was not lost. Even before he had knelt down to brush away the thick layer of dust that covered the brass sign on the door, Ernest knew what he would find: HAPPINESS.

Ernest looked down and realized that the fine dust now coating his shoes was almost certainly all that remained of Dulcia's happy memories. If this had been the mind of any other person, Ernest would have felt a deep sense of pity. Instead, he felt nothing. He kicked the rubble back over the door and continued forward, past the remains of the buildings that had once stored the memories and thoughts of fear, surprise, and excitement, until he reached the single tower, which, as he had already guessed, contained all thoughts and memories of anger. He stopped for a moment at the heavy wooden door of the vast building towering above him, its dark stone walls broken only by a few barred windows. How many of the memories housed inside those walls, Ernest wondered in disgust, were of him and his brother? Then he looked over at the scattered remains of the building opposite, the one that should have housed memories of love, and all his questions about how his mother really felt for him were answered. If he had had any doubt before, he had none now. Dulcia Genever was not a person worth saving.

Ernest walked back onto the road and continued forward. This time, however, there was no feeling of trepidation or fear, only a sense of resolve that was immune to the darkness of this city that he was walking through.

There was only one building on Locations Street, and lucky for Ernest, it was still standing. Whatever damage had been done to Dulcia's mind over the course of her life, her memory of events and places had not been affected. This discovery was a relief: he hadn't had a backup plan.

Ernest walked through the revolving doors into the large, high-ceilinged room that looked like an old, abandoned library. The folders in here were arranged on bookcases that ran in rows parallel to each other. At each end, a dark-green-enameled sign with gold lettering jutted out, indicating which letter of the alphabet the memories were stored under. Ernest breathed a sigh of relief. The only thing he knew, from what his mother had told him in the past, was the name of the school. He looked around, saw the sign for M in the distance, and walked over to it, the sound of his shoes hitting the dark wooden floor echoing eerily about him.

Housed at the far end of the long room, the files for the Myers Holt Academy took up an entire bookcase. Ernest, however, needed only one simple piece of information, and that, he hoped, would be filed under the summary sheet at the beginning of the Myers Holt folders. He pulled out the folder he had been searching for, a black file identical to the thousands of others lining the shelves, and opened it up. There, in bright-black ink that was as clear as if it had been written that morning, was the information he needed:

Myers Holt Academy
40 Montague Street
London WC1 6JO
United Kingdom

It was interesting, Ernest thought, that at that very moment, he had added this information to a similar folder in the Locations building within his own mind. He placed the folder back in the bookcase, unnecessarily, given what was about to happen, and made his way back toward the entrance, glancing every once in a while at the names of the folders he was walking past; Mexico, Machu Picchu, Manchester, Maureen Smith's house—all places that he had never heard his mother speak of and would certainly never hear of from her in the future.

Ernest stopped when he reached the doorway. He turned to face the bookcases, his back against the glass of the revolving door, and closed his eyes. There, in his own mind, was the memory of his twin brother, Mortimer, standing in front of him. Mortimer, who, despite having never shown Ernest any kindness, was the one person who had really known him. Mortimer, who should never have died. There were two people responsible for his death, and now the first of those was about to suffer the consequences.

This is it, he thought, taking a deep breath.

"THIS IS FOR MORTIMER!" he shouted.

Ernest opened his eyes, and staring directly at the bookcase in front of him, he willed it to ignite by placing in his mind an image of the bookcase in flames until, after a few minutes, smoke began to appear. Ernest watched, breathing heavily, as the files in front of him started to smolder, their edges slowly disappearing as the orange line spread outward. Suddenly, flames exploded into the room and made their way, fast and furious, along the bookcase. Ernest imagined them getting bigger, and the flames obeyed, rising up higher and higher, licking the ceiling and leaving trails of soot that circled in and out of each other until, having consumed the entire bookcase, they jumped onto the next one and then the next. Soon the flames joined together to create a single, giant ball of fire. Ernest turned and stepped calmly through the revolving doors, knowing that, as real as the scene appeared to be, this was not his body and he could choose to leave at any time he liked.

Ernest looked back and saw that the fire was barely evident from the street. Small flickers of flame flashed across the thin, rectangular windows. This, he knew, would not be enough.

Ernest stepped back off the sidewalk and onto the cobbled street until he was far enough away to be able to take in the entire building. He started with the door, staring at it until it exploded and sent a whirlwind of glass and metal up into the dark skies and then continued with the stone walls, imagining their destruction until they also began to burst, revealing the savage fire within.

Ernest continued along every street and alleyway in Dulcia's mind, making sure not to miss a single building or cabinet as he followed the route he had planned out a few days earlier. He left a trail of smoldering stone and metal behind him, and finally, there was only one building left. A tall, wide building in the midst of a blanket of flames and dark clouds with a simple sign on its front door: FAMILY.

Ernest considered, for a brief moment, entering the building and finding his own file—a final chance to see for himself what his mother really thought of him. But he decided there was no point in it. He didn't have to see a file to know that she didn't love him. For that reason only, anything else she might have thought of him became irrelevant.

Ernest let his eyes glaze over, and filling his mind with all the rage and anger he had been holding back within himself, he let his mind go to work. The building began to shake from its foundation upward and a long, low moan, as if the building were actually crying out, began to fill the air. Ernest watched while the walls started to bow outward as the force of his mind literally pushed at them from the inside and then, in one gigantic burst of energy, the stones broke free in a tremendous explosion that rocked the ground. As the stone disintegrated with the force of Ernest's Ability, giant fireballs appeared and shot upward and outward in all directions across the now-flattened cityscape of Dulcia Genever's mind.

Ernest turned and walked calmly back to the door leading out to the Reception. He put his hand on the knob, then stopped. He turned his head and looked out over the burning streets and dark mountains of stone one last time before stepping out and closing the door behind him.

Ernest stared at Dulcia, her eyes closed, sitting in the armchair next to the fireplace, exactly as he had last seen her before entering her mind, and wondered if what he thought he had done had really happened.

"Dulcia? Dulcia, wake up," said Ernest without getting up.

Dulcia opened her eyes slowly and blinked. She looked around the room, then back at Ernest. When she finally spoke, any concerns that Ernest had had about his plan not working were forgotten.

"Hello. Who are you?" Dulcia spoke in a gentle voice, apparently confused and with a softness that he had never heard.

"It's not important," said Ernest. He could tell her, he thought, that there was no way she would ever be able to remember anything anybody ever told her again, but there was no point.

"Where am I?"

"That's not important either," said Ernest as he helped Dulcia to her feet. "We have to go."

"Where are we going?"

Ernest didn't speak. Instead, he took Dulcia by the hand and led her out the door, along the corridor, and down the stairs. There, by the front door, he collected Dulcia's coat and helped her into it before leading her out onto the driveway where the taxi he had ordered was waiting.

The driver rolled down his window as Ernest opened the door, guided Dulcia into the back, and placed a plain white envelope in her hand.

"I've been waiting half an hour," said the driver, annoyed. "I was about to go."

"This should cover it," said Ernest, placing a wad of notes into the driver's hand.

The driver looked surprised, though still clearly annoyed. He opened his mouth to speak, but Ernest raised his hand to silence him. Then, his eyes glazing over, he implanted the suggestion he had prepared into the driver's mind.

Minutes later, the taxi drove away toward the destination that Ernest had instructed him to take Dulcia to—the only information the driver would remember of his journey.

Ernest stood and watched as the taxi disappeared from view. He wondered if he should feel something—relief, perhaps—but there was nothing except the urge to rush back inside to prepare for the second and final part of his plan: the death of his brother's killer, Christopher Lane. And now he knew exactly where to find him.

CHAPTER TEN

The lobby of the police station was busy and filled with the chatter of people waiting their turn to be seen by the single officer on duty behind the counter. Standing in line, looking confused, was a striking tall woman wearing a long black coat that matched the black of her eyes. In her hands she was clutching an envelope that had been handed to her at some point by somebody—she couldn't remember who.

"Next," called out the officer.

The woman approached the counter slowly, as if unsure as to what to say or do.

"Yes?" asked the young officer in a clipped voice. There was a long line behind the woman, and the officer was already late for his lunch break.

"Who are you?" asked the woman quietly.

The officer rolled his eyes. "P.C. Hyland. How can I help you?"

"I don't know. Who are you?"

The officer sighed. Another crazy one, he thought. He noticed the envelope in the woman's hands.

"Shall I take that?" he asked.

The woman looked down at the envelope, as if surprised to see it.

"I don't know."

The police officer held his hand out, and the woman passed him the envelope. She stood watching as the officer silently read the note, a look of shock passing across his face.

"Who wrote this?" the officer asked.

The woman looked confused. "Who wrote what?" she asked.

"This," said the officer, holding up the single piece of paper.

"I don't know. What is it?"

The officer stared at the woman for a moment, trying to work out if she was playing games with him, but she didn't react.

"I'll read it to you," said the officer. "'To whom this may concern. The person delivering this letter is Dulcia Genever. Your records should show that she is wanted for a number of crimes, including the attempted murder of Sir Bentley Jones and Prime Minister Edward Banks. I, her son, helped her to escape from Holloway Prison yesterday. You will now find that her mind is completely blank—I'm

sure the people involved will understand what I mean—
and that she is no longer a threat to society. I was forced
into carrying out my mother's plans. I am now being cared
for by relatives who know nothing of what happened. You
can be assured that, with Dulcia Genever in your custody,
the threat to anybody is gone. Yours sincerely, the son of
Dulcia Genever.'"

The woman looked blankly at the officer.

"Are you Dulcia Genever?" the officer asked.

"I don't know."

The officer lifted the hatch on the counter and stepped
out into the waiting area. Before Dulcia had a chance to
react, the officer had grabbed her wrists and placed handcuffs on them.

"Dulcia Genever, I am arresting you on suspicion of
absconding from prison. You do not have to say anything,
but it may harm your defense if you do not mention,
when questioned, something which you later rely on in
court. Anything you do say may be given in evidence. Do
you understand?"

Dulcia Genever looked up at the police officer.

"Where am I?"

The officer sighed. "I guess my lunch is going to have
to wait. Come with me," he said, leading Dulcia Genever
away. Vacant and confused, she shuffled timidly behind
him, completely incapable of understanding that she was
now going to be spending the rest of her life behind bars.

CHAPTER ELEVEN

The prime minister closed the door of his study and turned to face Sir Bentley.

"Are you sure?"

Sir Bentley nodded. "I've just been down to the station. It's her."

"Has she said anything yet?" asked the prime minister.

"She's talking, but . . . it's not her. Her mind is completely wiped. Empty."

"Inferno?"

"Yes, Basic Inferno. Nothing else has been put in her mind. It's completely blank. I didn't even need the Myers Holt pupils to confirm it. You could spot it a mile away— the woman knows nothing."

"So, what do we do? Can we charge her?"

"Yes—there were hundreds of witnesses. We don't need a confession to prove anything. We have the weapon she stabbed John Walker, one of our security guards, with, and just to check, we ran the fingerprints down at the station. It's a match."

"So that's it? It's over?"

Sir Bentley nodded.

The prime minister considered this as he poured one drink for himself and another for his friend and former schoolmate. "Well, Bentley, I think this calls for a quiet celebration."

Sir Bentley took the glass, clinked it against the prime minister's, and sipped.

"What about Myers Holt?" asked the prime minister. "What do you want to do? The children were enrolled to sort out this mess—if it's all finished with, do you want to close the facility?"

"I was hoping to keep it open, if you agree," said Sir Bentley. "We can go back to the way it was in the old days—but with the benefit of knowing the mistakes that were made."

"You want to use the children's Ability to help with police cases?" said the prime minister, checking.

Sir Bentley nodded. "It is very useful."

"Yes, I can imagine it is. It's just that . . ." The prime minister put his glass down on the cabinet and looked up at Sir Bentley. "Bentley, we cannot have a repeat of what happened when I was a pupil nor of what happened at the Antarctic Ball. It could have been worse, I know, but there's no taking away from the fact that a boy died that night. To be honest, I still can't believe we managed to keep it out of the papers." He paused for a moment and then sighed. "I understand how useful the Ability is and the good that can come out of it, but I just can't have any more blood spilled. If you can give me assurances of that, then I agree."

"You have my word," said Sir Bentley.

"Very well, then," said the prime minister after some thought. "To the future of Myers Holt," he said, raising his glass.

"To Myers Holt," said Sir Bentley. The glasses clinked, and the two men took a sip, both relieved that the nightmare had ended.

CHAPTER TWELVE

Chris and his friends celebrated the recapture of Dulcia Genever with a midnight feast under the moonlit Dome. For the first time in a long time, he slept soundly, knowing that the twin brother of the boy he had killed was now safe and happy and being cared for by relatives. To make matters even better, Ms. Lamb had, after three days of Chris polishing her boots and counting out sacks of small change, tired of the dunce corner—or perhaps she had just run out of ideas for punishments—and he had been allowed to return to his desk. Not only that, Hugh Valedictoriat had left permanently for personal reasons—Chris hoped it had nothing to do with him—and Sir Bentley, at the insistence of everybody (nobody, it seemed, had taken much of a liking to Boo Boo the bear), had decided not to hire a replacement. All in all, it had been a good week, filled with swimming, picnics, and interesting lessons. He had even had a long chat with Miss Sonata, who had been horrified to hear about his mother's relapse over the holidays and had promised that she would take it upon herself to make sure more help would be made available for her.

Best of all, Chris now had no fear of his Ability. The anger and anxiety he had been feeling had disappeared the instant he had heard that the boy was well. It didn't change the fact that he had killed the other boy, and he knew it was something he would remember for the rest of his life, but he was ready to move on. In fact, he thought as he made his way to the classroom with a smile on his face, he was actually looking forward to learning how they would be using their Ability to solve crimes.

"This is going to be excellent," said Rex. "I can see the headline already: 'Rex King, Crime-Solving Superhero.'"

Everybody turned to Lexi, waiting for her to fire back at Rex with a smart comment, but she didn't say a word.

"Are you okay?" asked Daisy.

Lexi looked up, her thoughts interrupted, and saw that everybody was staring at her. "What? Oh, yeah, I'm fine. Just a bit tired—I stayed up last night memorizing all the law books in the library. I think they'll come in useful when I start working as an agent."

"You already are a government agent," pointed out Philip.

"Right, yeah. I mean a proper one—you know, like James Bond."

"Really, Frizzo, when are you going to stop going on

about James Bond? That's all you've done since you came back to school. James Bond this, James Bond that. You should marry him if you love him so much," said Rex, sounding, Chris thought, a little jealous.

Lexi's eyes narrowed. "I don't love him—I just want his job. And anyway, he's not even real."

"Yeah, whatever," said Rex as Lexi walked away. "Lexi and Bond, sitting in a tree, k-i-s-s . . ."

"Rex!" shouted Lexi, turning back, her face flushed in anger.

Rex shrugged his shoulders. "Only joking. Don't be so irritable."

Lexi glared at Rex, then turned away and stormed off ahead.

Sebastian turned to Rex. "I can provide you with some advice on the subject of love," he said as they continued down the corridor. "You appear to have difficulties."

"First," said Rex, stopping in his tracks, "I'm not having any difficulties with anything. Second, and no offense, Romeo, but I don't think a twelve-year-old dressed up as a clown is going to know much about how to pick up girls."

"Rex! That's mean!" said Daisy, putting her hand on the arm of Sebastian's orange suit. "Don't listen to him, Sebastian. I think you look lovely."

Sebastian turned to Rex so that Daisy couldn't see him, and gave him a wink. "I'm available if you change your mind."

Chris laughed as Rex turned a deep shade of red and folded his arms.

"Come on, hurry up," said Chris to Rex, rushing out

through the doors of the Dome. "He's only joking with you. Let's get to class—Sir Bentley won't be happy if we're late."

Rex huffed and mumbled something under his breath but followed Chris without argument.

"Welcome, everybody," said Sir Bentley as they all rushed in through the classroom door. "Quickly, to your seats. We have a lot to get through."

Chris sat down at his desk and saw that sitting by the wall next to him were Ron and John. Chris could tell, even though he was wearing his sunglasses, that Ron was even more on edge than usual, his knees jiggling nervously and his arms folded stiffly. John, on the other hand, looked more relaxed and not at all uncomfortable, which was strange, thought Chris, given that he was about ten sizes too big for the chair he was sitting in.

"Hi," said Chris as he leaned over and pulled out his pencil case from his bag.

John nodded back at him, but Ron didn't respond. John pointed with his thumb in the direction of Ron. "He doesn't like being in a classroom. Bad experi—"

"Shh!" whispered Ron, nudging John in the side. Sir Bentley cleared his throat.

Chris turned back to face the front of the class.

"As you can all see, we have guests today. John and Ron will be joining us—I thought it would be good for them to see the kind of thing you'll be doing, especially as they'll be escorting you on your assignments."

Everybody except Ron seemed pleased about this.

"The police commissioner, Sir Neville Loosier, and I have been discussing how best to use your talents, and we have come up with the first set of cases for you to handle. Any questions?"

Nobody said anything.

"So, to your first assignment—a robbery."

Chris grinned at Philip. This was what they had all been waiting for!

Sir Bentley picked up a newspaper from his desk and held up the front page for them all to see.

"This," he said, pointing to a picture of what was, as far as Chris could tell, a loaf of bread, "is a piece of art created by one of the most sought-after artists of the moment, Kingston Khan."

Rex put up his hand.

"Yes?" said Sir Bentley.

"It's a loaf of bread."

"Well spotted, Rex. It is, in fact, made of clay. Inside, however, are approximately ten million pounds' worth of diamonds."

"I can't see them," said Lexi, squinting her eyes at the picture.

"No," said Sir Bentley. "Apparently, that's what makes it art. The artist calls it . . . hold on, I'll have to read this"— Sir Bentley turned the paper round and read the caption— "*The Guilt of the Rich.*"

"Eh?" said Rex, echoing exactly what Chris and the others were thinking.

Sir Bentley shrugged his shoulders. "Don't ask me to explain—I really have no idea. For the purposes of what we're doing, all you need to know is what it looks like and that it's very valuable indeed—Khan's last, um, sculpture, sold for twelve millions pounds. This one was valued in the region of thirty million—though probably a lot more since it won the Kitchner Prize last night—not long before it was stolen from the gallery."

"How was it stolen—wasn't there any security?" asked Chris.

"Yes, plenty of it. Unfortunately, there were no cameras where the four finalists' work was being displayed, but the gallery itself was under heavy security—that's why we think it must have been an inside job."

"What is the definition of this?" asked Sebastian.

"'Inside job,'" explained Sir Bentley, "means that the theft was carried out by somebody who either works for or has help from someone within the premises. The winner was announced at nine o'clock in the evening. The artwork was stolen approximately three hours later. By this time, most people had left, though Kingston Khan and the three runners-up were still in the gallery with a few others, including the gallery owners. Khan's sculpture and the work of the three other finalists were in another room, which was being guarded by two security guards. One of the runners-up of the prize, Valentino Brick, went in to check on his own piece and was attacked. When he came to, he alerted security, who immediately noticed that the winning sculpture had been stolen and raised the alarm. The guards stationed outside the room claim that they saw nothing, as did the guards at the gallery entrance who had been checking everybody coming in and out. They insist that nobody could have left with it. The police are stumped—the only explanation is that at least one of the guards is lying. Your task will be to interview all the people who were there last night and find out if any of them had anything to do with the theft. Questions?"

"What happened to the artist? Is he hurt?" asked Daisy.

"Valentino Brick? Nothing too serious, just a bit of a gash across his head. The police have spoken to him, but all he remembers is hearing a sound and turning around to see a tall man in a black jacket and balaclava. The next thing he remembers is waking up on the floor. He will be there, so you can check to see if there's anything he saw that he doesn't remember."

"Do they know we're going to be accessing their minds?" asked Philip, surprised.

"No, no," said Sir Bentley. "They all think that they're being interviewed by the police. Nobody knows anything about the purpose of your visit with the exception of the commissioner. We're just going to say that you are on a school visit, to the gallery. There are"—Sir Bentley picked up a notebook from the table and flicked through it until he found the page he was looking for—"eighteen people to Mind Access in all, including the four artists: all the people who were inside the gallery at the time of the robbery. So, when you enter these people's minds, where will you go to find this information? Anybody? Yes, Lexi?"

"In the Guilt building on Emotions Street?"

"Possibly. But that, of course, depends on the person feeling guilty about what they did and, sadly, that is not always the case. So, it could be there, but it's not guaranteed. Any other suggestions?"

"Calendar Street?" asked Philip.

"That would make sense except that we don't know exactly what we're looking for; nor do we know the exact time. We believe it's unlikely that the person who committed the robbery will actually be interviewed, so we're concentrating on looking for the person who helped the thief. Therefore, the only way to be absolutely certain is to have a look in the Crimes and Misdemeanors building on the Road of Significant Events. I'm surprised nobody worked that out."

Chris kicked himself for not thinking of this, but up until recently, that was not a part of the mind map that they had spent much time learning about.

"Where is that building, Chris?"

"Off People Street, the next right turn after Celebrations Lane."

"Good. Once in the building, you should find a filing cabinet labeled 'Thefts,' possibly more than one, depending on how busy the person has been, and inside, folders sorted in chronological order relating to individual thefts."

"We're going today?"

"Yes—time is of the essence in crimes such as these. Now, it's important for you to be aware that all the employees will have folders with thoughts about the theft. However, most of the memories will be about discussing it or reading about it in the newspapers. We're obviously only interested in memories that involve either that person stealing the piece or telling somebody how to do it. Understood?"

Everybody nodded.

"Well, there's not really much more to say. You'll all be given a report form to fill out for each person you access. You'll need to complete it even if the person had nothing to do with it—it's highly unlikely but possible you'll miss something that is significant to the police investigation team. Yes, Chris?"

"Are you coming with us?"

"Unfortunately not. I have work to do. Ms. Lamb will accompany you."

Sir Bentley ignored the groans from the pupils. "That's all. Ron and John will be taking you. What time are they expecting us?"

Ron's hand shot up in the air.

"No need for that, Ron," said Sir Bentley. "That's just for the pupils."

"Right, of course," said Ron, quickly lowering his hand. "Midday arrival. Departing Myers Holt at eleven thirty a.m. sharp. Rendezvous at the front door."

"Excellent. Well, free time until then, though I'd recommend you all take a moment to run through everything that I said in the lesson—I know you'll remember it word for word. You can ask Ms. Lamb any questions you think of on the way."

"Yes, sir," they all responded.

"Off you go, then," said Sir Bentley, waving them out.

· CHAPTER THIRTEEN ·

"Don't go anywhere you're not supposed to, don't talk unless you're spoken to, don't pick your noses, and *do not* do anything to embarrass me," said Ms. Lamb as their new minibus, driven by John, pulled up outside the art gallery.

"Yes, Ms. Lamb," they all said dutifully, though Chris couldn't help but roll his eyes at Philip, who smiled back.

"I'll park, then meet you inside," said John while Ron, who had completed his security assessment of their surroundings, opened up the passenger door to let them all out.

Chris walked up to the gallery, which, despite it having hosted one of the art world's most prestigious prizes the night before, was mostly empty, closed on account of the robbery.

Ms. Lamb approached one of the two police officers stationed outside the front and, with the same angry tone of voice that Chris had thought was reserved just for them, demanded to be allowed in.

"The gallery is closed," said the first police officer, a young woman in pristine uniform.

"Yes, I can see that," said Ms. Lamb, looking at the large sign on the door. "I am capable of reading. Now let us in—we are expected."

"I'm sorry, my job is to make sure nobody comes in or out without authorization."

"You won't have a job if you don't let us in right now."

Chris cringed, and they all looked away in embarrassment at the way Ms. Lamb was acting.

"If you don't leave immediately, we will be forced to take action," said the second officer, scowling.

"Don't be ridiculous," said Ms. Lamb, clearly not in the slightest bit intimidated. "Go and get Sir Neville Loosier right now—I know he's inside."

Both police officers suddenly looked very nervous at the sound of the commissioner's name.

Without another word, the first officer disappeared into the gallery, and a few minutes later, he emerged behind a tall man who had slicked-black hair and wore a gray suit.

"Commissioner," said Ms. Lamb, "these officers of yours should be dismissed for their incompetence."

If the commissioner was surprised by Ms. Lamb's request, he didn't show it. "Just doing their job," he said calmly as he waved them through the glass doors.

"It's good to meet you all," he said once they had

stopped in the large white reception area. He shook each of their hands in turn. "I've been looking forward to seeing your work."

"Where will they be working?" snapped Ms. Lamb.

The commissioner gave Ms. Lamb a disapproving glance before leading them down a long corridor, through a set of double doors, and into another white room.

"This," he said, turning to the pupils, "is where the incident occurred. The three pieces you can see are by the other finalists. I'll give you a quick tour and explain where everything happened, in case it helps."

Chris followed the commissioner as he walked over to a large ball of green yarn sitting on a white plinth.

"This," explained the commissioner, "is *The Sheep's Lament* by Emily Buckworth. She was in the restaurant at the time of the robbery, along with Kingston Khan—whose piece as you know, was stolen—and the other finalist, Ann Abernathy. This is her piece."

Chris approached the large photograph hanging on the wall and looked up at it, confused. It was, as far as he could tell, completely black.

"It's called *A Portrait of Death as a Young Man*," explained the commissioner.

"I don't get modern art," said Chris to Rex, who was standing next to him.

"I think it's brilliant," said Rex, though Chris wasn't sure if he was being sarcastic.

"Finally," said the commissioner as he pointed at a large white canvas with a single black dot in the middle, "this is Valentino Brick's entry. It's called *This Is the Center of the Universe.*

As I said, he was the only person in the room when the robbery occurred, and he was standing right . . . here."

Chris looked down at the splatter of blood on the floor, cordoned off by a square of police tape.

"That, I'm afraid, is all we can tell you. The attack occurred at midnight. I hope that you'll be able to tell me more after the interviews."

"Utter rubbish!" said Ms. Lamb.

Everybody turned to look at her and only then realized that she was not talking to the commissioner, but looking at the ball of green yarn.

"That, madam, is not a very pleasant thing to say."

Chris turned to see a man in a blue velvet suit with a wild mass of white hair standing at the room's entrance.

"I am entitled to my opinion," said Ms. Lamb curtly.

"Excellent suit," said the man, looking at Sebastian's pink suit.

Sebastian grinned. "I am much obliged. Yours is most tremendous also."

"At least someone here has good taste," said the man. He narrowed his eyes in the direction of Ms. Lamb.

"This, children, is Kingston Khan," said the commissioner.

"Sorry about your bread getting stolen," said Lexi.

"Well, not your fault, but thank you," said Kingston as he shook Lexi's hand. "My goodness—what spectacular green eyes!"

Lexi stood awkwardly, blushing, while Kingston stared at her intently, as if he were taking notes in his head.

"And this," said the commissioner, interrupting, "is Valentino Brick."

Chris turned to see a man dressed head to toe in black, his black hair plastered down across his head with what Chris imagined must have been an entire tub of hair wax. Just below his hairline, a large bandage was taped to his forehead, some dried blood visible on it.

"Yes, yes. You must all be very thrilled," said Valentino without looking at any of them. "I am a busy man, commissioner. How long do you intend to keep me here?"

"Just a little while longer, Mr. Brick. Thank you so much for your patience. I'll go and see how everything is getting on and see what we can do. In the meantime, Mr. Brick, we've arranged lunch for you in the restaurant. Now, children, would you follow me?"

"I'm afraid this is the best we could do," said the commissioner, leading Chris and the others into a small room crammed full of cleaning equipment. A large table had been placed in the center. Chris pushed his way past a line of mops and wedged himself into his seat.

"I believe you have the report forms?" asked the commissioner.

Ms. Lamb rolled her eyes, as if the question were absurd. "Of course."

"Very well, I'll leave you to it. The interviews will start immediately. I have a list here of all the names—Sir Bentley has already assigned which of you will be, erm, how do you say it?"

"Mind Accessing?" asked Philip.

"That's it. Sir Bentley has drawn up a schedule to make sure that nobody is too overworked. I believe using this

Ability of yours can be quite tiring. So . . . ," said the commissioner, reading from a piece of paper, "Chris and Daisy, you will go first."

Chris looked over at Ms. Lamb and saw that she was glowering at him. He looked away quickly but couldn't help a small smile. He was fairly certain that she wouldn't have used him at all, but now she was left with no choice.

"Yes, sir," he said as Ms. Lamb slammed a pencil and report form in front of him.

The first interviewee, one of the two guards, was clearly nervous as he took his seat in the next room, completely unaware that not only was he about to be interviewed by police but he was also about to have his mind accessed by a pair of children sitting only a few feet away.

It was, however, obvious to Chris within only a few minutes of searching through the man's mind that he had nothing to do with the robbery and that the real reason for his nerves was that he had fallen asleep at the job, peacefully dreaming about fishing for salmon when he should have been keeping guard over one of modern art's most expensive pieces of work.

Chris wrote down the little that he had found and handed his form in to Ms. Lamb, who took it silently and waited for Daisy to finish hers.

"Next," said Ms. Lamb, pointing at Sebastian and Lexi.

And so the time passed in silence as each pair took turns accessing the minds of the guards and then the gallery owners. Their efforts proved fruitless.

"This is ridiculous," said Ms. Lamb, reading through all

the reports. "Somebody must know something. You need to try harder."

Chris felt himself tense. Without actually making anything up, they couldn't change what they found.

The commissioner, who had been popping his head in at the end of every interview to find out about their progress, appeared once again.

"Nothing?"

Ms. Lamb shook her head. "No. Nothing at all."

"Well, the only people left are the four artists. We'll start with Valentino Brick—he's getting restless."

"Getting restless" was something of an understatement. Chris watched, in his mind, as Valentino entered the room next to them, shouting and waving his arms about in frustration.

"Are you doing this to wind me up?" he snarled at the commissioner. "I am an artist—I need freedom, and you are caging me in like a wild animal."

Chris looked over at Daisy, who smiled back at him. Fortunately, as Ms. Lamb couldn't see into the adjoining room, or into their minds, she just had to sit in silence and wait for them to do their work in their own time.

"Ready?" asked Daisy. Chris nodded and turned his head toward the far wall. He let his mind wander until all he could see was Valentino Brick, seated and silently mouthing abuse at the policemen in front of him. Chris let his eyes glaze over.

The first thing Chris saw, on entering Valentino's Reception, was an explosion of color. Unlike any other Reception he had visited, Valentino Brick did not appear to view his surroundings as a photograph. Instead, the policemen in front of him were blocks of dark colors, their faces red and melting, and their voices, which Chris knew were level and calm, sounded in here like screeching cats.

"This is so strange," said Daisy, walking up to Chris.

"If this is his Reception," said Chris, walking over to the spinning glass doors at the other end of the room, where thoughts of bold colors were pouring in, one after the other in a never-ending stream, "imagine what the other side of this is going to look like."

"Wait! Don't go without me!" said Daisy, running through the blocks of color to catch up.

"Ready?" asked Chris, eager to get inside.

Daisy nodded.

"Okay, one . . . two . . . three . . . go!"

Chris jumped in first as a gap appeared between the revolving doors. He had intended to run round to the other side, but the doors were moving faster than he had expected and he found himself slammed up against the glass and spinning around, colors swirling about him, until, suddenly, he saw his opportunity and pushed himself forward.

For a moment, Chris wasn't sure if he'd made it through. He didn't know where else he could be, but this was like no mind he had ever seen. Or not seen. There were no buildings, no streets. Just white. A pure and brilliant white that surrounded him so completely, he wasn't sure if he was looking at a wall or a distant sky. He put his hand up in front of himself and saw that it was perfectly in focus. So he wasn't in a cloud of fog, he thought. He looked around, squinting to try to make out anything at all, but there was nothing. He was still sitting on the white floor looking confused when Daisy came flying out from behind him and landed by his side.

"Where are we?" she asked, shielding her eyes with her hands and looking around.

He turned and saw the door behind him, as if hovering in midair, a whirlwind of colors swirling violently against the spinning glass panes.

"I don't know," he said at last. "Do you think his mind is empty?"

Daisy considered this and then shook her head. "It can't be. We heard him talk to the commissioner—it would have been obvious if his mind were empty."

Chris nodded in agreement.

"So, what shall we do—turn around and go back?"

"No way," said Chris immediately, "Ms. Lamb doesn't need any more reason to have a go at me. Let's just walk around a bit. There's got to be something here."

Chris stood up.

"It looks like you're floating," said Daisy, giggling.

Chris smiled. "Come on, let's go. I reckon we try to follow the map in our own minds. If we go straight," he said, pointing into the white, "we should walk onto People Street—the Family building should be in front of us. If we don't see anything, we'll turn right and see if we find anything—there's got to be something on Arts Avenue."

"Okay," said Daisy.

"Oh, and don't forget to keep an eye on the doors to Reception," continued Chris. "We don't want to get lost in here forever."

Daisy's eyes widened in horror.

"It's all right. It's not going to happen."

"Okay," said Daisy, walking over and taking Chris's hand. "Just don't leave me alone."

"I won't," he said, blushing, glad that Rex wasn't with them—Chris would never have heard the end of it. "Ready?"

Daisy nodded.

Chris took a deep breath and stepped forward. He was acting braver than he felt for Daisy's sake but, really, he had no idea what to expect, and he just hoped that he wasn't leading them into trouble. He looked down at his feet as he took one step onto the white floor, and then another and then . . .

Daisy pulled on Chris's arm suddenly, yanking him backward.

"What was that?" she asked.

"What was what?" asked Chris, confused. He looked around but could see nothing.

"Something just fell on your head."

"What? I didn't feel anything," he said, brushing his hand over his hair. Then he looked at Daisy, who was staring at his hand in horror.

"You're bleeding," she whispered.

Chris looked down at his hand, which was covered in dark red, and his heart jumped. He ran his hand again through his hair, but he couldn't feel anything. Even more confusing was that he hadn't thought it was possible to get hurt in somebody's mind.

"I don't think it's my blood," said Chris.

"Let's go back," said Daisy, pulling at Chris's sleeve.

"You go," he said. "I'm just going to have a bit more of a look."

"I'm not leaving you here!" said Daisy.

"Just two minutes," said Chris.

Daisy closed her eyes and took a deep breath. "Fine," she said. "I'm coming with you."

She took Chris's hand once more, and squeezing it tight, they both stepped forward.

Plop.

Chris's head snapped round, and there, on the ground, was a small dark-blue puddle. He looked up but could see nothing.

Daisy remained quiet as Chris knelt down to look at the puddle more closely. Then, as Daisy took a sharp breath, he reached out and touched it.

"It's paint," he said, surprised.

"Paint?"

"I think so," said Chris, rubbing the blue smear between his fingers.

He stood up and took another step forward.

Plop. Plop. Plop.

Chris looked around, amazed, as drops started falling in front of them, creating splotches of red, green, and pink. He took another step forward, and as he did so, the drops started to fall more frequently.

Chris watched, fascinated, as the rain of color began to fall, creating puddles on the ground that swirled as they landed on top of each other. He looked over at Daisy, who was staring down at a bright-green splatter on her dress.

"Don't worry," said Chris, "I don't think it will be there when we leave his mind."

"Okay," said Daisy, reassured. "Let's keep going."

The two of them took another step forward and then another and then, suddenly, the downpour started, as if a shower above them had been turned on to full power.

Chris and Daisy looked at each other in amazement as the rain grew in intensity. The drops now blurred as they fell hard and fast, covering them in a rainbow of paint. He watched as Daisy's blond hair quickly became a sodden mess of multicolored stripes that dripped down her face.

Daisy looked down at her dress and arms and then back up at Chris. He wondered what to say, not sure if she was upset or frightened, when suddenly, her face broke into a huge grin and she started laughing.

"This is *amazing!*" she shouted, spinning round in the rain.

Relieved, Chris laughed and jumped into a large puddle that was forming in front of him. The paint flew up and landed all over Daisy. She went to kick at the puddle to splash him, but she slipped and fell down, screaming with laughter.

Chris rushed over, the rain still falling hard and heavy, to help her up. Daisy took his hand, and then, with an evil grin he hadn't seen before, she pulled his arm and he felt himself tumble downward, face first, into a large puddle of swirling purple and turquoise.

"You're in trouble!" he said, reaching out to splash her, before realizing that she was no longer looking at him.

"What?" he asked, turning his head to see what Daisy was looking at. "Ohhhh . . ."

There, revealing itself as the rain fell, was a large building, its top half covered in colorful paint that was dripping down over the doors and windows of the bottom half.

"The buildings appear as you walk through the mind," said Chris to himself as he stood up and turned around to face where they had come from. He saw that the rain was falling only around where they stood and that, behind them, the trail of paint was quickly disappearing, leaving the floor crisp and white once again.

"It's the Family building, just like you said," called Daisy through the falling rain as she inspected the now-red-and-orange sign on the front door.

"Come on," said Chris, with renewed enthusiasm for their mission now that he understood what was happening. "Let's see if we can find the Crimes and Misdemeanors building."

Chris waited for Daisy to catch up with him, and they started walking in the direction of Crime Alley, the rain turning to follow them.

"Wow," said Daisy as they walked slowly forward, watching the paint fall in front of them to reveal the once-invisible buildings.

Chris wiped the paint from his face with the back of his hand and continued onward, taking Daisy by the hand to hurry her up.

They began to run, splashing through the colors, and the rain quickened also, leading the way.

"Down here," said Chris, turning right down a small alleyway that appeared only seconds earlier.

Chris stopped and looked ahead of him at the plain white background. He took a step forward and another until the rain suddenly began to reveal a building not much larger than Chris's own house.

Chris waited silently with Daisy by his side, both of them dripping wet as paint of every color poured down over them. They watched as the colors slid down the sides of the building's walls, revealing the doorway.

"How long have we been in here?" asked Chris as he walked up to the door and turned the handle.

"I don't know," said Daisy. "Maybe ten minutes?"

Chris opened the door. "We'd better be quick, then. Ms. Lamb's going to kill us if we keep them waiting."

He stepped back to let Daisy through first.

"Chris—look!"

Chris stepped inside and looked around. The room was crisp and white, with only a single bookcase that curved around the room from one end to the other. Unlike in any other building Chris had entered, here the memories were stored in folders of different colors that ran from the lightest shade, white, to black at the other end. And, Chris noticed immediately, there was not a single label to be seen. He turned to Daisy and realized that she wasn't looking at the room but down at herself—now miraculously clean, her dress back to its original pale pink and her blond hair clean and dry. He looked down at himself and saw that all traces of paint had also disappeared from him.

"I love this place," said Daisy, smiling. She walked up to

the bookshelf. "Now, what's the name of the stolen art? *The Guilt of the Rich*, is that right?"

"Yes, but that's not going to help you much," said Chris. "They're not labeled."

"Oh . . . you're right," said Daisy, inspecting the spines of the folders. "So, how do we find it?"

"Um, I'm not sure," said Chris, pulling out a folder at random—a deep green one with, he saw to his surprise, a picture of a car drawn on it. He opened it up, and immediately, the room around them darkened. At first, it wasn't clear to Chris what he was looking at, but as the memory began to move, he saw that Valentino was hiding under a table in a large, bright classroom decorated with painted handprints, numbers, and letters pinned to the walls. In the far corner, Chris watched as a small boy, about five years old, left the room. The door closed behind him, and Valentino jumped out and ran over to the wall of coats and bags. The memory scanned the name tags above the hooks until Valentino found what he was looking for: a dark-blue backpack with a train on it. The room spun round quickly as Valentino checked he was on his own, then, satisfied the coast was clear, his two chubby little hands came into view and reached out to unzip the bag. He peered inside, and there, wedged between a half-eaten sandwich and a banana was a bright-green toy car. Valentino reached into the bag, pulled out the car, and carefully tucked it in his gray trouser pocket. He raised his hands and zipped the bag closed. A little giggle filled the room as Valentino chuckled to himself and then skipped off in the direction of the door.

"Oh, I get it!" said Chris, closing the folder. The light returned to the room, and Daisy appeared before him, looking rather cross.

"What? That he's a thief?"

"Well, he was only little," said Chris.

"That's no excuse," said Daisy indignantly.

"Anyway," said Chris, "that's not what I meant. Did you see the color of the car?"

"Yes, green. Why—oh!"

Chris smiled. "He doesn't file things alphabetically, he files them by color."

Chris put the folder back onto the bookshelf and walked up to the lighter end of the bookcase.

"Do you remember the exact color of the bread sculpture?" he asked. "I think it was kind of orange, right?"

"Not that dark," said Daisy, looking at the file Chris was reaching toward. "Maybe this one?"

Chris nodded and watched as Daisy pulled out a folder. She looked at the picture on the front, a pencil, and shook her head. "Not this one. How many things has he stolen?" asked Daisy.

Chris didn't say anything. He was thinking about the time he had stolen the twenty-pound note from his teacher and that there were surely quite a few files in this building in his own mind. He made a mental note never to allow Daisy to have a look around there—she'd probably never speak to him again.

"Here it is!" said Daisy, shaking Chris from his thoughts. She held out a pale-orange, almost brown, folder with a picture of a loaf of bread on the front. Chris watched as

Daisy opened it. The room darkened, and before them appeared the gallery entrance, exactly as they had seen it earlier, except darker.

Chris watched as Valentino crept past the sleeping guard whose mind Chris had accessed earlier and then sneaked into the main gallery room, closing the doors behind him. Once inside, he turned around and looked at the four spotlit pieces until his eyes came to rest on his own creation—*This Is the Center of the Universe*—the large white canvas with a single black dot in its center.

"My baby," he purred softly, walking over to his work. Chris watched, confused, as Valentino began to stroke the canvas gently.

"That's a bit weird," said Chris.

"Very," agreed Daisy.

Valentino stroked the canvas a while longer and then, finally, turned to face the winner—the ceramic loaf of bread standing in the middle of the room on a square white plinth. The room immediately turned cold.

"So this," he hissed, "is what those judges think is art?"

Valentino approached the loaf of bread and stood over it with narrowed eyes, his mouth twitching. "What do those silly little people know about art? They wouldn't know genius if it hit them in the face. How dare they judge my work to be inferior to this . . . this . . . monstrosity!"

Chris watched carefully as the artist began to circle the plinth until, suddenly, he reached over and grabbed the sculpture.

"He's stealing it!" said Daisy. Chris was about to nod his head in agreement when, without warning, Valentino raised the ceramic bread up with both hands and smashed it against his forehead.

Chris and Daisy gasped.

"That's why he had the bandage on his head!" said Chris as Valentino surveyed the large fragments of sculpture lying on the floor amongst the hundreds of sparkling diamonds.

Then, with a low growl, Valentino lifted his foot and began to stomp on the pieces.

"This," snarled Valentino, "is not"—he brought his boot down again with a thud and a *crunch!*—"art!"

"He's crazy!" said Daisy.

Chris couldn't believe what he was seeing. He and Daisy watched in quiet fascination until the last piece of pottery was completely disintegrated, the diamonds now sitting in a pile of fine dust.

"That's better," said Valentino finally, his voice back to normal. He bent down and began to scoop the dust and diamonds into his hand and then into the pockets of his trousers until all the evidence had disappeared. Then, having checked the floor for any missed diamonds or fragments, he walked over to the room's double doors and opened them.

"I'VE BEEN ATTACKED!" he screamed, quite believably, Chris thought.

The sleeping guard jumped up, startled. *"What?"*

"I've been attacked by robbers! Call the police!"

The guard looked horrified as the enormity of what was happening hit him. He looked through the double doors at the empty plinth in the center of the room and rushed toward it, leaving Valentino alone.

Valentino looked around to check that he was on his own and then ran over to the entrance of the restrooms. Chris and Daisy both gasped as they watched the artist slide his hands into his trouser pockets and empty out a few million pounds' worth of diamonds into a bin.

The last thing Chris heard as he closed the folder was the quiet sound of giggling, the same giggling he had heard when the five-year-old Valentino had run off with his classmate's prized toy.

"I can't believe it," said Chris, turning to Daisy as the image disappeared.

"I can," said Daisy. "He was a horrible boy—I'm not surprised he turned into a horrible, jealous man."

"He didn't even keep the diamonds," said Chris.

"No—he just wanted to be spiteful. I'm glad he didn't win."

"Me too," said Chris, placing the folder back on the shelf and walking over to the door. "I wonder what will happen when we report back?"

"Well, maybe he'll finally learn his lesson," said Daisy with a forcefulness that surprised Chris.

"I like tough Daisy," he said, smiling.

Daisy blushed. "I'm not tough. It's just about right and wrong. Come on," she said, quickly changing the subject, "let's go back."

Chris nodded, then followed Daisy back out into the torrential rainbow-colored rain.

· CHAPTER FOURTEEN ·

"I did the world a favor!" screamed Valentino Brick as he was led out into the Kitchner Gallery's foyer in handcuffs. The two policemen jostled him toward the door, where a police van was waiting on the other side.

Chris and the other pupils stood silently against a wall and watched as Valentino was dragged past them, completely unaware that it was these twelve-year-olds who had uncovered his spiteful crime. Valentino was bundled out of the building, down the steps, and into the waiting police van, his screams of protest suddenly silent as the van doors shut behind him.

Chris looked round to see the commissioner approaching them, smiling. He waved them into a circle so that he could speak to them without anybody else hearing what he was saying.

"That was truly marvelous," he said, shaking Chris's hand, then Daisy's. "Not much surprises me, but this—well, this is something I won't forget."

Chris grinned and looked at Daisy, who was beaming also.

"You've outdone yourselves," continued the commissioner. "I look forward to the next assignment."

This time, he shook hands with all of them, then with Ron and John and, finally, Ms. Lamb, who, Chris noticed, was actually looking quite pleased.

As they drove back to the school in silence—John's usual blasting of country music having been banned by Ms. Lamb—any hopes that Chris might have had that his success at the gallery would earn him even one day of peace from Ms. Lamb were dashed.

"Wipe that smirk off your face," she said, turning round to glare at Chris. "It was the luck of the draw. Any of the other imbeciles would have found the same information if they had entered that man's mind instead."

Chris didn't say anything, but in the only way he could be defiant without getting into trouble, he didn't apologize for his success either; after all, he didn't feel he had done anything wrong.

"I demand an apology," said Ms. Lamb. Chris looked over at Philip, who was leaning forward so that Ms. Lamb wouldn't see him as he pulled faces. Although nobody said anything in his defense, and he couldn't blame them one bit—it would only have made the situation worse—he was nevertheless grateful to know that he had their support, and it made him feel stronger.

"I don't know what I'm apologizing for," said Chris as calmly as he could manage.

"You are apologizing for your smugness, you disrespectful little . . ." Furious, she stood up suddenly from her seat and immediately noticed Philip pulling faces. Caught red handed, Philip leaped back in his seat.

There was a moment of tense silence as Ms. Lamb glared at Philip, her eyes narrowed and her lips pressed tight in anger.

"How . . . dare . . . you," she said finally.

"I'm—I'm sorry. I wasn't copying you . . . I had an itch on my face . . . it was . . ."

"I know exactly what you were doing, boy," said Ms. Lamb, seething with anger.

"Can you sit down and put your seat belt on please?" called out Ron from the front.

Ms. Lamb ignored him as she turned to address the pupils.

"You are all," she said slowly as she stared at each one of them in turn, "disrespectful, lazy, good-for-nothings. I have given every one of you a pretty easy ride up until now, but from this moment on, I give you my word that I am going to make this year the least enjoyable, most unpleasant time that any of you have ever experienced in your pathetic, pampered little lives. And I'll begin by giving you all detention every day this week. Except for you . . ."

Nobody said anything as Ms. Lamb leaned down to face Chris. "I haven't liked your cocksure attitude from the day I set eyes on you. For that, you get three weeks' detention."

Ms. Lamb's heavily made-up face moved in closer, and Chris instinctively turned his head away in the direction of Philip and the window.

"Look at me when I'm talking to you!" she shouted, a bit of spit flying from her mouth onto the side of Chris's face.

But Chris didn't respond, for at that very moment, something caught his eye. He squinted as Ms. Lamb's voice faded out and everything around him disappeared— all except the face of a pale young boy standing by a lamp-post, staring directly at him, his eyes following him as the bus moved slowly forward. Was it true, he wondered, or was he just seeing things? Perhaps he wasn't as fine as he had thought. He blinked and shook his head, but the boy was still very much there. Chris's heart stopped, and then, realizing they were going to lose sight of him, he reached down, undid the buckle of his seat belt, and jumped up across a startled Philip to look out the window behind them as the minibus drove on.

"WHAT ARE—" shouted Ms. Lamb.

"It's the boy!" said Chris, ignoring her. "John! Stop the bus! It's that boy."

Chris jumped up onto the seat and looked out the back window, and he saw the boy suddenly turn and begin to run as the minibus slowed.

"What boy?" asked John, pulling over onto the side of the road and turning on the hazard lights.

"The boy—the boy whose brother I killed. The son of Dulcia Genever."

Chris barely heard the gasp from the other children as he ran to the front of the bus, his heart pounding.

"Turn around!" he shouted. "He was back there, by the parked cars!"

"Hold on," said John as he suddenly pressed down on the accelerator and spun the steering wheel around.

"Quick!"

After fifteen minutes of driving around with no sign of the boy, John finally sent Chris, shaking and pale, back to his seat.

Chris looked around at everybody as he sat down and saw that they didn't look nearly as concerned as he thought they should be. He knew it was because nobody believed that he had really seen him.

"It was him!" he said, protesting to nobody in particular. "I swear."

Ms. Lamb, who had insisted this was a waste of time from the moment John had followed Chris's instruction to turn around, looked delighted. "You are more troubled than even I had realized. I think I'll have a talk with Sir Bentley on our return—I'm sure he won't want any pupils at Myers Holt who believe they can see dead people."

"Not the dead boy!" said Chris, furious, "his brother. His twin brother."

"Don't you talk back to me," said Ms. Lamb. "You're in enough trouble as it is for wasting our time."

"The boy only said what he thought he saw," said John. Chris was grateful that John was standing up for him, but he couldn't help but feel annoyed that John didn't believe him either.

"It was him," he said, mostly to himself.

Ms. Lamb just sneered, and Chris, too angry to say anything, turned to face the window. He didn't say another word as they pulled up outside Myers Holt and went inside. As soon as the elevator hit the floor of the facility, Chris stormed off into his bedroom.

CHAPTER FIFTEEN

Maura had prepared an early evening picnic under the tree in the Dome for the students, which Chris ate in silence while Daisy and Philip made awkward attempts at conversation.

"This is my favorite time of day in the Dome—early evening," said Daisy brightly, looking up at the dusky-orange sky above them.

"Mine too," said Philip. "What about you, Chris?"

Chris didn't answer. He picked up an apple and took a large bite.

"Mum sent me the new Hunter Reid album. Anybody mind if I play it later?"

"Who's Hunter Reid?" asked Philip.

"A singer that Daisy's in love with," said Lexi.

"I'm not in love with him!" said Daisy, her face turning red.

"Well, better than being in love with a fictional character," said Rex.

Lexi glared at him.

"What about you, Chris—you want to listen to the album later?" asked Daisy.

Chris shook his head and took a sip of his drink as the group went silent again.

Chris was surprised at how normal they were acting—as if nothing had happened, as if one of their good friends hadn't just seen the brother of a boy he had killed watching him. They should have believed him—they were his friends—and he thought that was what friends did. No— they had all dismissed him as crazy. Perhaps they had thought that all along but it was only now coming out into the open.

He was about to stand up and leave when Ron and John came out from the classroom wing, deep in what looked to be an argument.

"What's wrong with them?" asked Daisy, clearly shocked. Although Ron and John were constantly bickering between themselves, none of them had ever seen the two men genuinely angry with each other.

"Call me that one more time and I'll . . ." shouted Ron.

"And you'll what?" replied John, his voice thunderous.

Chris watched, shocked, as John then leaned down so that his face was within inches of Ron's.

"L-I-A-R. LIAR!" he shouted.

Ron didn't move. Instead, he lifted the sunglasses from

his face and placed them on top of his head. Then, in a move Chris was sure he hadn't learned in the military, Ron raised his index finger and jabbed John in the eye.

"ARGH!" yelled John, clutching his face in his hands. Ron watched silently as John lowered his hands. Then, without warning, John leaped forward on top of Ron and the two men fell to the ground, wrestling each other.

"Somebody do something!" said Daisy, clearly upset.

Sebastian leaped to his feet. "Gentlemen—stop!" he shouted.

Ron and John both froze and looked up. On seeing the pupils, the men both jumped up and brushed themselves off, both looking slightly sheepish at having been caught acting so unprofessionally. They mumbled something between themselves and then nodded, shook hands, and walked purposefully up the hill.

"Sorry about that," said John.

"Why are you fighting?" asked Lexi.

"We weren't fighting," said Ron. "Just, um, a small disagreement."

"Looked like a fight to me," said Rex.

"Thing is," said John, "Ron and I have an issue from a few years back that we've never managed to sort out. It comes up once in a while."

"Every day," corrected Ron, looking annoyed.

"Whatever," said John, not looking at Ron. "Anyway, when we heard about all the other stuff you can do with that Ability of yours today, we thought that maybe you could settle the matter once and for all."

"We can do that," said Lexi. "Right?"

Everybody nodded except Chris, though he didn't stand up to leave—he didn't want to have to explain himself to Ron and John.

"Good," said John. "Then Ron can apologize and it'll all be over."

"Apologize? I think you're the only one around here who's going to be apologizing."

"We'll see about that, Ron," said John.

"Yes, John, we will. . . ."

Sebastian raised his hand. "Stop. We will conclude this. Explain the situation."

Ron took a deep breath. "Just gone midnight. Fifth of July 1990. Iraq."

"We arrived back to our tent after doing some military work," continued John. "Can't tell you much about that except that it was just the two of us and we hadn't slept in three days. Anyway, cut a long story short: I fell asleep and woke up to find that Ron had stolen from me."

Daisy gasped. "Really, Ron?"

"*No!* Of course not!" said Ron, furious.

"Well, you tell me who, then? We're in a tent in the middle of the desert. Nobody else for miles around. I go to sleep and it's there. I wake up and it's not."

"What's not there?" asked Rex. "A gun?"

Ron and John both turned to Rex, looking confused.

"Why would I steal a gun?" asked Ron, "I had plenty of my own. No, John here thinks I took his chocolate bar."

"A chocolate bar?" repeated the pupils in unison, shocked.

"Yes, well, it might not sound like much," said John,

sounding defensive. "But it's the principle of it. You don't steal from your partner—if you can't trust him with something as basic as food, how can you trust him with your life?"

"He's got a point," said Rex.

"And then, to make matters worse, he lies about it."

"I didn't lie about it—I just didn't do it," said Ron.

"No? Who did, then? Tell me that. Do you think a wild desert animal found our tent, unzipped it, unwrapped the bar, and then ate my chocolate?"

"Well it wasn't me, so unless you—"

"Why don't we just find out?" asked Lexi.

Ron and John nodded.

"What do I have to do?" asked Ron. He lifted his sunglasses, and from the way his eyes were darting about, it was clear that he was nervous.

"Nothing," said Philip. "Just sit down and we'll find out."

Rex stood up to make room for Ron on the bench.

"Who's going to do it?" asked Ron.

"We'll all do it," said Lexi, scooting around so that she sat cross-legged on the grass in front of him. "Right, Chris?"

Chris didn't know what to say. He could feel John looking at him, and he nodded slowly.

"All right," said Ron, "just don't go anywhere else."

"We won't," said Rex. "Midnight to morning, yes?"

Ron nodded.

Chris was in no mood for running around minds with the others. He saw the others' faces go blank and decided that there was no need for him to do it as well, but then he noticed that John was looking at him, a puzzled expression on his face. Before John could say anything, Chris let his mind eyes glaze over, and within seconds, he was standing in Ron's Reception surrounded by the image that Ron was looking at: himself, John, and the other pupils staring intently at him. Chris could sense Ron's nerves as he moved forward toward the door at the other side of the room. The others turned and saw him, but nobody said anything as Rex reached over to the handle.

"This should be interesting," said Rex, opening the door.

A blaring alarm suddenly exploded to life, making them all jump.

Beeeeeeep . . . beeeeeep . . . beeeeeep . . . waaaaaaaaaaa!

"What is that noise?" shouted Daisy, her hands to her ears.

"It's an alarm," replied Philip.

Chris stepped out onto the orange dirt path and looked around at the featureless gray concrete buildings.

"Over there!" called Sebastian, pointing in the direction of Calendar Street.

Chris followed the others from a short distance behind as they broke into a run, eager to get into the building they were looking for and away from the deafening wails of the sirens.

Chris, hands up to his ears, ran past the first buildings along Calendar Street and watched as Rex checked the signs by the doors until he found the one he was looking for. He nodded and opened the door, rushing in as the others quickly followed behind him. Chris was the last one in. He closed the door behind him. Immediately, the sound of the sirens disappeared. Everybody breathed a sigh of relief.

"Nice of you to join us," said Rex.

Chris didn't respond.

"No wonder he's so jumpy with all that going on in his head," said Daisy. *Always the one to change the subject,* thought Chris.

"Come on," said Philip, "let's get this done and get out. Just being in here makes me jumpy too."

"I concur," said Sebastian, walking over to the first of the filing cabinets and checking the label.

Chris went in the opposite direction from the others and began checking the filing cabinets until, finally, Philip shouted out from the corner of the room.

"Here! I found it!"

Chris walked back over as Philip opened up the top drawer of the filing cabinet that was marked JUNE-JULY-AUGUST 1990.

"July third . . . fourth . . . Here we go," said Philip, pulling out a green file. He held it out in front of him, opened it, and watched the memories come flying out, lining themselves up in a row in front of them—a long snake of hovering images made up of colorful dots jumping around each other.

Sebastian, who happened to be standing at the beginning of the line, reached out and touched the first image. The memory exploded open in front of them, larger and larger, until all that Chris could see in front of him was the inside of a large green tent and two enormous backpacks resting by the closed entrance. The wind swept gently against the sides of the tent, causing the canvas to ripple slowly from left to right. The sun filtered through the fabric, casting a green glow about the sparse surroundings.

They all watched as Ron began to wake slowly until, suddenly, a deep booming voice broke through the morning calm.

"Where's my chocolate?"

Chris saw Ron look round and come face-to-face with a much younger, and very angry, John.

"What are you talking about, John?" said Ron, pushing John away as he sat up.

Sebastian reached out and touched the memory. Immediately, it disappeared, collapsing back into a flat image of green and brown dots bouncing around each other at the front of the line. Sebastian pushed his hand against the image, and it moved back into the others before disappearing into the green folder, which then fell to the floor with a thud.

Chris picked it up and placed it back in the drawer as the others watched him.

"So he didn't do it," said Daisy. "The chocolate was already stolen when he woke up."

"Or he doesn't remember doing it," suggested Philip.

"Upstairs, then?" asked Lexi.

The top floor was much like the first except darker and dirtier. There, the thoughts and memories that were long forgotten were stored. It was also the place, as Chris had learned over the course of his studies at Myers Holt, where most dreams were stored—assigned to forgotten cabinets almost immediately on waking.

"Over here," said Daisy, opening up a drawer.

Chris watched as Daisy pulled out a file that was, not surprisingly given the amount of time that had passed, much larger than the one downstairs.

"There is something contained here from earlier in the day," said Sebastian, excited, as he stared at the front of the line of hovering memories. "It is labeled 'three a.m.'"

Sebastian touched the swirling image, but this time, instead of seeing the inside of a dark tent, as they were all expecting, a kitchen appeared. Chris looked around the small room with its cream cabinets and wooden countertop and shook his head, confused.

"He's dreaming," said Lexi, pointing to the pink haze that surrounded all memories of dreams.

Of course, thought Chris, but he didn't say anything. Instead, he watched silently as Ron stood up and walked over to a counter. He looked down, and there, lying unopened, was an enormous bar of milk chocolate.

"Mmmmm, chocolate!" said Ron, sounding giddy with excitement.

Ron's hand reached out and began to frantically unwrap the bar, stuffing the chocolate into his mouth.

"I don't get it," said Lexi as they watched Ron munching contentedly. "He's dreaming it—it wasn't him."

"Maybe, even though he was sleeping, he knew that someone was eating it, and he dreamed about it," said Philip, collapsing the image down and placing it back into the drawer.

They had all started to walk back downstairs and were

desperately trying to find an explanation when Philip drew a sharp breath.

"What?"

"I've got it! I know what happened! He was sleepwalking!"

"Well, did you find out?" asked Ron as soon as he saw that everybody had stopped using their Ability.

"Yes!" said Daisy, excited.

"Are you ready?" asked Rex. "The reason that the chocolate bar got eaten was that . . ."

"Ron was sleepwalking," said Chris flatly.

"Thanks for ruining the reveal, Christopher," said Rex.

Chris shrugged unapologetically.

"I was sleepwalking?" asked Ron. He was too shocked to notice the tension between Chris and the others.

"He didn't remember it at all. It was stored where all the forgotten memories are kept," explained Daisy.

"I don't know what to do with that," said John finally. "It's not like I can have a go at you about something like that."

"Yeah, guess not," said Ron. "Still, sorry about eating your chocolate in my sleep, John."

"It's all right, Ron." John turned to the children and nodded. "Thanks for that."

"You are most welcome," said Sebastian.

"Game of cards?" asked Ron as he walked off down the hill.

"In a moment," said John. "You go set up. Chris?"

Chris tensed, wondering why he was being singled out. "Yes?" he asked.

"Remember how you asked me last term about how a car engine works and I said I'd show you?" asked John.

Chris knew he had too good a memory now to forget something like that. "No, John. It wasn't me."

"Course it was," said John, standing up. "Remember?"

Chris had no idea where this was going, but it was obvious that John wanted him to say yes.

"Er, maybe."

"Right, then. I'll show you now if you've got five minutes."

"Oh, it's all right . . . ," said Chris. Then he looked round at the others, all watching him, and decided he'd rather spend time with John than with them. "Actually, yeah—now's a good time."

Neither Chris nor John spoke until they were standing outside Myers Holt, next to the school car.

"John," said Chris as John walked over to the driver's-side door.

"Yes?" John opened the door and began to lower his gigantic frame into the seat.

"I never asked you about car engines."

John looked over the roof in Chris's direction. "I know," he said as he disappeared into the car and closed the door.

Chris wasn't sure what was going on. Did John want him to get in the car? Wait outside? Then the window next to him rolled down.

"Get in," called John from the other side.

Chris hesitated, because he now understood why John had brought him here. And Chris was in no mood for talking.

Sure enough, as soon as Chris took his seat, John turned to him.

"You want to tell me what's going on?" he asked.

Chris shook his head, his shoulders hunched. "Not really."

"All right, then. How about I guess what's happened and you just nod if I'm right."

Chris thought about this for a moment, then nodded.

"I think that maybe you had a bit of a falling out with your friends today. Yes or no?"

He nodded.

"You're angry with them."

Chris nodded again.

"Because they didn't believe you about seeing that boy."

Chris tensed. "You didn't believe me either."

"I never said that," said John.

"No. But that's what you were thinking," said Chris, his heart beginning to race, his words coming out faster. "You all think I'm crazy. Nobody understands what—"

"Chris. Stop," said John firmly. He turned his head to face forward. "I know you better than you think, son. And I know you're not crazy."

"How do you know?" asked Chris. His eyes began to fill with tears. "Maybe I am crazy. Maybe I was imagining that boy—I'm not sure of anything anymore."

"I know you're not crazy because I know what you've been through—I've been there myself."

Chris swallowed, trying to push away the lump that was forming in his throat. "What do you mean?" he asked.

John stayed looking straight ahead. "I know what it's like to kill someone."

Chris's eyes widened. Of course; John had been in the army.

"I know about the nightmares," continued John. "I know what it's like to see the face of the person you killed everywhere. I know how it feels when the people around you can't understand what you're going through because they can't—not unless they've been in the same position."

Chris felt a tear roll down his cheek. "Does it ever stop?"

"No. It doesn't ever go away."

"I didn't think so," said Chris.

"But," said John, turning to face him, "it does get easier. You need time. And you need your friends."

Chris lowered his head.

"It's not their fault that they don't understand. You just have to accept that. They can't, and I hope they never will. That doesn't make them any less your friends. It doesn't mean they don't care. If you want to move on from this, then you need them. And they need you. It'll be hard at first, but I promise you, it does get easier."

"I hope so," said Chris.

There was a moment of silence as Chris thought about everything John was saying.

"That's all I had to say about that," said John finally. "I hope you'll think about it."

Chris nodded. And then he thought of something that had been playing on his mind since Sir Bentley had read out the letter the boy had written.

"Can I ask you something?"

"Anything at all," said John.

"Do you think it would be wrong to wipe my mum's mind?"

"What do you mean?"

"I mean wiping her mind the way Dulcia's mind was wiped by her son."

"I don't know. What do you think?" asked John.

Chris shrugged his shoulders. "I'm not sure. I wouldn't do it like that boy did—I'd just wipe away all the sad memories so that she would be happy again. But then I think that I'd have to get rid of the memories of my dad from her mind, and that seems wrong. No matter how unhappy I was, I wouldn't want anybody to take away the memories I have of him."

"You've thought about this a lot, haven't you?"

Chris nodded. "Do you think the boy feels bad for wiping his mother's mind?"

"Maybe. I can't answer that. It couldn't have been an easy thing for him to do, that's for sure."

"I wish I could ask him. I know he hates me for what I did to his brother, but I think we have a lot in common. It's not the same, but his mum was messed up. Like mine."

"Maybe there are things that are similar, but that's true of you and anybody else. And your mums—now, I haven't met yours, I admit, but I'm thinking they're not the same, not unless your mum goes around stabbing people."

Chris smiled and shrugged his shoulders. "I suppose."

John sighed. "Look, son. If there is one thing that will drive you crazy in life, it's spending your time thinking about the what-ifs. There are just some things you can't change—meeting the boy, the way your mum is, things like that. You could wipe her mind, but you'd have to live with that for the rest of your life, and I think that would be harder than just learning to accept your life as it is. And finding the best in it. You know what I mean?"

"Yes," said Chris, "I think I do." He looked John in the eye. "Thanks."

"You're welcome," said John, giving Chris a pat on the shoulder. "That'll be fifty quid."

Chris gave a small laugh as John leaned over and opened the glove box. He pulled out a booklet and handed it to Chris. "Should take you a few seconds to memorize—in case anybody quizzes you on your car knowledge."

Chris knew, straight away, that John was right, and he went back into school feeling lighter knowing that he wasn't alone. By bedtime, Chris had made up with everybody, even Rex. He hadn't had to say much. In fact, Chris had been shocked at how quickly they had forgiven him and he had forgiven them. The next morning, they all played in the pool before breakfast, as if nothing had ever happened.

Less forgiving was Ms. Lamb, who kept to her word about giving them a difficult time. In the days that followed their visit to the art gallery, her unpleasantness, as difficult as it had been to put up with before, was now intolerable. She rearranged the school timetable (on the pretense that they needed extra training for their upcoming assignments) so that they now spent most of every day with her shouting at them, ordering them to repeat work over and over again ("The pen is too black! The corner of the page is creased!") and keeping them all in after their lessons were over to write out pages and pages of lines. Finally, and most upsetting for Chris, who had got used to the shouting and the tedious chores, she tore up Chris's newspaper with the picture of Valentino Brick in handcuffs on the front page, sent to him and signed with thanks from the commissioner.

By lunchtime on Friday, after a particularly brutal session where Ms. Lamb had spent three hours drilling them relentlessly over how to extract truth from fiction in a person's dreams, Chris and the others had just about had enough. They sat in the dining room, eating their soup, and griped about Ms. Lamb.

"There's only one good thing about leaving here—and that's never having to see that witch again," grumbled Philip.

"I agree," said Chris.

"I cannot envisage her ever having been a child, can you?" said Sebastian.

"Yep," said Lexi, "she would have been the one snitching on everybody."

"And ripping up other people's work if it was better than hers," said Philip.

Chris was about to join in when Miss Sonata appeared in the doorway.

"I hope you've got enough energy for a new assignment," she said brightly. "Something's come up."

Chris, who had been wondering when they would next get to solve another crime, sat up and nodded. The others did the same.

"Wonderful," said Miss Sonata. She pulled out a chair at the head of the table and sat down.

"There have been a series of fires started at post offices around North London in the last week," began Miss Sonata. "An appeal last night on television brought a number of possible suspects to our attention, but we have no evidence to charge any one of them and they all deny any involvement. We've got them all at a police station not too far from here—we'll take you there and see if you can find anything. I'll give you all the details on the way."

"What about dinner?" asked Rex.

"It shouldn't take too long," said Miss Sonata. "You really don't have to come, though, Rex if you'd prefer to stay here."

Rex jumped up, alarmed at the thought of being excluded. "No—it's fine. I'll grab a snack from the dining room."

"Excellent. Everybody else coming?"

They all nodded enthusiastically.

"Good, let's go!"

The case was solved within twenty minutes of their arrival. This time, however, Chris was not the one responsible for solving the crime—it was Lexi and Sebastian, who happened to access the mind of the culprit, a man harboring an unnecessary amount of anger for a parcel that had been lost in transit. Lexi and Sebastian gave their information to the commissioner, who sent his men immediately to a storage locker that the pupils had identified. There, the police found a mountain of canisters filled with gasoline and a laptop containing photographs of every one of the targeted post offices. Not long after that, the man confessed.

By the time they left the post office, three hours later, Chris and the others were all starving—something that always happened after intense use of their Ability. Even the snacks that Maura had packed for them hadn't been enough to stop their stomachs growling. They bundled into the minibus, eager to get back to Myers Holt.

Chris listened as next to him, Lexi, who was giddy with excitement at solving her first real crime, chatted with Miss Sonata and Daisy. Meanwhile, over at the front of the bus, Ron, John, Sebastian, Rex, and Philip discussed the best way to subdue a shark with bare hands.

Chris leaned his head against the window and looked out at the charcoal skies of London, the streets glistening from the rain that had fallen earlier that day. They moved slowly, the traffic thick with people trying to get home to start their weekend, and Chris distracted himself by watching the pedestrians on the sidewalk. Occasionally, for no good reason other than to kill time, he would access the mind of somebody when the minibus stopped at a red light, but he found nothing of interest—just a lot of people thinking about food, much like he was.

The minibus drove slowly past the British Museum, and Chris entertained himself by trying to spot the tourists, then he would access their Receptions to find out what language they were speaking to find out whether he had been right. He had just correctly identified a group of Italians when, out of the corner of his eye, he spotted him.

Chris sat up abruptly—was he imagining things again? He pressed his face up against the glass and stared as the minibus moved slowly forward. There, standing just round the corner from the museum entrance was the pale young boy whose brother he had killed, wearing a dark-blue jacket, his black hair slicked down. He knew what John had said, about seeing the face of someone you killed everywhere, but this was different. The boy was just a few feet away, and his face was unmistakable. He was talking to somebody, a clean-shaven man dressed in a suit and a long black overcoat. Suddenly, the minibus started moving, and Chris was jolted out of his stupor.

"Stop the van! It's that boy again!" yelled Chris.

Everybody in the bus immediately stopped talking to look at him, except for John, who kept on driving as he argued with Ron, who was sitting beside him.

"I tell you, Ron, jab it in the eye first. . . ."

"*Stop!*" shouted Chris, who could now only see the faint figure of the boy beginning to walk away from the man.

Miss Sonata, alarmed, leaned over to Chris as John, who had heard Chris now, pulled over to the side of the road.

"What's the matter, Chris?"

"Dulcia Genever's son! He was there—back there by the museum—talking to a man. It was him!"

Chris's eyes darted around the bus and found that everybody was staring at him as if he had lost his mind.

"Over there—back there. John, please, turn around!"

John hesitated. "Chris . . ."

Chris's could feel his face turning red. "I know what we talked about, but I promise you—I'm not imagining this! It's him."

"You're sure?" asked John.

Chris nodded. "I really am."

"All right." John turned back to face the road. He indicated right and pulled out into the traffic at a frustratingly slow speed.

"Hurry! He's going to get away," said Chris, running to the back of the bus and pushing himself in between Rex and Philip. He peered out the window, but he couldn't see either the boy or the man, both lost within the crowds of commuters and tourists.

By this time, everybody on the bus was looking out the window to search for the boy, and then Chris found him once more.

"There!" said Chris, pointing to the back of a boy with a dark blue jacket on. "Quick!"

"Are you sure it's him?" asked Miss Sonata.

"*Yes!* I saw his face. Please! Quick!"

John looked in his mirrors and pulled out into the opposite lane, causing the oncoming cars to honk their horns loudly as they swerved to get out of the way.

"I see him—over there!" shouted Chris.

"Let me out, John," said Ron. He leaped over to the door of the bus.

John, who was still on the wrong side of the road, suddenly veered back to the left, finding a gap that hadn't really existed between two cars, and pressed a button. The doors flew open, and Ron leaped out, deftly swerving out of the way of an oncoming bicycle, then ran down the road toward the boy.

Chris, his heart pounding, turned, and ran down the length of the bus and out the doors after him, closely followed by the others, despite Miss Sonata's protests.

Chris gasped as he saw Ron, up ahead of him, leap forward. Chris watched as Ron grabbed the boy by the collar and began to turn him round when a large group of tourists suddenly emerged from the museum, obscuring his view. Chris pushed his way through them, ignoring their angry shouts, and emerged to see Ron looking very pale as he talked to two furious-looking adults standing beside the boy. Chris ran forward, and as he did so, the boy turned to look at him.

Chris's heart sank. The boy facing him had an olive complexion, and his hair, though also black, was short and spiked at the front.

"I really do apologize," Chris heard Ron say as he approached. "A case of mistaken identity."

"We must call the police," said the father of the boy, in a thick Spanish accent.

"No, really. No harm done. Just a misunderstanding," said Ron, trying to calm the situation.

"A stranger grabs my boy—this is a crime here, too, no?" asked the mother, waving her hands in anger. "I should slap you."

Interrupting them, Sebastian stepped forward and then, in Spanish, began to apologize for the misunderstanding. Chris, who now had a good grasp of Spanish from his studies, listened as Sebastian explained that one of the pupils from the school trip had gone missing and they thought it was him. Calming slightly, the parents huffed but seemed to accept the explanation. And then, to Ron's relief, the father suddenly grabbed the confused boy's hand and led him off down the street.

Chris was suddenly very aware that everybody had turned to look at him.

"It wasn't him," he said.

"No, Chris, it wasn't," said Ron, his arms folded and a deep frown on his face.

"I mean I did see the boy, it's just that that wasn't him," said Chris, but he could tell by the look on Ron's face that he didn't believe him. Chris turned to the others. "You believe me, right?"

Sebastian, Lexi, and Philip all looked down at their feet awkwardly, but Rex just spun his finger by his temple. "Cu-ckoo," he said. Chris imagined it was what everybody else was thinking.

Chris opened his mouth to argue, and then he changed his mind. What was the point? he thought. They had obviously made up their minds that he was crazy the first time he had seen the boy. This time, however, Chris knew without any doubt that it had been him. The only question now was why.

"Come on everybody, excitement's over," said Miss Sonata. "Let's all get back to school."

Chris, followed the group back across the road and into the waiting bus.

"It's all right, son," said John as Chris walked past him, his head hung low.

Chris waited on the ground floor of Myers Holt with Miss Sonata and the others for the elevator to arrive. He didn't know what to say, and clearly, neither did anybody else. They waited in silence until the doors of the elevator opened and Ms. Lamb stepped out wearing a tight green coat and holding her purple umbrella. She looked at Chris and immediately curled her lip at him before turning to Miss Sonata.

"Successful?" asked Ms. Lamb, referring to their assignment.

"Yes, thank you, Gertrude."

If Chris hadn't felt so awful at that moment, he would have almost certainly burst out laughing at hearing Ms. Lamb's name for the first time.

"No incidents at all?"

Miss Sonata shook her head. "None at all. The children did a superb job."

Chris couldn't have been more grateful that she didn't mention the incident with the boy.

"Surprising," said Ms. Lamb, "considering they are all so useless."

Miss Sonata didn't respond. Instead, she let Ms. Lamb pass and wished her a lovely weekend.

"Yes, and you," said Ms. Lamb without looking back.

CHAPTER SIXTEEN

At nine o'clock the next morning, Chris was summoned to have a chat with Sir Bentley and Miss Sonata. Any hopes that he might be able to convince them of what he had seen vanished as soon as they started talking and made it clear that they were concerned not for the whereabouts of the boy but for Chris's state of mind. Chris figured that continuing to insist that he had been right might make them question if he was mentally able to cope with the work at Myers Holt, and so he decided to keep quiet. Instead, he did his best to appear embarrassed about the misunderstanding, and finally, reassured, they let him on his way. Chris decided right then that the next time he saw the boy—and he was certain he would—he would investigate it himself.

Once he had come to that decision, Chris relaxed slightly. Although it played on his mind constantly, by Sunday he was, in the eyes of the others, back to his normal self. And, in a sense, he was. Chris had spent a long time thinking about the situation and decided there was nothing he could do until the next time they left the school. He knew that while they were deep underground in the facility nobody would be able to make their way in physically—Ron, John, and the tight security would make sure of that—or by using their Ability. As Sir Bentley had explained to them on their first day, the entire place was lined in lead, completely blocking anybody from using the Ability to look in to, or out of, Myers Holt.

So sure was he of this that by Monday morning the only thought on Chris's mind was how he would survive another full day of lessons with the odious Ms. Lamb. The pupils all walked slowly into her classroom, dreading the inevitable shouting and name calling that they were about to be subjected to, but Ms. Lamb wasn't there. They took their seats, surprised, and waited in silence.

And then, after ten minutes of waiting, something miraculous happened. Something that had not once happened in all the time that the pupils had been at Myers Holt. Ms. Lamb walked into the classroom . . . smiling.

"Good morning, children," she said brightly, not mentioning, if she noticed, that all the pupils were staring at her with a look of total bewilderment.

"I hope you've all had a pleasant weekend."

Nobody answered.

"Good, good," she said, the heels on her knee-high

leather boots clacking on the floor as she made her way over to her desk. She bent down, the skirt of her tight green suit stretching painfully as she searched through the drawer for something.

"Aha!" she said, pulling out a stack of white paper. "Here we go."

Chris looked over at Philip. "What's wrong with her?" he mouthed.

Philip raised both hands and shrugged his shoulders.

Chris watched, expecting Ms. Lamb to snap back to her old self at any moment as she handed each pupil some paper.

"I thought we could brighten up the classroom," said Ms. Lamb, carrying over a large box of colored pencils that Chris himself had sharpened during his time in the Dunce Corner.

Chris watched as Ms. Lamb placed a handful of the pencils on each pupil's desk before finally coming to his. Chris looked up, wondering if she was going to find some way to insult him even in her good mood, but no. She placed the pencils on his desk, just as she had done for the others, and walked away with a smile on her face, not once having looked at him.

"I'm not in the mood for teaching today," she said, sitting down at the chair behind her desk. "So why don't you all use this lesson to draw the most interesting mind you've entered during your time at Myers Holt. Make it detailed and, um, colorful—whatever will keep you entertained." She pulled out the newspaper and folded it over so that the crossword was faceup, then picked up a pen.

"Off you go," she said, waving her hand at them dismissively. As Chris picked up his pencil to draw Valentino Brick's mind, he wondered what on earth was going on. It wasn't that he wanted to be shouted at, obviously, but this change in Ms. Lamb was so out of character that it had completely unsettled him. The more he thought about it, the more convinced he was that this was a ploy to catch them out in some way and that any minute now, she would somehow reveal this to be a cruel trick. He looked round at the others, who were beginning to draw in silence, and saw from the looks on their faces that they were all thinking the same thing. In fact, the class had never behaved so well.

Half an hour later, having worked in total silence, Chris approached Ms. Lamb's desk nervously. He stood by her side as she scribbled a word into the crossword until, finally, she noticed him standing there.

"Yes?" she asked, not sounding in the least bit angry at the interruption.

"I've finished my work," said Chris, placing the paper on the desk, aware that the eyes of all the other pupils were on him.

Ms. Lamb picked up the paper and inspected it. Finally, she looked up and placed it on the corner of her desk.

"Good. Do you have a book to read?"

Chris nodded. "Yes, in my bag."

"Very well, then, go and do that for the rest of the lesson." Ms. Lamb looked back down, picked up her pen, and began to work on her crossword once more.

Chris was too shocked to move. No tearing up of his

work, no shouting, no insults—it just didn't make any sense.

"Yes?" she asked, realizing that Chris was still there.

"Um, nothing," he said, about to turn and walk away when Ms. Lamb suddenly sighed and looked up at him.

"Look. I don't like any of you any more than I did last week, but I've decided, you stay out of my way, and I'll stay out of yours. Understood, Chris?"

The whole class gasped as Ms. Lamb, oblivious to the shock on everybody's face, looked back down and continued her crossword puzzle.

"I can't believe she said your name!" said Lexi as they all ran up the hill to sit under the tree.

"She's never said any of our names before—not once," said Daisy.

They all sat down on the picnic blanket that Maura had laid out for them and started picking at the food.

"For someone who didn't get screamed at or forced to write lines, you really do look very unhappy," said Rex, noticing Chris's puzzled expression.

"It's just so strange," said Chris, cutting up a piece of cheese. "I don't trust her."

"I agree," said Philip. "Something's up."

"I do not say this often," said Sebastian, "but I concur with Rex. I think you should just be happy—perhaps she has simply understood the error of her ways."

"I don't know," said Lexi, "maybe Chris and Philip are right—maybe there is something more going on."

"Thanks, Lexi," said Philip. "Somebody with some brains."

"She just wants there to be something up so that she

can pretend to be a superspy and work it out like her boy-friend, James Bond," said Rex.

"How many times do I have to tell you that I don't love him: He's a made-up character in a book," said Lexi, glowering at Rex.

"Even more embarrassing that you want him to be your boyfriend, then," said Rex, taking a large bite of his sandwich.

"Stick up for me, Chris!" said Lexi.

Chris, who had been tucking into his lunch and ignor-ing the usual bickering between Lexi and Rex, looked sur-prised at being brought in to the conversation.

"Er, stop picking on Lexi," said Chris.

Rex looked at Chris as if he might punch him. "Why don't you mind your own business," he said.

"Come on," said Chris, not in the mood for arguing with Rex, "I'm just saying be nice—you're always being mean to her."

"That is because he is in love with her," said Sebastian, matter-of-factly.

"SEBASTIAN!" shouted Rex and Lexi, both looking equally horrified.

"You may protest, but this is the truth. I have seen this behavior many times in the literature I have been reading: The man likes the lady, so the man is horrible to the lady. I don't comprehend—we do not do this in Spain."

Chris laughed but was quickly silenced by a deathly look from Rex.

"The only reason I'm not nice to her," said Rex, standing up, "is that she's annoying, she's always making sarcastic comments, and she doesn't know when to *shut up*."

Lexi put her hands on her hips and gave a smug smile. "Takes one to know one, Freckles," said Lexi.

Rex held his breath as he stared down at Lexi and then turned and stormed off before suddenly turning back on himself, picking up a selection of food in silence, and then storming off once more.

"Ah, young love," said Sebastian, grinning. He took a sip from his orange juice and then lay back on the grass to bask in the artificial sunlight.

"Anyway," said Daisy brightly, always the first to try to clear the air after an argument, "which mind did you all draw?"

"I selected Kingston Khan, of course," said Sebastian, "but it was a complication to draw all the buildings made of mirrors—there was no silver pencil."

"Did everybody draw the artists' minds?" asked Daisy.

Everybody nodded. They were by far the most interesting places they had all visited: Kingston Khan's mirrored city, Emily Buckworth's funfair, where all the memories could only be reached by slides that shot upward instead of down; the blackness of Ann Abernathy's mind, where all the buildings were lit up in bright neon outlines; and, of course, Valentino Brick's rain-of-paint mind.

Chris was the first to walk into the classroom the following morning, followed quickly by the others, who were all as eager as he was to see if Ms. Lamb's peculiar transformation had been a one-off. It hadn't.

"Good morning, children," said Ms. Lamb. Chris hid a grin as he saw that she was wearing a bright-orange flower in her hair to match the sparkling orange eyeshadow plastered in two deep circles around her eyes.

"Good morning," they all murmured back as they took their seats and waited to hear what she had in store for them.

"So," said Ms. Lamb, standing up from her chair, "what would you all like to do today?"

Chris didn't know what to say, but Rex, as always, had an answer ready.

"We could just spend the morning playing games."

Chris couldn't believe the nerve of him, but Ms. Lamb didn't raise an eyebrow.

"Fine, play games."

"I'd like to do some work on data retrieval from criminals' minds," said Philip. "Sir Bentley said we're going to start prison visits soon."

"Be quiet, Einstein," said Rex, who was never one to take on any more work than absolutely necessary.

"You can do that, too," said Ms. Lamb, looking neither pleased nor annoyed by the request. "That's chapter twelve in *The Ability Training Manual*—you don't need me to read it for you, do you?" For a moment, a hint of the old, unpleasant Ms. Lamb was evident.

"No," said Philip, unzipping his bag.

"Very well. Now, as long as you leave me in peace, do what you like. Well? Off you go."

Chris jumped up and helped Lexi and Daisy push the tables together as Sebastian and Rex rushed off to the Map Room to collect the games before Ms. Lamb could change her mind. Philip, disapproving of this lack of interest in learning, sat back in his seat, in his pressed three-piece suit with his hair neatly parted, and began to read.

"Who's keeping score?" asked Chris.

"Anybody except Rex," said Lexi. "He can't be trusted."

"I didn't cheat," said Rex, trying not to raise his voice. "Just because you can't take losing."

Lexi didn't look convinced. "Fine. Let's see who wins when Sebastian's the one keeping score."

Sebastian looked around. "We have no paper. Anybody?"

They all shook their heads and then turned to look at Ms. Lamb, who was bent over and writing on the folded newspaper in front of her.

"You be the one to ask," said Sebastian to Chris.

"Uh-uh, no way—she may be pretending to be nice, but you all know she hates me. You do it."

Sebastian sighed and stood up reluctantly. Chris and the others watched as he made his way across the room and stopped at Ms. Lamb's side.

"Yes?" said Ms. Lamb without looking up.

"We, eh, require some paper, Ms. Lamb."

"Bottom drawer. Help yourself."

Sebastian bent down, opened the drawer by Ms. Lamb's orange-stockinged legs, and pulled out some paper. He closed the drawer and stood up but didn't move.

"Yes?" asked Ms. Lamb once more, a slight hint of irritation creeping into her voice.

"We require a pen also."

Ms. Lamb, without saying a word, handed him one of the pens on her desk and went back to reading her newspaper. Sebastian stared down at the desk for a brief moment before turning and rushing back to the table, his eyes wide.

"What's the matter?" asked Daisy.

"I know what has been the cause of her change!" he whispered. "Her affliction is not sinister, it is an affliction of the heart," said Sebastian.

"Pedro, how many times do I have to tell you: English," said Rex, shaking his head.

Sebastian leaned in more as a curious Philip edged his way into the group. He waited until they were all huddled together before making his announcement.

"The woman is in love."

Chris and the others stared at Sebastian for a moment, and then, in unison, they all burst out in hysterical laughter.

"That," said Lexi finally, tears rolling down her eyes, "is the single funniest thing I have ever heard in all my life."

Rex, his face bright red, looked up to say something else but then burst into a loud guffaw, which just made the others dissolve into another bout of giggles.

Sebastian glanced over at Ms. Lamb, but her head remained down—she didn't seem to have noticed the noise.

"It is true, I tell you," said Sebastian urgently. "Go up and observe for yourselves. She is doodling hearts on the page of the newspaper."

Chris, who was still half laughing, shook his head in disbelief. "That doesn't mean she's in love."

"Yes," said Daisy, "I doodle hearts all the time," she said.

"Listen to me!" interrupted Sebastian, frustrated that

nobody was taking him seriously. "I tell you, she is in love. And the reason that I know she is in love is that she was scribing her name above the hearts, with an arrow and another name underneath."

The whole group gasped.

Sebastian smiled, pleased to have their attention.

"I can't believe it," said Daisy. "What's the name?"

"Count Dracula?" asked Rex.

"Quasimodo?" asked Philip, grinning.

"No," said Sebastian, leaning forward, "the man is named . . . Chucklebunny."

For a moment, there was a total, stunned silence. And then the whole group collapsed once more into hysterical fits of laughter.

That afternoon, Chris and his fellow pupils were running through the crowded streets of New York City, using their Ability to solve a complicated series of clues that Professor Ingleby had devised for them in their think-tank training, when Rex suddenly had an idea.

"Chris should enter her mind!"

Chris, who was in the process of lowering himself into an open manhole, looked up, surprised. "What?"

"Maintain your focus!" shouted Mars, Rex's think-tank teacher.

Rex rolled his eyes but didn't say anything again until they were all standing at the bottom of the sewer tunnel. With his hands over his nose, he whispered loudly to the others—forgetting, it seemed, that Mars was able not only to hear what he was thinking but to read his mind.

"Chris is the only one who can enter Ms. Lamb's mind without her noticing. He should go in there and find out if she really is in love."

"Are you crazy?" asked Chris, shocked. "Can you imagine if she found out? She'd kill me. And I mean that literally."

"She won't find out," said Rex, moving quickly down the tunnel toward where they believed the Egyptian artifact had been hidden by Professor Ingleby, "you're too quick."

"He's right," said Lexi, leading the way with a flashlight.

"It would be interesting to find out what kind of a nutcase would choose Ms. Lamb as his girlfriend," said Philip.

"There it is!" said Daisy suddenly, pointing at a small chest barely visible from its hiding place, a hole in the bare brick wall.

"Excellent—how long have we got left before time runs out?" asked Chris.

Sebastian checked his watch. "Five minutes to return to Times Square—I believe this is achievable."

"Let's go!" shouted Lexi, grabbing the chest.

They all ran off back in the direction they had come from, all thoughts of Ms. Lamb momentarily forgotten.

It was only after the lesson was finished, he had said good-bye to Cassandra, and the think tank had faded into darkness that Chris let himself think about what the others were asking him to do. He was torn. On the one hand, they were his friends and they really wanted him to do this—even Daisy didn't seem to think it was that bad. On the other hand, it was a terrible thing to do—to enter the mind of somebody to find out something so private.

If he was caught, there was nothing at all he would be able to say in his defense. The problem was that the others didn't feel the same way about the Ability as he had before he had killed the boy, and he knew that they wouldn't understand if he didn't play along. He couldn't explain that he didn't find using the Ability as funny as they did anymore, or that he didn't enjoy the games they played with it. He still went along with it all—the food fights, the pranks between themselves—but that was harming nobody. It just didn't feel as good as it used to, not now that he had seen firsthand how deadly those powers could be. It was only when he thought about his conversation with John, and how he had told Chris how important it was not to fall out with his friends, that he knew he really had no choice.

Chris stepped out of his glowing red think tank to find the rest of the group waiting for him.

"Well?" asked Rex.

Chris sighed. "Fine, if it will get you all off my back, I'll do it."

"Yes!" said Rex, patting Chris heartily on the back as the others cheered.

What have I let myself in for? thought Chris, suddenly feeling very nervous.

CHAPTER SEVENTEEN

Agreeing to enter Ms. Lamb's mind was one thing, actually doing it was something else altogether. As Chris walked into the classroom the next morning, he felt his stomach doing somersaults, and he wondered whether he would be able to go through with it. Then he saw his classmates grinning excitedly and waving him over, and he swallowed hard. He was just going to have to do it.

"Good morning, everybody," said Ms. Lamb in a bright-green outfit that included a thick smear of matching lip-stick and eyeshadow. And a lime-green beret.

"Ribbit," croaked Rex in a whisper.

"What was that?" asked Ms. Lamb, her eyes narrowing.

Rex sat up, looking alarmed. "Erm, er . . ."

"Yes?" asked Ms. Lamb.

"I was just saying how nice you look today, Ms. Lamb."

Chris put his hand over his mouth as Ms. Lamb appeared to consider this. Chris watched, ready for an explosion of fury, but Ms. Lamb suddenly started making a strange sound. It took a moment for him to work out that she was in fact giggling. "Why, yes I do, Rex. Pleased that you noticed. Now, why don't you all play some more games or something today—I'll be getting on with some paperwork."

She sat at her desk and leaned down to rummage through her bag. Chris turned to see Rex wiping his brow with the back of his hand. *Phew!* he mouthed.

Chris stood up and pushed his desk toward the others as they had planned.

"I can't believe you just did that," said Philip as they arranged their chairs around the now-large table in the middle of the classroom.

"It just came out," said Rex. "Took me by surprise too."

"Well, you got away with it. In fact, I think your charm disarmed her."

Lexi giggled. "Maybe Chris will find that she's actually in love with Rex."

"I didn't know your nickname was Chucklebunny," said Philip.

Rex pulled a disgusted face. "That's not even funny," he said.

Chris walked around to the back end of the table and took his seat directly facing Ms. Lamb: the others all sat in a line opposite him to obscure her view of him.

"Doesn't this look a bit strange?" asked Chris, suddenly feeling like he was at an interview.

"Actually," said Philip, moving his chair around, "you've got a point. Maybe I should sit next to you. It makes sense. That way, if she looks up, I can give you a kick."

Having come prepared, Sebastian took out a board game from his bag and laid it out in front of them.

"Right, forty seconds, that's all we need," said Lexi, referring to the time that it had taken Chris during a practice run the previous night to enter Rex's Reception and then get across his mind—the point during which the ears rang to warn the person that somebody was entering their mind. It was precautionary—they all knew that Chris was quick enough to cross a Reception without alerting the person's mind to the intrusion, but they had all decided it was best to be safe, just in case.

"Okay, everyone ready?" asked Rex.

Everybody nodded and then turned to Chris.

Chris looked round at all his friends. "Is this really a good idea?"

"Chris!"

Chris sighed. "Fine, fine. I'm ready."

"Good. Three . . . two . . . one . . . *go!*"

Immediately, they all started shouting loudly.

"I WANT TO BE RED!"

"NO, I WANT TO BE RED!"

"GIVE ME THE DICE!"

"NO, I'M STARTING!"

Chris saw Ms. Lamb look up at the noise for a moment before lowering her head and getting on with her work.

Lexi looked up at Chris. *Do it now!* she mouthed.

Chris nodded, turned back to face Ms. Lamb, and let his eyes glaze over.

Chris had been inside Ms. Lamb's mind once before, in his first week at Myers Holt, where he had sealed his fate as her most hated pupil by finding out her fear of being lonely. That time, his first visit past anybody's Reception, the cityscape had been filled with blocks—a three-dimensional replica of the colorful mind map that he had committed to memory only moments earlier. Now, as he opened the door from her mind's Reception and looked out over the cityscape, he noticed how much progress he had made over the course of his training. The city of Ms. Lamb's mind now revealed itself to be a much darker place than he had first encountered, a mass of menacing Gothic buildings of all shapes and sizes. The skies, however, were blue, a reflection of her good mood, thought Chris, which only made the soot and dirt on the buildings more obvious.

Chris walked quickly down the cobbled streets of this silent city and tried to ignore the menacing stone gargoyles that sneered down at him from the tops of the buildings. He turned left onto Emotions Street and walked quickly to where the building housing memories and thoughts of love should be. At first, Chris thought that it wasn't there, but as he approached it he saw that it did exist. Being only the size of a small garden shed, however, it had been hidden by the looming towers of Dislikes and Jealousy on either side of it. He hurried over to the rickety wooden door and looked at the small carved stone sign hanging

from a rusty hook over the faded red paint: FAIRLY STRONG
LIKES.

This, thought Chris, smiling, was clearly as close as Ms.
Lamb got to feeling love. He opened the creaking door
and entered it. There, in the center of the tiny room, was a
dark wood filing cabinet with a single drawer, which Chris
pulled open.

Hanging inside were only two green files. The first was
labeled MEDUSA THE CAT and the other simply CHARLES.

Chris picked up the files and ran his finger over the top of
them. There were, he estimated, about ten pages of swirling colors. Chris was surprised: He would have expected
somebody to have more than ten memories of somebody
she was in love with. He opened it, and the pages flew up
into a line. He walked up to the last one, dated the previous
night, and touched it. The memory, Chris saw, was of Ms.
Lamb in what he assumed was her own living room, but
as far as Chris could tell, nobody was there with her. Chris
looked around, fascinated, at the dark purple walls and the
black sofa covered in clumps of fine gray hair that Chris
assumed belonged to a cat called Medusa, and tried to commit everything to his own mind so he could tell the others.
He was just taking in the collection of sappy love films on
her shelf when he heard the phone ring. Ah, thought Chris,
the memory is of a phone conversation. He saw Ms. Lamb's
hand reach out and pick up the phone.

"Yes," said Ms. Lamb, the familiar angry voice sending
a chill down Chris's spine.

"Hello, Gertrude. It's Charles," said a dark voice, it's
booming low tone filling the room.

"You're late. You were supposed to call me at seven. It's five past seven now."

There was a bit of a pause and some muffled noise coming from the other end.

"Is somebody with you?" snapped Ms. Lamb.

"Um . . . no, of course not . . . , my darling."

Immediately, Chris felt the air around him warm slightly.

"Oh, Chucklebunny," said Ms. Lamb, suddenly talking in a sickly little girl's voice that made Chris's skin crawl. "I forgive you, sweetie. Just don't do that again. It makes Gertrude sad."

Again, another pause.

"Okay. Er, do you want to go on a date on Friday?"

"Does Zeus like a glass of nectar?" said Ms. Lamb, sitting up with excitement.

"I don't know, does he?"

"Yes!" said Ms. Lamb. "That's a yes, of course, Chucky. Where are you taking me—a romantic dinner?"

"No. We're going to a concert."

Ms. Lamb leaned back as an old hairy cat jumped up on her lap. "Wonderful! Classical, opera?"

"No. They're called . . . the Death Screamers."

"Pardon?"

"I said the Death Screamers. They're playing at the Hell Club in Camden."

"The Death Screamers? I've never heard of them. What kind of music do they play?"

"Heavy metal. Are you coming or not?"

"Oh . . . it's not really my kind of music, but . . . well . . . yes! Of course, my honey bear."

"Fine. I'll pick you up at eight."

"Wonderful. And, Chucksie?"

"Yes?"

"It's going to be your lucky night. I've already decided that you may kiss me, and if you're really good, you can give me a foot massage."

Silence.

Finally, the man spoke. "I'll pick you up at eight."

"Eight o'clock. I'll be ready and waiting, Chucklebunny."

"It's Charles . . . and I need your address."

"Of course, how silly of me. It's three Albany Street, Notting Hill. Apartment eighteen."

"See you then . . . , dear," said the man.

"Bye . . . oh, I can't hang up. You hang up."

The phone went dead.

Chris closed the memory, shuddering at the thought of anybody having to touch Ms. Lamb's feet. He walked over to the other end of the line to find Ms. Lamb's first memory of Charles and was surprised to see that it only dated back to Friday evening, less than a week earlier. Intrigued, Chris opened the memory, and a setting he knew very well filled the room. Chris watched as Ms. Lamb walked away from the elevator and toward the front door of Myers Holt. She turned around, and there, for a strange moment, he saw himself looking sullen, Miss Sonata and the others beside him. Chris recognized it instantly as the moment they had met Ms. Lamb upon returning to Myers Holt after Ron had chased the wrong boy outside the British Museum.

"Have a lovely weekend," said Miss Sonata.

"Yes, and you," said Ms. Lamb, opening the door and

stepping out into the rain. She clomped down the steps and had started to walk to the right when, suddenly, a man slammed into her.

"You stupid, clumsy oaf!" shouted Ms. Lamb.

"I'm so sorry," said a deep voice. Chris immediately identified it as being the voice on the other end of the phone to Ms. Lamb. *This is the beginning of the romance,* thought Chris, enjoying the thought of how much the others were going to love hearing about this.

The man took Ms. Lamb's hand, and before she had a chance to snatch it away, he raised it gently to his lips, his head bowed, and gave her hand a small kiss.

Chris grimaced.

"Oh . . . my," said Ms. Lamb, "how . . . unexpected." Chris could feel, from the sudden warmth in the room, that Ms. Lamb was blushing.

"Please forgive me—let me take you for a coffee to apologize."

Ms. Lamb looked up, her hand still in his, and then the two of them locked eyes.

Chris watched as the man's face came into view, and he froze. As Ms. Lamb lost herself in the man's hazel eyes, Chris could only stare in shock. His heart suddenly pounding furiously, Chris wondered if he was mistaken, but the more he stared, the more certain he was: This was the man that Chris had seen on Friday evening with the pale boy in the street.

And now, not long after he had seen that, there was the man bumping into Ms. Lamb. Chris was absolutely certain: This was no coincidence. He dropped the folder to the ground and ran out the door.

. . .

"What did you see?" asked Daisy, excited.

Chris, still shaken, said nothing. His mind was racing, and he took a breath to try to calm himself.

"Chris? What occurred?" asked Sebastian.

Chris could tell, by the sound of his voice, that Sebastian was concerned about him. The others too probably. He wanted to share with them what had happened, but a thought stopped him: Just because he believed something did not mean that his friends would. They hadn't believed him when he said he'd seen the boy talking to the man in the first place—they were almost certainly not going to believe that he had seen that same man again in, of all places, Ms. Lamb's mind. Even knowing that it was true, it was still hard to believe.

"Argh, I can't stand it!" said Rex finally, interrupting the silence. "Tell us what you saw. Is she really in love?"

Chris nodded. "Yes."

Lexi shook her head, exasperated. "And?"

Chris knew they were starting to get annoyed with him. Could he tell them? he wondered. He wanted to. He had so many questions that they could have helped him with: Why did Charles meet with the boy? Were they plotting something? Was Ms. Lamb now involved in that plot? And, most important, did they also think that the plot might be about taking revenge for the killing of the boy's brother?

"Chris!"

But he couldn't risk it. What if they thought he was going crazy again and told one of the teachers? He didn't want to go through the worry of whether he was about to be expelled once more. And he didn't want to fall out with his friends again either. He had enough information to find out the answers for himself. So, finally, just at the point that Rex looked to be getting ready to punch him, Chris began to talk. He told them about everything—the somber stone buildings of her mind, her shedding pet cat Medusa, and the interior of her living room. He repeated, word for word, the telephone conversation between Ms. Lamb and her Chucklebunny and watched them recoil in horror, just as he had, when he mentioned the promise of a kiss and a foot massage. Then, finally, he told them about how they met, recounting every detail except for one: the moment he had recognized Charles as the same man who had been talking to Dulcia Genever's son. When he finished, they all laughed, clapped, and cheered, and Chris, glad that they were happy, excused himself and went back to his bedroom.

That night, Chris was sitting in an armchair in the Map Room, still trying to make sense of what he had seen, when he felt a light tap on his shoulder.

"Chris?"

Chris turned his head and saw Daisy looking down at him. "Hi," he said.

"You okay?"

Chris nodded. "Yeah, I'm fine, thanks."

"You sure? Don't you want to join us for the pool tournament?"

Chris shook his head. "I'll give it a miss, thanks."

Daisy looked at him for a moment, then shrugged her shoulders and walked off.

Chris was about to get back to thinking about the plan

he was formulating when he heard Daisy's voice from behind him calling out to the others.

"I'm not going to play this one," she said.

"Makes no difference to me. You would have lost anyway," said Rex.

Daisy ignored Rex. "Chris," she said, loud enough that everybody could hear.

Chris leaned his head round the side of his armchair. "Yes?"

"Will you help me in the library? I can't find a book I need for my ancient Greek revision."

"I'll help you," called Philip, "I memorized the whole library catalogue the other day."

"Oh, um, it's okay thanks," said Daisy, "Chris isn't playing in the tournament, so he can help me. Can't you, Chris?"

Chris sighed and stood up.

"I don't really feel like talking, Daisy," said Chris as Daisy guided the library platform down to the bottom level.

"Just five minutes," she said as she opened the platform gate and walked over to the large sofa by the unlit fire. "Okay?"

Chris watched as she took off her shoes and then curled up on the sofa, her feet tucked underneath her. He rolled his eyes and walked over, sitting down at the other end. "Look, Daisy, really . . ."

"What's the matter?"

The question surprised Chris. "Nothing. I just didn't feel like playing pool, that's all."

"It's not that, Chris. I know you, and you haven't been fine since you left Ms. Lamb's mind."

Chris had always considered himself a decent liar—he'd had to become one to dodge questions about his situation at home, always fearful that somebody would find out and take him away from his mother. But, for some reason, he couldn't bring himself to lie to Daisy.

"You won't tell anyone?" he asked.

Daisy shook her head.

"Promise?"

"I promise, Chris. I won't tell anybody if you don't want me to."

Chris took a deep breath.

"Ms. Lamb's boyfriend Charles is the same man I saw with the boy outside the museum last Friday."

Daisy stared at Chris, her eyes widening as she processed what he was telling her.

"Are you sure?" she asked finally.

"One hundred percent. There's no doubt about it. Charles was talking to that boy, and then, less than a half hour later, he was asking Ms. Lamb out on a date. I know that nobody believes me, but I'm telling you, Daisy, it was definitely him. I know what—"

"I believe you," interrupted Daisy.

"Why? Nobody else does."

"Because I know you wouldn't lie to me. If you said you saw him, I believe you."

"Oh," said Chris, blushing.

"So, what happened?"

Chris told her about Ms. Lamb and Charles's first meeting outside Myers Holt and the moment he had recognized the man's face.

"But, I don't understand. Why?"

Chris took a deep breath. "I think the boy wants to get revenge for the death of his brother. And I think he wants to take that revenge on me. Who better to help him than Ms. Lamb? She'd jump at the chance to get rid of me."

"You think she'd do that?"

"Definitely—don't you?"

Daisy thought about this for a moment before finally nodding her head slowly. "Yes. I think she would."

Chris breathed a huge sigh of relief. He could have kissed her for believing in him. Then he blushed for even thinking it.

"So what happens next?" asked Daisy, not appearing to notice Chris's red face.

"I'm going to follow her on her date," he said.

"You can't go out of school—last time you did that, you got caught, or have you forgotten? Why don't you wait until she comes back to school on Monday? You can access her mind then."

Chris had already considered this. "I don't want to wait until then. It might be too late." He wondered if that sounded a bit overdramatic. Fortunately, Daisy seemed to be taking him seriously.

"I don't know, Chris. It's such a risk. You could get caught. Worse, you could get hurt." She reached out and touched him on the arm. "I don't want that to happen."

"I have to do this, Daisy."

"But why, Chris? Why can't you just tell somebody?"

"You know they won't believe me. It's not just that. I . . . well . . ."

"Yes?"

"I need to meet the boy. This man is my only chance of finding him."

"Why would you want to do that?" asked Daisy.

"I need to tell him I'm sorry for what I did," said Chris, feeling himself begin to get upset. "I want him to know that I didn't mean to kill his brother."

Daisy put her head in her hands. For a moment, neither of them spoke, until, finally, Daisy looked up.

"You're going to do this no matter what, aren't you?"

Chris nodded.

Daisy considered this for a moment, and Chris held his breath, hoping his trust in her wouldn't backfire on him. Finally, she spoke.

"I won't tell anybody, but you've got to let me help you. I don't want you to get caught, and if something goes wrong and you don't come back, I'll be able to get help."

Chris hadn't expected this. "Are you sure? I mean, I don't want you to get into any trouble. How will you help me?"

"I can activate the elevator for you. That way, it will be my thumbprint on record, but I'll make sure I stay with everybody for the evening so nobody will suspect anything. I'll tell them you've gone to bed not feeling well. Then, at some point—you can choose when—I'll wait for you upstairs to take the elevator back. If you don't turn up exactly at that time, then I tell the teachers everything."

Chris wanted to hug her. "Thank you—you're amazing."

Daisy blushed before quickly changing the subject. "So . . . want a game of chess?"

· CHAPTER EIGHTEEN ·

Chris and Daisy spent much of the next two days huddled together in deep discussion as they finalized their plan to get Chris out unnoticed and back to school safely afterward. They had mapped out Chris's route to the concert by bus and worked out all the timing—including the time that Chris had to return by: eleven o'clock, after which Daisy would raise the alarm. Although Chris considered Philip to be his best friend, and he still was, Daisy was different. Having grown up without a sister or any friends that were girls (or boys, for that matter, but anyway . . .), Chris was surprised how easy he found it to talk to Daisy; he could share his thoughts and concerns with her, things that he couldn't have discussed with anybody else.

On Friday evening at ten minutes past seven, as

everybody else chatted loudly over dinner, Daisy gave Chris a small nod. He put his head in his hands and rubbed his eyes as hard as he could. Daisy stood up suddenly.

"Chris, are you okay? You don't look well."

Chris looked up weakly. "I'm . . . uh"—*cough*—"okay," he said, wishing that he were a better actor.

"Are you sure? Your eyes are really red," said Philip.

"I'll go and get Maura," said Lexi, standing up.

"No!" said Daisy and Chris, in unison.

"Really"—*cough*—"I'm fine," said Chris as he made his way over to the door. "It's just a cold or something. I'm going"—*cough*—"to just go to sleep early. I'll be fine tomorrow."

"Maura has prepared her homemade apple pie," said Sebastian. "Do you not wish to partake?"

Chris shook his head.

"Wow," said Rex. "You must be really ill. Keep away from me, Germ Boy."

Chris raised his hand as pathetically as he could manage and waved good night to everybody, then turned and walked out of the door, coughing.

"I'll just go and see if he's okay," he heard Daisy say, as he walked quickly down the corridor.

"Did you know kissing was invented to spread germs?" shouted Rex.

"Oh, be quiet," said Daisy, running out of the door to catch up with Chris.

Daisy stood at the bottom of the ladder to Chris's bed and handed him the spare blankets they had taken from the linen cupboard earlier that day. Chris stuffed them under the duvet until both he and Daisy agreed that it looked like there was a person under it. Satisfied, Chris jumped down and started to make his way to the door when Daisy stopped him.

"Don't forget this," she said, pulling out a small pink purse. "There's four pounds eighty in there. It's all I had."

Chris put it into his jacket pocket. "Thanks," he said, "I'll pay you back."

"Don't worry about it," she said as they both peered out into the hallway to check that it was empty. Seeing that it was, they jumped out at the same time, and as quietly as they could manage they ran down toward the entrance foyer and sat down on the long seat by the elevator doors.

"Can you see it?" asked Daisy.

Chris turned his head to face the wall, let his mind go blank, and immediately was able to look directly into the office of Ron and John's quarters.

"Yes," he said quietly, without looking away.

Chris heard Daisy stand up next to him as he watched Ron and John through the wall next to him, sitting back in their armchairs as they watched a film on the small television set.

Knock. Knock.

Chris watched as John picked up the remote and pressed pause. Ron pulled his sunglasses down from the top of his head and jumped up to answer the door.

"Sorry to bother you," said Daisy, "but there's a bit of a problem we need your help to sort out."

Without answering, Ron leaned over her, peering up and down the corridor before suddenly turning and running to his locker, where he began to quickly and efficiently prepare himself for action.

"What is it? An intruder? A fight? You've found a suspicious device?"

John watched calmly from his armchair as Daisy walked into the room looking alarmed.

"No—stop! Nothing like that. I . . . I just have a question I wanted you to answer."

Ron stopped dead.

"Oh," he said, sounding very disappointed. He placed the flashlight and walkie-talkie back in the locker and unbuckled his utility belt as John gave a small laugh.

"What's the question?" asked John, turning his head to look at Daisy.

"We were all just trying to work out something," said Daisy, and then she began to describe a scenario involving a school of jellyfish, a submarine, and an army of ninjas.

Chris, meanwhile, set to work. As Daisy distracted them, Chris looked over to the control panel for the cameras, positioned on the opposite side of the room from the television, and pressed the pause buttons for the elevator camera and the ones upstairs and looking outside. Chris zoomed out with his mind and looked at the video screens. He breathed a sigh of relief. Everything looked normal, the only clue being the tiny clocks at the bottom of every picture. Chris would just have to hope that they wouldn't choose to take a closer look.

"No, Ron, you're mistaken. You'd have to take care of the jellyfish first, then the ninjas," said John, who was now, Chris noticed, standing up. Chris looked over at the blue light in the corner, the one that alerted Ron and John to anybody using the elevator, and found the small wire coming out from the box. Concentrating, he watched the wire begin to twitch slightly and then pull against itself slowly, getting tighter and tighter until the connector suddenly popped out loudly and landed on the table with a small clank.

Chris snapped his head round to get a view of Ron and John and saw, to his great relief, that they were completely distracted by the argument that was beginning to develop.

Chris turned to face Daisy, who was standing impassive as the two men argued in front of her, and as quickly as he could, he entered her Reception.

"It's all done," he said, passing the message into her mind.

Daisy looked around at the screens, nodded, and turned back to Ron and John.

"Okay, well. Never mind," she said brightly. "I'll go back and tell the others that you don't know."

Ron looked aghast. "Of course we know—just John here is not listening to reason. We'll talk to you in the morning."

"Okay, thanks!" said Daisy, rushing out of the room and closing the door behind her, smiling as the two men continued their argument in loud voices.

"They're going to be arguing all night," said Daisy as she turned the corner to meet Chris. "We did it."

"We haven't done anything yet," said Chris, remembering the last time he had left the school building without permission. That time, he had thought he was in the clear from the very beginning, only to find Sir Bentley waiting for him upon his return. Tonight, although he was being much more careful and had the added bonus of Daisy's help, he still wasn't going to let himself get complacent.

The two of them rushed over to the elevator doors and stepped into the dirty, cramped kitchen. Chris moved to let Daisy pass and watched as she pressed her thumb over the kettle's switch, as they had agreed.

"Run as fast as you can once you get outside," said Daisy as the room they were in whooshed upward. "I'll go straight back downstairs and use my Ability to fast-forward the tapes. As long as nobody suspects anything, there'll be no reason to check the tapes."

Chris, who already knew all this, nodded. He zipped his jacket and waited for the room to come to a stop.

"Go now—and be careful," said Daisy.

Chris turned to run, and then, just as he was about to step out of the doors, he stopped.

"Thank you, Daisy. I really appreciate—"

"Thank me when you get back," interrupted Daisy. "Now go!"

Chris smiled and broke into a run.

Chris stepped off the bus and onto the busy pavement. He had worried, when he and Daisy had been planning the night, that people would notice a twelve-year-old milling about on his own, but the throngs of people were too busy enjoying their Friday night to notice him, let alone to try and work out if he was accompanied by an adult.

Chris walked quickly through the noisy streets toward the club—a route he had memorized and walked through in his mind many times already. At Daisy's suggestion, they had worked out where Ms. Lamb and Charles would probably be arriving from and chosen a bus stop on the opposite side of the club, a little farther from the venue than necessary, so as to minimize the chances of Chris bumping into them. Nevertheless, Chris was on full alert as he made his way past the takeout restaurant and pubs, weaving in and out of the slow-moving crowds, always keeping an eye out for the sight of Ms. Lamb, Charles, or the pale boy—but thankfully, none of them appeared.

The Hell Club, it turned out, was hard to miss. A gigantic uninspiring lump of a building, it sat in the middle of a patch of green that was barely visible beneath the thick black soles of the hundreds of people waiting to enter.

"Oi! Get out of the way, runt." A large hand suddenly appeared on Chris's shoulder, and he turned his head to look up and saw an enormous man with a tall green mohawk wearing a jacket made almost entirely of metal studs.

Chris didn't say anything as the man pushed him to the side and stomped past him, followed quickly by a terrifying group of people wearing skeleton masks. Chris felt very young, very conspicuous, and, he had to admit, a little bit scared. That surprised him, and he tried to remind himself that he had the protection of his Ability if he needed it, but it wasn't as much comfort as he had thought it would be, having never found himself in a crowd like this one before. Completely surrounded, Chris was finding it impossible to get a good view, and he was getting increasingly nervous that he might find himself face-to-face with Ms. Lamb without notice. Deciding on a change of plan, he retreated quickly to the other side of the road and slipped into a dank-smelling doorway that was hidden behind a line of people waiting to buy fish and chips.

Chris leaned back on the door and, unable to see over the heads of the people talking in front of him, let his eyes glaze over and used his Ability to look around unnoticed in order to plan his entry.

The crowds, Chris noticed, were quickly beginning to get agitated. As his mind scanned over the top of the tightly packed group outside the venue, he saw a couple of bottles being thrown in the direction of the entrance, and then the chanting started.

"LET US IN! LET US IN!"

Chris's mind moved over to the entrance and saw four large security men jostling with the front row of the chaotic line, all the people pushing their way forward in the direction of the closed doors.

Chris watched, for a moment forgetting that he was supposed to be coming up with a plan, as the door suddenly opened and the face of a surprised-looking attendant appeared briefly before disappearing under the stampede of people rushing forward.

It was quickly obvious to Chris that any concerns he might have had about finding his way in were unnecessary—the system for checking tickets, if there ever had been one, was completely forgotten as the crowds, yelling, whooping, and making strange screaming sounds, pushed their way in. Chris looked past the thick black outer walls of the building and was suddenly transported into an enormous, darkly lit room that was quickly filling with people spreading out across the entire floor, as if the crowd were a river that had broken its banks. Chris looked around to find a hidden vantage point—he was certain that anywhere in the venue would be close enough for him to access Ms. Lamb's mind, no matter where she should choose to stand. His mind swooped upward, and there, up some stairs, Chris found the perfect place—between a pillar and some sound equipment, next to a staircase that led down to an exit door. Just in case.

Now that he had a clear plan, Chris's nerves vanished. He let his mind return to his actual surroundings and noticed that the crowd was beginning to thin. Chris knew he didn't have much time if he wasn't going to find himself walking up to the entrance alone. Even his Ability wouldn't be able to prevent raising the suspicions of all the passersby if they were to see a schoolboy walking unaccompanied on a Friday night into a heavy-metal concert. He had to act quickly.

"Excuse me," he said, surprising the couple standing in front of him, who had been deep in conversation. They stepped back, and Chris ran through, scanning the people from left to right until he found a group large enough to hide among.

Chris ran over and slipped into the middle of the moving group, who were shouting and pumping their fists in the air. Chris kept his head down and tried to walk at the same fast pace as them, but the group stopped suddenly and the man behind him stumbled on top of him.

Chris felt the wind knocked out of him as he fell to the ground. Disoriented, he tried to push himself up but then felt two large hands grab him and lift him back on to his feet.

Chris looked up and saw a huge and terrifying man with a tattooed face staring down at him.

"Very sorry about that," said the man. "Are you okay?"

Chris nodded, his breath slowly coming back.

The man, apparently not thinking anything of a boy suddenly joining his group, put his hand on Chris's shoulders and began to lead him forward, protecting him from the crowd, which was getting increasingly aggressive as it neared the entrance.

"Stick with me. It'll get better once we get past the doors," the man shouted as the crowd closed in around him.

Chris heard a frantic voice to his right as the crowd rushed forward.

"TICKETS, PLEASE. I'M SUPPOSED TO BE TAKING TICKETS! TICKETS?"

Ignoring the voice, the man, who still had two hands firmly on each of Chris's shoulders, pushed his way toward the doors. Chris was carried forward by the people around him, bodies pushing against him so that he could barely breathe, but then, suddenly, the crowd began to disperse. Chris stumbled forward, taking deep gasps of air, as the tattooed man leaned down to face him.

"You okay?"

Chris nodded.

The man smiled and put two thumbs up in the air.

"Good. Enjoy the show!"

Chris didn't have a chance to thank him before he

walked off chanting "DEATH SCREAMERS" as he made his way to the front of the stage to join his friends.

Chris quickly darted over to the wall and made his way up the stairs onto the gallery level, where already at least a hundred people were milling about, shouting loudly over the booming background music.

Checking that nobody was looking, Chris sidled up to the pillar he had seen from outside and slipped behind it, quickly crouched down on the sticky black floor, and found himself looking down on a perfect view of the floor below through the railing next to him. He checked his watch. It was eight thirty.

The venue was now packed to capacity, and Chris scanned the tops of the peoples' heads looking for Ms. Lamb but she was nowhere to be found. Sure that she was not already inside the venue, he kept his eye on the entrance directly below him. Suddenly, the crowd erupted into a deafening cheer. Chris turned his head and saw a mass of flashing lights coming from the stage as four men appeared wearing black leather trousers with what Chris hoped was fake blood covering their heads and bare upper bodies. They rushed toward the front of the stage and started screaming at the crowds. Chris didn't have to guess how they had come to choose their name.

Chris watched, fascinated, as the drums started beating, the electric guitars began screeching and the entire crowd below him began to jump as one. The lead singer raised his arms and began to sing.

"RIVERS OF BLOOD! TEARS OF DOOM! . . ."

The whole crowd sang along, shouting at the tops of their voices. A man rushed up on stage and dived backward onto the crowd. Chris leaned forward, watching as the man was carried around the room by the crowds beneath him, the music being played louder and faster until, finally, he was set down by the entrance, cheering and jumping.

Chris watched as the man began to muscle his way back into the crowd, probably to do it again, when suddenly Chris spotted them. There, only a few feet below him, was Charles, wearing an elegant black coat, and Ms. Lamb, dressed, Chris noted with a shudder, in a tight black leather minidress and black boots that were laced up to her knees. Both of them had a look of horror on their faces, as if neither of them could quite believe what they were hearing. Chris wondered how long they had been there.

He ducked back to hide, then, figuring that they wouldn't be able to see him in the darkness, even if they were to look up, he inched forward and pressed his face up to a gap in the railing.

Ms. Lamb looked to be arguing with Charles, gesturing toward the doors they had just come through, but he ignored her and, dragging her by the arm, pushed her forward into the crowd until they were completely surrounded.

At least, thought Chris as his eyes glazed over, there's no chance of her hearing any ringing in her ears with all this music and screaming. He tried to relax as the view around him faded away.

· CHAPTER NINETEEN ·

The music blared just as loudly within Ms. Lamb's Reception as it did outside it. Chris looked around at the jumble of current thoughts that were flying around in the vast room: her dislike of the music, her desire to leave, a disturbing image of her locked in a kiss with Charles, and her coveting the clothes the women in the crowd were wearing. He ran through them all, adrenaline coursing through his veins as he made his way toward the now-familiar wooden door on the other side of the room, eager to find out what he needed to know. Chris turned the handle, opened the door, and stepped out into his teacher's mind.

Everything went silent. The music that had been blaring in his ears only a second earlier had completely disappeared, replaced with the *thump thump* of his heart pounding. Chris, suddenly finding himself at the edge of the vast Gothic city, took a moment to calm down as the dark clouds swirled furiously above him. He looked out over the dark, twisted spires and spotted, in the distance, the building he was looking for—an imposing towered fortress surrounded by a moat.

Chris ran through Ms. Lamb's mind with no effort, his Ability sending him breathlessly over the cobbled streets, his sneakers silent as they padded against the dark gray stone. As he ran, he thought about exactly where he was going to go, and in which order, until he found what he was looking for. Knowing so much about her mind already, Chris had decided with Daisy that this would be the best place to start. Then, if he had no success, he would try Charles's mind. Either way, Chris just wanted to find something, anything, that would prove he wasn't losing his mind.

On reaching Language Lane, the road leading up to the Career building, Chris slowed. He looked around as he walked, surprised at the number of languages Ms. Lamb had a knowledge of: German, ancient Greek, Latin, and even Esperanto. He walked past them all until, finally, he reached the end of the road, which opened out over a vast green expanse, a large fortress sitting prominently in the middle, surrounded by a wide band of still, black water. For a moment, Chris thought about swimming across, as opposed to taking the easy route over the lowered draw-bridge, but, of course, he didn't. As he stepped out onto the wide wooden walkway it occurred to him how strange it was that even within the total privacy of someone's mind, he never broke the rules of normal behavior. He could have sung loudly all the way, cartwheeling along the empty streets, but instead he always acted in the same way he would have if he had been walking outside in the real world. He smiled to himself and made a mental note to ask the others if they did the same.

Chris noticed that the front door of the Career building was open halfway across the battered wooden drawbridge. He didn't think too much of it. If there was one thing he had learned in his time at Myers Holt, it was that no two minds were the same. Nevertheless, it was the first time he had seen an open door inside somebody's mind that he himself hadn't opened, and he slowed down instinctively as he neared it instead of rushing straight in as he would normally have.

Chris walked up to the end of the drawbridge and stepped out onto the dust floor. He was about to take another step when, suddenly, he froze. There, right in front of him and leading all the way up to the door, were a series of faint but unmistakable footprints. Somebody else had already been here.

As Chris ran forward and pressed himself up against the stone wall of the fortress, he tried to think of the possible explanations. Perhaps the footprints had been there for a long time, maybe even years. He had no idea how much the landscape might change over time, but without any wind or harsh weather, he couldn't imagine it changed much.

He sidled up to the open door and peered into the small crack between the hinges, but it was too dark and the gap was far too narrow—he could see nothing. As he tried to steady his breathing, Chris tried to work out his options. He came up with only two: Leave now or face whoever was inside, if, indeed, there was anybody in there at all. Chris took a deep breath. If he wanted to find out what was going on, he had no choice. Telling himself that whoever had visited was surely long gone, he leaped out from behind the door and into the dark room.

Crash!

A bookshelf to the right fell to the floor as somebody jumped back in surprise. Chris stood frozen as the figure stood up slowly.

"You!"

Chris couldn't breathe. Even before the figure stepped into the light coming in through the doorway, he knew exactly who it was. Chris had only heard the voice once, but the words "You killed my twin brother" had haunted him ever since.

"What are you doing here?" asked the boy. His face was paler than Chris remembered it, and he seemed as surprised by this meeting as Chris was.

"You're Dulcia's son."

"I was Dulcia's son," said the boy, without expression.

"What's your name?" asked Chris.

The boy's eyes narrowed. "My name is Ernest, and you—you are Christopher Lane—my brother, Mortimer's, killer."

It was Chris's turn to look shocked. "How do you know my name?"

"I have the Ability too. Remember?"

Chris nodded, his mind swimming with a hundred different thoughts. He tried to remember the speech that he had rehearsed in his mind so many times in case they should ever meet, but now that he was here, face-to-face with the boy—Ernest—Chris couldn't remember a single word of it.

"Where are you? Are you at the concert?" asked Ernest.

Chris nodded slowly, not sure if this was information he should be giving out. "Are you?"

Ernest nodded also.

"Why?" asked Chris.

"I needed the noise to get in here, obviously. Why are you here? Were you looking for me?"

Finally, here was the opportunity he had been waiting for, but for some reason, his mouth was dry and he couldn't speak. Ernest stared at him until, eventually, Chris found his voice.

"I wanted to tell you how sorry I am."

The boy stared at Chris in silence.

"For what happened to your brother," Chris continued.

"Sorry?" hissed Ernest. "That's it? You think that's enough—that you can just tell me you're sorry and I'll forgive you?"

"I don't know what else to say," said Chris. "It was an accident."

"It was no accident," said Ernest, stepping forward to face him. "I saw what you did. You murdered my brother, and nothing you say will ever change that."

"He was trying to hurt people—I had to do something."

"You didn't have to kill him."

Chris had no response. He couldn't argue with that—after all, he had thought the same himself.

"Don't you have anything else to say?" asked Ernest as Chris stood silently in front of him with his head bowed. He wondered how he could have been so foolish as to think that saying sorry would make anything better.

"What can I do to show you how sorry I am?"

Ernest looked straight into Chris's eyes, and with no hesitation he answered him. "I want you to die too. An eye for an eye."

Chris's eyes widened as he took in what Ernest was saying.

"It hasn't been easy," said Ernest, taking a slow step forward. "But, finally, I worked it out."

"What do you mean?" asked Chris.

"It doesn't matter," said Ernest, continuing to inch closer. "As it turns out, you've made things very simple by showing up tonight."

With that, Ernest rushed toward Chris. Chris jumped out of the way and prepared to defend himself—forgetting that you couldn't get hurt inside somebody's mind—but, to his surprise, Ernest ran straight past him and out the door. Chris was about to turn and run after him when he noticed that the memory Ernest had been accessing was still open, a single image hovering in the air. Chris, momentarily distracted, looked at the paper and felt himself go weak. There, perfectly in focus, was a page from the school files about him, giving his age, his mum's name, his address, his previous school, and his friends, as well as more personal information, about his mother's depression, his father's death. It was everything that Ernest could ever possibly need to know to get to Chris if he wanted to.

Chris didn't stop to think. He turned, running as fast as he could out the doorway and over the drawbridge.

"STOP!" he shouted, his voice echoing out over the city as Ernest, now a tiny figure in the distance, sprinted down Language Lane.

Ernest looked back but didn't stop running as he turned the corner onto Science Road, disappearing from view.

Chris, panicking, began to run as fast as he could after him, but as he turned the corner himself he saw Ernest already at the door leading back into Ms. Lamb's Reception.

"ERNEST—STOP! I WANT TO TALK TO YOU!"

Ernest placed his hand on the handle of the door and paused briefly. He stopped, then turned to face Chris, who was running as fast as he could to reach him.

"Good-bye, Christopher."

With that, Ernest turned and ran out.

Chris ran up to the door, a few seconds behind him, and jumped back into Ms. Lamb's current thoughts, where the sound of the band suddenly reappeared, screaming in his ears.

"THE GRIM REAPER! THE GRIM REAPER! YOUR SOUL'S KEEPER, YOUR SOUL'S . . ."

Chris looked around desperately but saw no sign of Ernest—he must have already left Ms. Lamb's mind. Chris ran through Ms. Lamb's Reception, determined to get back into the real world as fast as he could. Ignoring the music and the thoughts swirling about him, Chris kept his eyes straight ahead, and when the door to the outside was finally within reach, he lunged forward.

"HE WON'T APOLOGIZE . . . FOR HIS BLOODSTAINED LIES! THE GRIM REAPER, THE GRIM REAPER! WAAAAHHH!"

Chris's head was spinning as he felt himself return to the club, the deafening sound pressing in around him as he tried to focus on his surroundings. His heart was beating, and the fear and adrenaline from using the Ability, combined with the intense heat of the room, had him dripping with sweat. He wiped his forehead quickly with the back of his hand and lifted himself up unsteadily to his feet.

Chris looked around as the lights from the stage began to flash, sending the audience into darkness and back again, over and over, faster and faster. Although it felt like he had been gone for hours, the floor was just as packed, the bodies all jumping with the same, if not more, intensity than they had before he had entered Ms. Lamb's mind. Chris, however, was not looking at them or even at Ms. Lamb or Charles, though he spotted them briefly from the corner of his eye, standing in the same place as he had left them. All Chris was interested in, at this moment in time, was finding Ernest, no matter who saw him. His life, he knew, depended on it.

Chris stood up and, leaning over the railing, looked out over the gallery below him, trying to find Ernest amidst the pulsating lights and the tightly packed mob. His eyes darted about—around the audience, along the back wall, and across the stage. Chris gasped as he spotted him—he was standing behind a security barrier next to the stage.

And Ernest was staring directly at him.

Chris didn't have a chance to think, let alone use his Ability. Suddenly, he was lifted off the ground with a violent force, as if an invisible rope had been tied around him and suddenly yanked forward. Chris felt himself falling.

Chris landed on his back, in the middle of the crowd.

"YEAHHH!!!"

Chris looked down, panicked, as the people beneath him, their arms high in the air, began to push him from person to person, away from the stage. Chris struggled to lift his head as he was jostled clumsily over the heads of the audience, trying desperately to keep his eyes on Ernest, who was now fighting his way through the jumping mass of bodies toward him.

"LET ME DOWN!" screamed Chris but nobody heard him as the hands below him bounced him from person to person. The band wailed and screamed, and the crowd began to chant. "DEATH SCREAMERS! DEATH SCREAMERS!"

Chris turned his head and saw Ernest nearing the edge of the crowd, not far from where he was being carried. Suddenly, the guitars stopped and the drummer on the stage began to pound out a heavy beat. The crowd beneath him began to jump higher, and he felt himself being thrown up over and over. Chris flailed about uselessly like a rag doll until, at last, he reached the edge of the crowd and was hurled backward. He landed on the black floor with a loud thud and looked up.

This time, it was his turn to take Ernest by surprise. He saw Ernest pushing himself out from the crowd, and before he had a chance to look for Chris, Chris let his eyes glaze over.

Chris watched as Ernest was thrown backward but just as he was about to hit the wall, his body came to a sudden stop and Chris felt Ernest's Ability come into force. Chris looked at Ernest, his eyes as intent as Chris's own, and the two of them began to try to push the other away, their Abilities wrestling against each other so that they were locked in a standstill.

And then, from somewhere deep inside him, Chris found his strength. He closed his eyes, let his mind go clear, and felt an overwhelming surge of power rush forward with such intensity that Chris could have done nothing to stop it, even if he had wanted to. He opened his eyes and saw Ernest flying back in the air, his eyes full of fear and then a look of defeat as he smashed into the wall and dropped to the ground.

Not again, thought Chris, suddenly feeling sick. He looked at Ernest lying still on the floor and struggled between wanting to check he was okay and running away. Then, just as he had decided that he had to check, Ernest dragged his arms forward and pushed himself up onto his knees.

He looked up at Chris, his eyes wide and angry, but he didn't attempt to fight back. In that split second, both boys knew whose Ability was stronger, and Chris could tell, from the look on Ernest's face, that it was over. Chris had won.

Chris turned away and began to walk toward the entrance, leaving Ernest staring at him from the ground when, suddenly, he heard the sound of ringing in his ears. He turned and saw Ernest, his eyes closed, facing him.

"I will get my revenge, Christopher Lane. When you least expect it."

Chris watched Ernest's eyes open, and then, suddenly, he felt himself jerked backward, as if a hand had grabbed the back of his collar.

"What are you doing here?"

Chris looked up to see Ms. Lamb's furious face looking down at him. He saw a blur rush past him and snapped his head round to see the back of Ernest running out the doors into the black night.

Chris looked up at Ms. Lamb, who still had him by the scruff of the neck.

"The boy!" he said, pointing in the direction of the doors. "Dulcia's son—he's here."

Chris looked over at Charles, who was staring at him strangely.

"Ask him. Charles—tell her. Tell her about the boy!"

"How do you know his name?" interrupted Ms. Lamb, *"Have you been spying on me?"*

"Charles!" shouted Chris, begging him to tell the truth.

Charles hesitated, clearly not sure what was happening. Finally, he seemed to arrive at a decision.

"I don't know what you're talking about. You've made a mistake. Gertrude—I'm leaving."

Without waiting for a response, he turned and walked away.

For a moment, Ms. Lamb looked torn between following Charles or staying with Chris. Finally, with an angry huff, she grabbed onto Chris's sleeve and pulled him toward the exit.

"You are going to regret this, Christopher Lane," she said, ignoring Chris's desperate pleas.

CHAPTER TWENTY

As Chris sat in the back of the taxi, exhausted and defeated, while Ms. Lamb screamed relentlessly at him, Ernest was limping down a dead-end road with Charles toward a parked limousine.

Ernest knocked on the window, and the chauffeur jumped up.

"Unlock the doors," he said as Charles stood silently next to him.

The chauffeur nodded and leaned over.

Click.

Ernest limped over to the door and opened it. He reached inside and pulled out a black leather briefcase.

"Your money," he said, handing the briefcase over to Charles.

Charles looked confused. "That's it? It's over?"

Ernest nodded. "Yes, that's it. You've done everything that I needed—the money is yours."

"So . . . I don't have to see that woman again?"

Ernest shook his head. "No. You don't have to have anything more to do with her. I got all the information I needed from her."

"What do you mean?" asked Charles.

"It doesn't matter," said Ernest. "I needed to find out something, and I could only do it by getting her somewhere loud enough where she wouldn't hear me."

"I don't understand," said Charles, opening up the briefcase.

"You don't need to. You did everything I asked, and now the money is yours. It's all there—you can count it."

Charles reached in and leafed through one of the many wads of notes to check that they were real. And then he paused, as if something had occurred to him. When he looked up, he had the same hard look on his face as when Ernest had first approached him, a homeless petty criminal sleeping rough in a doorway.

Charles snapped the briefcase closed and stared down at Ernest with dark eyes. "You never told me how awful that woman was. I had to put up with being called Chucklebunny, for Pete's sake. I reckon that's worth more than what you've paid me."

Ernest looked up, and his eyes narrowed.

"I gave you new clothes, a haircut, and a briefcase full of money. What more do you want?"

"Double what we agreed, and we'll call it quits."

"And if I say no?" asked Ernest.

Charles slowly leaned forward as he cracked the knuckles on his hand. "I don't think that would be a very good idea."

Ernest held Charles's stare as he replied in a slow, cold voice. "Are you threatening me? Because I'm fairly certain the police would be very interested to hear about a certain night in Kensington three years ago."

Charles's eyes widened in surprise.

"Not to mention," continued Ernest, "some useful information relating to a recent string of robberies in Hampstead."

"How . . . ?"

"Be very careful, Charles. You don't know who you're messing with."

Charles opened his mouth to speak.

"There's nothing more to say," interrupted Ernest. "You've got your money—enough to live on for the rest of your sorry life. Now get out of here."

Charles looked at the twelve-year-old boy standing in front of him, and suddenly looking very nervous, he turned, briefcase in hand, and ran off into the night.

CHAPTER TWENTY-ONE

Chris, as he soon found out when he returned to Myers Holt, wasn't the only one in trouble. Ms. Lamb had already phoned Sir Bentley from the taxi, and he had summoned Daisy, Ron, and John to the office also. Chris looked over at Daisy, who was sitting in an armchair sobbing.

"It's not Daisy's fault!" he said. He thought quickly as Sir Bentley raised his eyebrows in disbelief. "I made her do it—I put the suggestion in her mind."

Daisy snapped her head round in his direction. Chris looked down at his feet and let his eyes glaze over so that everybody standing round him wouldn't see as he sent a message into Daisy's mind.

"There's no point in both of us getting into trouble—I feel bad enough as it is. Please say I did it."

"Is this true?" asked Sir Bentley.

Daisy seemed to think about it for a second. Chris held his breath until, finally, she nodded her head.

"And I did it to Ron and John, too—they couldn't have known about me turning the cameras off."

Ron and John looked at each other in shock.

"But I didn't hear any ringing in my ears," said John to Sir Bentley.

Sir Bentley sighed. "No, the boy's very quick—you wouldn't have heard it. So," he said, looking over at Chris, "you did this all on your own?"

"Yes, sir."

"Very well. Daisy, Ron, John—you can all leave. Ms. Lamb and I will deal with this."

"The boy, his name is Ernest—Dulcia's son," said Chris as the door closed behind him.

"Oh, for goodness' sake!" screeched Ms. Lamb, "the boy is a figment of your imagination. Just admit it—you were spying on me."

"Only because I wanted to find out why you were meeting up with Charles. I saw him with the boy, Ernest, last Friday."

"That is the most ridiculous thing I have ever heard!" said Ms. Lamb.

"IT'S TRUE!" shouted Chris, his anger getting the better of him.

Sir Bentley stood up suddenly and glared at Chris. "*Stop!*"

Both Ms. Lamb and Chris immediately went silent.

"Now, let's be calm about this. Christopher—I want to know exactly what happened."

Chris, wishing that Ms. Lamb weren't sitting next to him, decided to tell the whole truth.

"I know it was wrong, but Ms. Lamb was acting strange," he started, trying to ignore Ms. Lamb glaring at him, "and we wanted to find out why. So I entered her mind . . ."

"You did what?!"

Sir Bentley raised his hand to silence Ms. Lamb. "Let the boy finish—we have to get to the bottom of this."

Ms. Lamb didn't say anything else, but Chris could hear her seething beside him as he explained how he had recognized Charles.

"It was too much of a coincidence—I'd only just seen him with Ernest. I thought maybe they were trying to recruit Ms. Lamb to get back at me."

"Get back at you? For what?" asked Sir Bentley as he raised his hand to Ms. Lamb once more. Ms. Lamb, who was on the edge of her seat and seemed on the verge of exploding, sat down.

"For killing his brother."

"And was she?" asked Sir Bentley. "Was she involved?"

"Sort of," Chris said.

"Liar!"

"Gertrude, please! If you prefer, I can do this alone."

Ms. Lamb humphed. "No—I want to hear these lies."

"Ernest went into Ms. Lamb's mind too," continued Chris, "to get information about me. That's where I met him. He wants to kill me!"

"So you actually spoke to him?" asked Sir Bentley.

"Yes."

"Nonsense," said Ms. Lamb.

"And what happened?" asked Sir Bentley, ignoring Ms. Lamb.

Chris explained everything that had happened—surprising Ernest, their conversation, the chase, and then the fight in the club.

"Did you see the injured boy?" asked Sir Bentley.

"No, of course not," replied Ms. Lamb, "he's lying. He was just leaving when I found him. There was nobody else there. And then he had the nerve to try to involve Charles, who, of course, didn't know what was going on."

"Ernest ran out when you grabbed me," said Chris, raising his voice.

"How convenient," said Ms. Lamb with a sneer.

Sir Bentley put his head in his hands, and both Chris and Ms. Lamb sat in silence, watching him as he processed everything that Chris had said. Finally, he looked up at Chris, and when he spoke, he did so calmly but firmly.

"Christopher. You say you have seen this boy three times now. The first two times, there were many people with you, and not one person was able to back up your claims. Tonight, you admit that you entered Ms. Lamb's mind because you thought she was acting a little strange. That is inexcusable. If you had really been that concerned, you could have spoken to one of us. I think it's quite clear that you entered her mind to find out about her personal affairs. Now you get caught following Ms. Lamb on a private excursion, at night, on your own in the middle of London, and then, when you're found out, you tell us that you saw the boy—"

"But I did! Please, sir, I know—"

Sir Bentley raised his hand to stop him.

"Enough. In your defense, I think that you are having an exceptionally hard time following the death of that boy—more so, perhaps, than any of us had realized. The other times you thought you saw the boy, for example. And the matter of Mr. Valedictoriat."

Chris flinched. "You know about that?"

"I know the state the room was in the next day. I know that he asked to be reassigned a day later. I put two and two together."

"Oh," said Chris, looking down. He had been right—Mr. Valedictoriat had left because of him.

"We have a responsibility to you for the things that have happened," continued Sir Bentley, "and I intend to make sure we take care of you, but your actions tonight were completely irresponsible. You have left me no choice."

Chris, although he had expected it, felt his heart sink.

"You are suspended."

Chris's eyes widened in surprise.

"Suspended? Is that all?" shouted Ms. Lamb.

"Yes, we must take some of the responsibility also, Gertrude. The suspension will be for one week to reflect the seriousness of what you have done. It will give you some time to consider your behavior. We'll call your mother first thing in the morning, and then John and Ron will drive you home. Now go to bed," said Sir Bentley.

Chris nodded and stood up. He turned to say something, but Ms. Lamb interrupted him.

"Get out of here!"

Chris saw the anger in both his teachers' faces and

decided that there was nothing more to be said. He turned and walked out the door.

The others were waiting for Chris when he walked into the Map Room. Chris could feel the tension in the air, and even a small smile from Daisy didn't make him feel any better. Finally, Rex spoke up.

"I just don't get it—why did you lie to us?"

"I didn't lie," said Chris weakly, feeling like his whole life was unraveling before him, "I just didn't think you'd believe me."

"Well, we wouldn't have," said Lexi. "We saw the boy last week, and it wasn't him. You've obviously lost it, but that's not the point. You should have told us."

"Do you all think that?" asked Chris, looking around.

For a moment, nobody said a word.

"I believe you," said Daisy, finally.

"Of course you do," said Lexi. "Nobody wants to think her boyfriend has gone nuts."

"He's not my boyfriend!" said Daisy.

"But he is nuts," said Rex.

"I'm still here, Rex," said Chris, feeling himself flush with anger, "and I'm not crazy—I know what happened."

"You are all making my head hurt," said Sebastian, all of a sudden. "He is crazy, you are crazy, everybody is crazy. Now—I wish to discover what occurred. Chris?"

Chris looked up at Sebastian, not sure whether to be grateful or not.

"What's the point?" asked Chris. "You won't believe me anyway."

"I want to know," said Daisy.

Chris looked around as everybody stared at him. He wondered if he had lost his friends for good—the only true friends he had ever had, and decided that the only way to gain their trust again would be to tell them everything.

"Well. Do you believe me?" asked Chris as he finished telling them about his meeting with Ernest.

Chris's heart sank. He knew, from the way everybody was shifting uncomfortably, what was coming before anybody spoke.

Finally, Rex put his hand on Chris's shoulder. Chris shrugged it away.

"Look, mate, we believe that you believe it, if that makes you feel better."

"It doesn't," said Chris flatly.

"You're obviously a bit messed up about killing that boy," continued Rex. "It's nothing to be ashamed of, right?"

Lexi, Sebastian, and Philip nodded.

"Thing is, we were with you when you saw the boy the other two times. He wasn't there. It was just another kid. You're seeing things."

"Chris," said Philip, "you know I don't like to agree with him—"

"Thanks, Einstein," interrupted Rex.

Philip ignored him.

"But Rex is right. Think about it—the only person who has seen the boy is—"

"Me, I know," said Chris, feeling completely deflated.

"But the rest of the story's good," said Rex, continuing

on from Philip, "hilarious, in fact. And, look, you're obviously not quite right in the head at the moment, so we forgive you about lying to us. Right, everyone?"

Lexi, Sebastian, and Philip all smiled and nodded. Chris sat looking glum as Philip gave him a friendly slap on the back and stood up.

"I'm going to bed," he said.

"Me too," said Lexi.

They all stood up, except Chris.

"Don't worry, Chris," said Daisy, turning to follow the others out of the room, "it's just a lot for them to believe."

"I suppose so," said Chris. He remembered what John had said to him, and as hard as it was, he knew that Daisy was right—he just wished he could think of some way of proving it to them.

Sir Bentley was on the phone talking when Chris walked into his office the next morning. He motioned for Chris to sit as he finished his conversation and then put the phone down.

"Christopher, we've been trying to call your mother this morning, but there's been no answer."

Chris looked alarmed. "She has to be there—she doesn't go anywhere."

"Maybe she's asleep, then."

Chris shook his head. "She would hear it—the phone is next to her bed, and there's one in the living room."

"Well, then, I'm sure she's popped out to the shops or something. Anyway, as soon as we get hold of her, we'll take you home, but until we do, you'll stay here. I have to go do some work, but somebody will come to get you later."

Chris's mind was racing. "You don't understand, Sir Bentley—there's no way my mum wouldn't answer the phone. She doesn't leave the house. Something . . ."

Just then, Chris froze, and suddenly, everything was clear.

"Yes?" asked Sir Bentley, seeing the expression on Chris's face.

"It's Ernest. Ernest has taken her!" said Chris, looking panicked.

"Now, now. Why would he do that?" said Sir Bentley.

"He was looking at my school file in Ms. Lamb's mind when I interrupted him—my mum's name and address were in it," said Chris, practically shouting with worry. "This is his way of getting me to come to him."

Chris could tell that Sir Bentley thought he was acting crazy, but he didn't care anymore. He jumped up and reached over to pick up the phone.

"Christopher, calm down!" said Sir Bentley as Chris frantically dialed his home number.

Chris waited, and then the phone began to ring. And ring. Sir Bentley looked at Chris as he listened, but he made no attempt to stop him. Finally, Chris gave up. He put the phone down.

"I have to go home."

Sir Bentley shook his head. "You can't go back to an empty house. Wait until we hear from your mother, and we'll get a car to take you there."

"You don't understand—he's taken her!" shouted Chris. He felt as if he were about to burst with anger and frustration. *"I need to go home."*

Sir Bentley stared at Chris, who was now pacing up and

down the room, frantically running his hands through his hair.

"Please," said Chris finally, stopping suddenly, tears of frustration beginning to form, "please let me go home. I need to go home."

Sir Bentley sighed. "Fine. I can see that you're upset. If it will give you peace of mind, I'll get Ron and John to take you. You can wait until lunchtime with them, and if by then she hasn't shown up, you have to come back to school. Do you understand?"

Chris nodded as Sir Bentley stood up. He knew that his mother wouldn't be there—but perhaps Ernest would have left him some way of getting in contact—he was, after all, the person that Ernest wanted to see.

"Please, hurry up," he said as Sir Bentley led him down toward Ron and John's quarters.

Chris rode the elevator in silence, squeezed tightly in between Ron and John and Sir Bentley, who was explaining to the two guards about what he wanted them to do. John, to his credit, said nothing. He just put his hand on Chris's shaking shoulder.

"It's all right, son," said John.

"We'll go get the car," said Ron as he walked quickly over to the front door, John by his side.

"We'll wait out front for you," said Sir Bentley, following behind with Chris. They were just about to step out the front door when Sir Bentley put his hand on Chris's shoulder. "While we're waiting, why don't you use your Ability to check whether she's there yet."

Chris looked up at Sir Bentley, shocked that he hadn't thought of this himself; in his panic, he had completely forgotten that once outside of the lead-lined facility, he could use his Ability to remote-access other locations. He stepped outside and, head bowed, eyes closed, he let his mind soar upward and then westward, over a map of London that he had long ago memorized, until, seeing his own house, he let his focus drop as quickly as he could until he was standing on the street outside. Chris looked up and focused on every room in turn—the image of each flicking quickly from one room to the next as he checked for his mother. The final place he looked in was the living room. Chris scanned the room, shocked at the state his mother had allowed it to get in—half-eaten plates of food, mugs of half-drunk tea everywhere, and photo albums of his father lying open next to the armchair that his mother fell asleep in most nights. Most worrying, however, was that the television was on.

"She's not there—I checked every room," said Chris, opening his eyes.

"I'm sure she'll be home any moment," said Sir Bentley, leading Chris down the steps as John pulled up in the car. Ron jumped out from the passenger side and ran round to open the door.

"Remember," said Sir Bentley to Ron, "wait until midday—if she hasn't shown up by then, bring Christopher back here."

"Yes, sir," said Ron.

"I'll leave you to it," said Sir Bentley. He turned to Chris. "Take care. I'm sure she'll be fine, and we'll see you in a week. Use the time to get some rest and relax a bit—I think you need it."

Chris nodded, wishing they would just get going.

Sir Bentley thanked Ron and John and turned back up the steps and through the front door.

"Are we in a hurry?" asked Ron as Chris climbed into the back of the car.

"Yes—please."

"Right, John—you heard him, he's in a rush."

John, whose enormous frame was squashed up against the steering wheel, looked up at Ron. "I'm already in the car."

Ron waved him out. "Get out, then. The way you drive, we won't get there till midnight."

"And the way you drive, we won't get there at all," answered John, nevertheless getting out of the car.

Chris put his seat belt on as Ron jumped into the driver's seat and adjusted the seat until he was so far forward he was practically lying on the steering wheel, his head pressed up against the windshield.

"Ready?" he asked.

Chris heard the click of John's seat belt. "Yep," said John.

"Then let's"—Ron turned the key in the ignition and released the handbrake—*"go!"*

Ron put one foot on the clutch, pressed all the way down on the accelerator with the other until the engine was screeching, and then, like a greyhound released from his trap, the car exploded into life.

Chris was thrown backward with the force as Ron began

to race through the backstreets of London, tires screeching as he negotiated the tight turns. John, who was clearly well used to Ron's driving, calmly navigated the way.

". . . And left, left, left. Sharp right . . . straight on . . . red light . . . I said red light, Ron. . . . Too late, never mind . . . straight on . . ."

"Won't you get a speeding ticket?" shouted Chris as they flew down the restricted bus lane.

"MI5 vehicle—they've got our number plate," said Ron as he veered round a line of stationary traffic onto the other side of the road, not once hitting the brake.

Chris sat back and looked out the car window at the blurred scenery. He wished he could enjoy the ride, but his mind was only on getting home and finding out what had happened to his mother.

Finally the car pulled up outside Chris's house. Before Ron had even turned off the engine, Chris had unbuckled himself, opened the door, and leaped out. As he ran toward the house, his eyes glazed over and the front lock clicked open.

"Wait for us," said Ron as the door swung open and Chris rushed inside.

The living room was exactly as it had been when he had visited it in his mind—the television guides thrown about the floor, the unopened mail scattered on the sofa, the television on. He was about to turn when Chris felt two large hands grab his shoulders.

"Don't touch anything," said John as Ron stepped in from behind him and started running around to check behind the furniture, "you've obviously been burgled."

Chris felt himself redden. "Um. No . . . it's always like this."

"Oh."

John let go of Chris, who then turned and sprinted down to the kitchen, which was filthy and stacked high with at least a week's worth of mugs and dishes. Again, there was no sign of his mother.

"What's up here?" called John, his feet thumping up the stairs.

Chris ran to the front of the house and looked up. There, on the landing, was a long ladder leading up into an open hole in the ceiling.

"The attic," said Chris, confused—he hadn't even thought of looking there.

"Stay here," said Ron, pushing past Chris and jumping, catlike, onto the ladder. "I'll check that it's safe."

Chris stood next to John and watched in silence as Ron scrambled silently up and then disappeared into the hole above. For a moment, there was complete silence and then, out of the darkness, Ron's head appeared.

"Chris," he whispered, "I think you'd better come up here."

Panicking, Chris climbed the ladder and stepped out onto the wooden floor. The attic was lit dimly by a single bare bulb hanging from the center of the vaulted ceiling. Chris looked around, but all he could see were piles of boxes and chests.

"Behind there," whispered Ron, pointing to a stack of cardboard boxes.

Chris stepped forward cautiously, stepping over an old

rolled-up rug and round the back of the boxes, and found what Ron was pointing at.

There, lying on the floor, was his mother, surrounded by a pile of open photo albums.

"Mum?"

There was no response.

Chris knelt down next to her and placed his hand on her shoulder. "Mum? Wake up."

He felt his mother stir and watched as she slowly opened her eyes. She looked around, getting her bearings, and then she turned to Chris.

"What are you doing here?" she asked.

Chris didn't know what to say. The truth—*I thought you had been kidnapped*—suddenly seemed too ridiculous to say out loud.

"Apologies for disturbing you, Mrs. Lane. We wanted to check that you were home," said Ron, stepping out from behind the boxes. "We tried calling this morning."

"Who is he?" asked Chris's mother, glaring at Ron.

"He's one of the security guards from school," said Chris. He still felt as if he'd been punched in the stomach. Nothing was making any sense, and his head was spinning from confusion.

"Ron Stiller," said Ron. He stepped forward and leaned over to help Chris's mum to her feet.

"Get your hands off me," she said, flinching away.

Ron jumped back, startled by her anger. Chris wished that the ground would swallow him up.

"Come on, Chris," said Ron gently. "Let's wait downstairs."

Chris looked at his mum, her hair disheveled, not speaking as she put the albums back into a box, and then turned away.

"Put a cup of tea on," said his mother as she walked into the living room. She glared at Ron and John without greeting them and sat down in her armchair.

"John Walker," said John as he walked over and offered his hand.

Chris's mother looked up at him and shook his hand coldly. "I'm here. You can go now."

"Mrs. Lane," said John, clearly uncomfortable, "the reason we needed to get hold of you . . ."

Chris was already feeling awful enough—he couldn't hear anymore. He looked over to Ron and signaled to ask if he wanted a drink. Ron shook his head, and Chris walked away, leaving John to explain Chris's suspension.

Chris turned the kettle on and opened the cupboard to find that there were no clean mugs—the only surprise about that was that he'd bothered checking. He turned on the tap and picked up one of the dirty mugs from the counter.

Distracted, Chris began to wash the mug, wondering how he could have got it so wrong. He had been so sure that his mother had been taken, but now that he had seen that wasn't the case, he felt no relief, just embarrassment at having been proved wrong, once again, and worry about what, exactly, Ernest might be planning instead.

"I've talked to your mum," said John, appearing at the kitchen doorway.

Chris picked up a tea towel and began to dry the mug. "What did she say?"

"Not much. I didn't go into detail—just said you'd got into a bit of trouble at school and you've been sent home for a week, and she said it's fine to leave you here."

Chris looked up as John pulled the door behind him closed and walked over to the sink.

"Chris, you don't have to stay. I think Sir Bentley will understand if we explain. . . ."

Chris shook his head. "It's all right. I'm used to it."

"Are you sure? I don't think your mum is feeling well. . . ."

"Honestly, John, I'm fine. She's been like this for years—I don't even remember what she was like before."

John thought about this for a moment and then, finally, sighed. "All right, but you know you can call if you need anything. We'll be here in no time—you saw how Ron drives."

Chris gave a weak smile. "Thanks."

"All right, we'll leave you now. We'll be back next Sunday at six. But if you change your mind or you need anything at all, just pick up the phone."

Chris nodded. Then, just as John was about to walk out, Chris spoke.

"I'm sorry, John. I really thought something had happened to her."

John gave him a smile. "Don't you worry about that, son—it's not been an easy couple of months. You rest up—this will all be forgotten when you get back to school."

With that, John walked out of the kitchen. Chris waited until he heard the front door close, then picked up the hot mug of tea, delivered it to his mother in silence, and went up to his room.

In the week that followed, until Ron and John returned to take him back to school, Chris never once left the house, more certain with every day that passed that Ernest was about to appear. The feeling that somebody was watching him during the day intensified at night, and Chris would wake up in a cold sweat from nightmares in which he was being chased by an unknown assailant, only to wake up and wonder if it was actually true.

Meanwhile, an increasingly unkempt Ernest sat alone within the vast and oppressive confines of Darkwhisper Manor and watched Chris's paranoia with a sense of cold satisfaction. Using his Ability, Ernest spent his days and nights barely sleeping as he tracked Chris in his mind— watching him wake in terror from his nightmares, then check the house before returning for a couple of hours of fitful sleep, only to repeat the process a couple of hours later. It was strange, he thought, how things had a way of working out. He had always known that his Ability lacked the power of his brother's, but he hadn't anticipated how strong Christopher Lane's powers might be until their meeting at the concert. That night, as he had returned home, limping and bruised, he had been devastated at not having accomplished what he had set out to do. Now he realized, as he watched Chris suffering with the anticipation of his attack, that the delay was in fact going to be the greatest part of his revenge. He would still honor the promise he had made at his brother's grave—Christopher Lane would die for what he had done—but Ernest was going to take his time about it. For, however strong Chris's Ability might be, Ernest had something far more powerful: patience. The element of surprise would be his strongest weapon, and that the long wait he was planning was only going to distress Chris further was simply an added bonus. As he watched Chris, confused and exhausted, leave his house a week later to return to school, Ernest smiled to himself. Let the waiting game begin.

. CHAPTER TWENTY-TWO .

Five Months Later

"Good evening, and welcome to a breaking news special with me, Anya Li. Tonight, scenes of jubilation as Lucy Horsham, the seven-year-old daughter of the Earl and Countess of Hampshire, is found alive in a barn in the New Forest. We go straight to our correspondent Felix Dunbar, who is live at the scene with the details. Felix, what can you tell us?"

"Thank you, Anya. In the last ten minutes, police have confirmed that they have located seven-year-old Lucy Horsham, alive and well and apparently unharmed. It's the end of an agonizing six-day ordeal for the friends and family of Lucy, who was kidnapped from her home, Lawrie Hall, in the early hours of Saturday morning. The successful conclusion is all the more surprising given that the police admitted yesterday that they had no reliable leads and that, aside from the ransom note left at the scene demanding one million pounds for her return, they had received no further information. It was thought that the extensive press coverage and the enormous public interest in the case—thousands of people have spent the last few days searching for the girl—might have sent the kidnapper into hiding, as no further demands had been received. Only this morning, as we reported earlier, a press conference was held appealing for the public's help. At that time, there was certainly no indication that any further information had become available, and many were beginning to lose hope that Lucy would be found alive. Tonight, however, a man and a woman are in custody on suspicion of kidnapping and blackmail—we have unconfirmed reports that they are they owners of the farm on which Lucy was found. It is another successful outcome in what has been an astonishing few months for the British police, the rate of serious crimes solved since January of this year being the highest in recorded history. We'll bring you more of this case as it develops, but for now back to you, Anya, in the studio."

Chris stood up, grinning, and switched the television off as Daisy, Lexi, Philip, and Sebastian let out a cheer.

"What's the matter?" asked Chris, seeing the frown on Rex's face.

"Well . . . it's good that they found her, but where's the thanks? We're doing all the work, and the police get all the credit. It's not fair—I should be on television."

Lexi rolled her eyes. "First, we're not doing all the work—we can't solve anything without the police doing the groundwork. Second, you agreed when you came here that you wouldn't tell anybody about what we do."

"I know," said Rex, looking glum, "but what's the point of this all if I don't get any credit? I could be famous."

"Oh, I don't know," said Philip, "maybe the point is that we've saved that girl's life. Or that fifteen people have had their convictions overturned following our information. Or maybe the eighty percent reduction in burglary since we started helping the commissioner, or the three hundred twenty-two arrests since we started working with the police. Or—"

"Yeah, yeah," said Rex, "I get it. Just saying—it would have been nice to see my picture on the front pages, that's all. We've got two weeks left, and then that's it—we'll all just go back to normal school and be normal pupils, and all this will be just some strange memory that nobody will believe, even if we tell them."

The room went silent as everybody considered this: the until-now-unspoken fact that their time at Myers Holt was coming to an end, and with their thirteenth birthdays fast approaching, so would their Ability. It was not something that any of them wanted to think about.

"Thanks for depressing us all," said Philip, slamming his book closed.

"Oh, come on, everybody, it's not that bad—we'll all still be friends, right?" said Daisy, trying to sound cheerful.

Nobody answered.

"And we won't have to have any more lessons with Ms.

Lamb," continued Daisy. "That's a good thing too. Right, Chris?"

"I guess," said Chris, who would have gladly put up with his daily dose of insults from Ms. Lamb in exchange for more time at Myers Holt. At least, he thought, he was going to be starting at a new school—Miss Sonata had arranged for a place for him at the same boarding school as Philip, starting in September.

"Daisy is correct—all good things must come to an end," said Sebastian, "but we have much to look forward to. We will most certainly be the highest achievers in our new classes—even Rex will be recognized as a genius."

"*Finally* be recognized as a genius," corrected Rex.

"And we won't have to listen to Rex moaning anymore," said Lexi. Rex turned to glare at her, but Lexi smiled back. "Only teasing, Rex. You know we'll all miss you."

"Like an ingrown toenail," said Philip, also smiling as he stood up. "Come on—this is too depressing. Let's go for a swim."

The last five months had seen a lot of changes for the pupils of Myers Holt but for none more so than Chris. The school timetables had been rearranged soon after Chris's return from his suspension so that they could dedicate their days to solving the crimes that the commissioner presented them with at a briefing every morning. In the evening and on weekends, barring any police emergency, the pupils would cram in as much studying as they could—all suddenly aware that the more they did now, the less effort they would have to put into their learning when they no longer had their Ability to help them. With their new schedule had come daily outings from the school—to police stations, prisons, crime scenes, and even, on one occasion, a submarine. At first, Chris had been almost paralyzed with fear every time he stepped out of the school's front door—certain that Ernest was about to appear at any moment. Slowly, however, that fear had begun to subside as the days passing without incident turned into weeks and his memory of the meeting with Ernest began to fade. If Ernest had wanted to attempt to kill him, Chris had eventually come to reason, then there had been plenty of opportunities given that they now spent so much time outside the safety of the school. It was clear, Chris thought, that on the night of the concert he had shown his Ability was no match for Ernest, and Ernest had decided to abandon his plans for revenge. As the weeks turned into months and Chris became increasingly convinced that he was right, he began to spend less and less time worrying about Ernest until, one day, he stopped thinking of him altogether.

Chris lay floating in the clear blue waters of the Dome's swimming pool as his friends splashed around him and thought about their earlier conversation in the Map Room. Daisy and Sebastian were right, he thought: In spite of how much he was going to miss Myers Holt, there was still so much to look forward to. Whilst nothing had changed at home—despite Miss Sonata's best efforts, his mother had refused any help—at least he would be going away to boarding school in September with Philip and wouldn't have to live at home.

As it was, he had not once seen his mother since his suspension. He had jumped at Philip's parents' invitation to stay with them during the Easter holidays so that, with the exception of a few brief and very awkward phone calls, he had had no further contact with his mother. Lucky for him, Philip's parents had enjoyed hosting Chris, and he had been invited to stay with them over the summer holidays. Miss Sonata had said she would check with his mother, but Chris was sure that she would agree—he now had no doubt that he was not welcome at home any longer. It was sad but true. He might have a mother who didn't want him around, his time at Myers Holt might be coming to an end, and his Ability would be disappearing in a few months' time, but at least, he thought as he waded over to join the others, he had his friends. And that was more than enough to be grateful for.

That afternoon, Chris sat at his desk in the classroom while Ms. Lamb shouted at him for using blue ink instead of black on his last report form, and he let his mind go blank. They were using a trick that Lexi had thought of a few weeks earlier: using their Ability to talk to each other unnoticed in class. Now that Ms. Lamb's lessons were mostly just an opportunity for her to find fault with their work—their training having long been completed—this way of talking between themselves was a welcome distraction.

"I think we need to come up with a way of saying good-bye to Ms. Lamb when we leave—something for her to remember us by. What do you think?" asked Rex, using his Ability.

"Brilliant idea. Chalk on her back?" suggested Chris.

"Amateur," said Rex.

"I agree," said Philip. "It's got to be something a bit cleverer."

"And as for the way you conducted yourselves on the minibus! Singing . . ." Ms. Lamb continued her rant, not noticing that despite everybody looking in her direction, nobody was paying any attention.

"We could hide round the corner," suggested Daisy, "and scare her when she comes into the classroom."

"You haven't got the hang of this at all," said Rex. "We've got one chance to get back at her for being so evil to all of us—that's it. We've got to make it good."

"Hide her boots?"

"Put salt in her coffee?"

"Bucket of water on top of the door?"

"Chris could pretend to fall in love with her," said Lexi. There was a brief silence.

"Best. Idea. Ever," said Rex, sounding delighted.

"Are you crazy?" asked Chris, horrified but trying not to let it show on his face. "Never. Not in a million years."

"All right, all right, calm down," said Rex, "Let me think . . . hmm . . . oh . . . wait . . . I've got it!"

"Christopher?"

Chris jumped up and saw Miss Sonata standing at the doorway, staring at him.

"Oh, um. Sorry, Miss Sonata."

"I told you," said Ms. Lamb, "they don't pay any attention."

"Christopher, can I have a word in my office?"

Chris nodded and stood up. He grabbed his bag and

walked out the door, but not before noticing the evil smile on everybody's faces as they listened to Rex in their minds.

"Christopher, I don't want to alarm you," said Miss Sonata as they walked through the Dome, "but we've been trying to get hold of your mum since yesterday to deliver the food shopping, and there's been no answer."

"She's probably just sleeping in the attic," said Chris, "like last time."

"I'm sure that's the case. Nevertheless, it's been twenty-four hours. I even went round there this morning, but there was no answer at the door, so I thought maybe we could go outside and you could use your Ability to check the house and make sure she's okay, that she's not unwell or anything like that."

Chris nodded as he followed Miss Sonata into the elevator.

"I'm sure she's fine," said Chris as they stepped out of the lift and walked down the corridor. "You've met her—she's probably just ignoring the phone."

"Well . . . you're probably right, but I'd still like you to make sure," said Miss Sonata.

Chris shrugged his shoulders and opened the front door. He stepped out onto the top stair, surprised at the cool chill of the air despite it being June, and turned to Miss Sonata.

"Now?"

"Whenever you're ready, Christopher."

Chris closed his eyes and let his Ability take over.

The first room that Chris entered in his mind was his house's living room. Even knowing how neglectful his

mother was of all household chores, Chris was shocked by
how filthy she had allowed her surroundings to become.
Sometime in January, when Miss Sonata had first learned
of his mother's relapse, his mother had been offered
a weekly cleaner, to be paid for by Myers Holt. She had
refused, saying that it would be an invasion of her privacy,
and the matter had been dropped. Chris had seen what a
mistake that had been when he had returned home during
his suspension and found the rooms that his mother used
in total disarray. Now he could see that not a single plate
or mug had been lifted from its place in five months, and
the entire room was covered in a thick layer of dust.

Chris shook his head in disgust as he let his mind wander to the kitchen. There was no sign of his mother there,
either, just empty packets and bags from the weekly shopping that had been dropped off to her and a bin that had
obviously not been emptied for a very long time. Chris was
glad that he couldn't smell the room. Nevertheless, he had
no intention of hanging around, so he let his mind slip past
the doorway, out into the hallway, and up the stairs. There
was no sign of her. Even more peculiar, the attic hatch was
closed, and there was no ladder leading up to it. Chris was
surprised—he had been sure that the reason for her not
answering the phone was the same as last time, that she was
hiding up there surrounded by photographs of his father.
To be certain, Chris let his mind soar up through the ceiling
and into the cold attic space. He checked carefully, behind
every box and in every corner, but his mother was not there.

Chris's breaths started to quicken with panic as he
checked the other rooms upstairs and found them empty

as well. He hadn't expected to feel so concerned, but it was his mother and, in spite of the way she had treated him, there remained, it seemed, a part of him that cared about her and remembered that she had once been so different. Chris began to check the house again, behind every piece of furniture, in the understairs cupboard, and even in the garden shed but found nothing. And then, with a sudden jolt, he remembered those words: "When you least expect it."

"When was the last time you spoke to her?" Chris asked Miss Sonata.

"Two days ago—when I was arranging the time for the shopping to be dropped. Why? What's happened, Chris?" asked Miss Sonata. "Is your mother okay? Is she hurt?"

"She's not there."

Miss Sonata smiled gently, but Christopher could see the concern in her eyes. "I'm sure she's fine—she probably just went out for a moment."

Chris looked at Miss Sonata. "In all the time that you've known my mum, has she ever left the house?"

Miss Sonata shook her head.

"She never goes out," said Chris before Miss Sonata had a chance to respond. "She's been convinced for years that if she does, something bad will happen."

"I agree, Christopher, it's unlike her. What do you think the explanation could be?"

"The boy—Ernest—he said it would be when I least expect it."

Miss Sonata took a deep breath and sighed. "Look, Christopher. That boy—"

"Ernest. Miss Sonata, please listen to me," said Chris,

panic rising up in him. "He took her because he wants to get to me—I saw him looking at my home address in Ms. Lamb's mind. I know that's what he was thinking."

"There would certainly be no need for him to take your mother. It just doesn't make any sense—and why would he wait all this time? If he wanted to make you suffer for the accident with his brother, he could have done that a long time ago."

Chris looked at Miss Sonata, and his eyes widened with understanding. "Suffer. That's it! He wanted me to suffer. He knew nobody believed me. He knew that it would drive me crazy expecting something to happen at any time. That's why he waited. Miss Sonata, I need to go home."

"For what, Christopher? What on earth do you expect to find?"

"I don't know. Maybe Ernest left me something—a clue. I can't tell with my Ability—there's too much stuff lying around to sort through."

"Why don't we give it a few more hours," said Miss Sonata, trying to lead Chris back in through the front door. "Then, if she still hasn't come home, you can give Ron and John your keys, and I'll send them round to check the house."

Chris shook himself free. "I'm sorry, Miss Sonata, I have to go right now. If my mum is in trouble, I need to find her."

Chris stepped down the stairs and was about to run, not thinking about how he was going to get home, when Miss Sonata called out to him.

"Christopher, you are not going anywhere like this. Wait five minutes—John and Ron will take you."

• • •

Chris jumped out of the car before John had even turned off the engine, and ran up the front path. He pulled the keys out of his pocket and fumbled with the lock.

"Argh!" said Chris, throwing the keys to the ground in frustration as he narrowed his eyes in the direction of the lock.

Click.

"Honestly, don't think I'll ever get tired of seeing that trick," said Ron to John as the door swung open on its own.

"MUM?"

Chris ran inside and stopped at the foot of the stairs.

"MUM? ARE YOU HERE?"

There was no answer.

Chris noticed Ron peering over his right shoulder as he looked up the stairs.

"I've already checked the attic," said Chris, annoyed that Ron would think he'd make the same mistake twice. He ran up the stairs and checked the bedrooms as Ron and John checked downstairs. It was no surprise to Chris that she wasn't there.

"Right," said John as Chris came down the stairs shaking his head, "why don't we all have a nice cup of tea and wait for her—I'm sure she'll turn up in a moment."

"She doesn't go out!" said Chris, feeling as if he were speaking a language that nobody could understand. "Mum doesn't leave the house. Ever."

John sighed but didn't look annoyed. "It's all right, son. I'm sure she's fine, but there's not much we can do at the . . ."

"Uh . . ."

Chris and John both turned to the living room door to find Ron standing in the doorway, a strange look on his face.

"I think you'd both better come and have a look at this."

Chris looked down at the newspaper cutting lying on his mother's armchair, and his heart stopped.

Dominating the front page was a large photograph of Hunter Reid, the clean-cut American teenage music sensation, under this headline:

LET THE FAINTING BEGIN!

HUNTER REID ARRIVES IN THE UK

TO PROMOTE THE LAUNCH OF HIS NEW ALBUM

Chris barely registered this, however. All he could look at was the message that had been scrawled across Hunter Reid's white jacket in thick bright red pen.

Chris,
If you want to see your mother again, meet me here. Same place as last time.
Ernest

A large red arrow pointed to the center of Hunter Reid's forehead.

"I don't believe it. You were right," said John slowly, as he read the message over Chris's shoulder.

Chris should have felt vindicated at last—finally, here was the proof that he wasn't going crazy, but he felt nothing.

"I don't get it," said John. "What does he mean, 'same place'?"

Chris picked up the paper without talking and stared at the page.

"Look," said Ron, pointing. "That's what he means."

The three of them looked down at the caption below the photograph:

Thousands of fans have already lined up outside the Maximum Music Store on Oxford Street, where Hunter Reid will be signing autographs tomorrow from 2:00 p.m.

"Have you been to Maximum Music? Did you meet him there?" asked Ron.

Chris shook his head. "That's not what he means," he said quietly.

Ron and John waited for an explanation, but none came. Finally, John grabbed Chris by the shoulders and turned him round to face him.

"Chris, son. Look. We're here to help you, so you need to tell us everything. Do you understand?"

Chris nodded, still in a daze. "He means meet him inside Hunter Reid's mind—in the same place that I met him when we were in Ms. Lamb's mind."

"Oh," said John. "At the signing?"

"Yes."

"Well, that's not much use right now," said Ron, frustrated. "Is there anything else? Anywhere you can think of that we could go?"

Chris shook his head.

"No. What about where Ernest lives? Do you know?"

"I haven't got a clue," said Chris. He folded up the

newspaper page slowly and put it into his pocket. "I'll have to wait till tomorrow."

"We're going with you," said Ron. He and John followed Chris as he walked in a daze out of the living room and toward the front door.

Chris lay on his bed that night, staring up at the glowing moon on his ceiling. In the bed across the room, Chris knew that Philip was also awake, but he, like everybody else, didn't know what to say to Chris, who had not said a word since John had broken the news to everybody on their return to Myers Holt. Chris's silence seemed to have unnerved everybody but he was not doing it intentionally. It was as if he were standing in a thick, dreamlike fog that had dulled everything around him—the sounds, the sights, the smells, and even his feelings. He knew he should have been panicking, and he was surprised that he wasn't. He supposed it must have been because he knew he couldn't do anything until he met with Ernest. In the meantime, he was sure that his mother was safe: Ernest needed her alive to get at him, and now he just needed to make sure he was rested enough to handle whatever lay in store for him. He closed his eyes and fell into a dreamless sleep.

CHAPTER TWENTY-THREE

Chris spoke once the next morning—to ask that none of the other pupils accompany him. Sir Bentley had agreed. Chris guessed that, given how everything had turned out, nobody felt in a position to argue with him anymore. The four-man police escort that Sir Bentley had arranged was waiting at the cordon that had been erected by Oxford Circus Station to contain the thousands of screaming girls who had gathered to get a glimpse of Hunter Reid. John and Ron spoke with them in hushed urgent tones making arrangements, while Chris hung back and looked out into the crowds searching for Ernest—a pointless exercise given that the crowds were thick and extended the length of the wide street up to the entrance of Maximum Music.

"Right, Chris," said John. "This is a bit more hectic than

we had thought so we're going to have to rely on your help to find him. The singer is going to be arriving in twenty minutes, and we'll make sure you're right there. When you find him, just let us know where he is and we'll take it from there. Yes?"

"Okay," said Chris as John handed him a glittering gold pass hanging on a fluorescent green cord, which he put over his neck. He saw a group of girls staring at the large VIP emblazoned on the front of the pass with pure envy.

"Are you famous?" shouted one of them, as the police officers lifted the red cordon to allow Chris, Ron, and John through.

"Er, no," said Chris, keeping his head down as he walked between Ron and John in their black suits with their sunglasses on. Rex would love this, he thought as the four police officers in front of him cleared the crowds to make way for him to pass. Chris, however, just kept a strong grip on the pass to stop the many reaching hands from snatching it off him and concentrated on finding Ernest.

The crowds of girls became increasingly angry as Chris made his way along the street until, by the time he was escorted through the glass entrance doors, he was surrounded by the sound of deafening boos.

"Go to the back!"

"We've been waiting all night!"

"Oi! Who do you think you are?"

Chris tried to ignore their fury as John and Ron, both straight-faced and staring intently around them, walked alongside him. Chris was thankful for their protection and breathed a sigh of relief as he was ushered past another cordon and through a side door.

"I've never seen anything like it," said John as they followed a police officer down a corridor.

"You can wait in here," said the officer, leading them into a room.

Chris walked in to find the place buzzing with the sound of people, all wearing white T-shirts with Hunter Reid's face on it, frantically making preparations. Chris jumped out of the way to let a woman carrying a large box filled with plastic Hunter Reid dolls pass.

"Why don't you stand at the back," said John. "We'll stay here by the door so we can keep an eye on everything and give you a shout when we're ready to go."

Chris nodded and weaved his way through the people and tables until he reached a small bit of cleared area near the far wall. Pushed up against it was a blue sofa, and on it was Hunter Reid, his blond hair gelled up, wearing silver trousers and a black vest, sitting quietly with his headphones on. He looked much younger than Chris had expected.

Chris searched for another chair, but not seeing one, he walked over to the corner and leaned up against the wall to wait.

"You can sit here."

Chris turned and saw Hunter Reid looking at him as he pulled the headphones out of his ears.

"Oh . . . thanks," Chris said. He walked over to the sofa and sat down awkwardly.

"Hi, I'm Hunter," said Hunter. He smiled as he put his hand out to shake Chris's.

"Hi—Chris," said Chris, shaking his hand, and then, not knowing what else to say, he sat back, facing forward.

"It's crazy, isn't it?" said Hunter after a moment.

"What do you mean?" asked Chris.

"All this," he said as he nodded at the room full of panicked people.

"Must be nice."

Hunter shook his head. "No, it's just business. It's not about me, it's all about the money."

Chris was surprised. "What about all those girls?"

"They don't really like me—they just like the whole fame-and-money thing. Next week they'll be screaming for someone else," said Hunter, sounding quite matter-of-fact about it.

"Really? They seem to be really into you."

Hunter thought about this for a moment and then shrugged his shoulders. "Yeah, maybe. And some of them seem really cool, but I never get to hang out with them—I don't stay in one place for long enough."

"Don't you like the whole singing thing, though?"

"Yeah, it's my life—I love it. I just wish they'd let me sing what I wanted to sing."

"Oh right. Um, what do you want to sing?"

Hunter leaned in, as if he didn't want anybody else to hear. "Heavy metal."

"Really?" asked Chris in surprise.

"Yeah. You into it?"

Chris gave a small smile. "I went to see the Death Screamers once."

Hunter broke into a wide approving grin. "Awesome!

They're amazing! 'The grim reaper! The grim reaper! Your soul's—'"

"Hunter?"

Hunter looked up at the young woman who had interrupted him. She was wearing one of the white T-shirts with Hunter's face on it and holding a clipboard.

"Everything's ready."

Hunter sighed and turned to Chris. "It's been cool hanging out, man."

He pulled out a card from his pocket and handed it to Chris.

"Here's my card. Give me a call if you're ever in LA—"

"Thanks," said Chris. He slipped the card into his pocket and smiled. "Good luck with the heavy metal thing."

Hunter grinned and gave Chris a double thumbs-up as he was shepherded away by the clipboard lady.

He's really nice, thought Chris, suddenly feeling a bit guilty about entering Hunter's mind without him knowing.

"Time for us, too," said John, suddenly appearing in front of him as the room quickly emptied behind Hunter. Chris stood up and followed Ron and John out the doors and down the black corridor. Ahead of him, Hunter stepped out into the shop floor, and the crowds erupted into frenzied high-pitched screaming.

Although there was no need for Chris to hide, he still needed somewhere away from the hustle and bustle of the moving crowds to concentrate and, ideally, to save energy while using his Ability. But he also had to have a clear view of Hunter, who was now sitting at a table signing photographs of himself and smiling for pictures.

"Over there," said John, leading them toward a triangle of empty space beneath the escalator. Chris followed behind him, all the time wondering if Ernest was watching.

"Right," said John, "here's the plan. You do your Ability thing, and we'll keep an eye out for him. If you think there's going to be any trouble, give us a thumbs-up and we'll have you out of here before that boy can so much as blink. Got it?"

"Yes," said Chris.

"Right, then, do whatever it is you do, and don't worry— we're here if you need us."

Chris nodded but didn't say anything as he prepared himself. He concentrated on breathing calmly as he stared at Hunter, who had his arm around a hysterical girl as her mother took their photograph. Chris felt his mind start to clear and his eyes begin to lose focus, and then everything in his mind went white.

The bright light disappeared as suddenly as it had appeared, and when it did, Chris saw that he was standing inside Hunter's Reception. The sound of the screaming crowd filled the large, white cavernous room as Chris walked through the floating thoughts filled with the pop star's sense of boredom and over to the door on the other side. He opened it, took a deep breath, and stepped out into the mind of Hunter Reid.

Chris looked down from the grassy knoll that he had walked out onto and gazed around at the city. Every mind he had entered up until that point had been different: Each had its own, singular style, a defining characteristic that shaped the buildings and streets, such as Ms. Lamb's

Gothic architecture or Valentino Brick's mind of paint. Hunter Reid's mind, however, was a confused blend of two completely contrasting environments. The Family building in front of him, for example, was a small and modest family home, not unlike Chris's own house, whilst the two buildings on either side of it were tall, sleek blocks of glass, corporate-looking structures that looked as if they were threatening to swallow up the tiny house in between them. Beyond People Street, the juxtaposition was even more obvious—some streets quaint and suburban, others a soulless parade of glass and steel. Chris, having found his bearings, looked in the direction of where he was heading, and even though it was far in the distance, he immediately found the building he was looking for: a gigantic block of blue-green glass sitting in the middle of what looked like a vast, empty parking lot. He started walking quickly toward it, constantly checking over his shoulder in case Ernest should suddenly appear behind him.

The imposing block that was Hunter's Career building loomed high behind the small row of houses on Language Lane. As he reached the end of the small road and prepared to step out into the tarmacked clearing, his heart suddenly began to beat faster as he realized that his mother's fate and his own were very soon to be decided.

The first thing Chris noticed when he turned the corner was that there was nowhere to hide. If Ernest was standing somewhere in the large glass building ahead of him, then he was surely watching him at that very moment, though the dull sunlight bouncing off the windows meant Chris couldn't see anything inside. The only thing that gave him any comfort as he started to run as fast as he could across the gray expanse, was that it wasn't possible to come to any physical harm in another person's mind. Nevertheless, the thought of Ernest tracking him unnerved him, so when he finally reached the entrance, he let out a sigh of relief.

The door was closed. This in itself didn't mean any-thing—Ernest was surely capable of closing doors behind him—but Chris had the feeling he was on his own.

"Ernest?" said Chris. His voice echoed around the vast room filled with sleek chrome filing cabinets, but there was no answer.

Chris walked across the polished floor, checking every aisle until he was sure that the room was empty.

"Ernest? Are you here?"

Chris climbed the glass steps of the modern staircase to the second floor and checked the entire room. Ernest wasn't there, nor was he anywhere to be found on the top floor. Certain by now that he was on his own, Chris walked up to the floor-to-ceiling glass wall and looked out at the impressive views of Hunter's mind to see if he could spot Ernest approaching, but the city was silent and still and it suddenly occurred to him that he would have no idea what to do next if Ernest didn't show up. Eventually, with still no sign of Ernest, Chris sat down on the cold, smooth floor facing the window and prepared himself for a wait.

Without a watch or any clock in Hunter's mind, Chris began to lose sense of time. It could have been five min-utes or thirty—he had no idea. All he did know was that if Hunter stood up and left, he would be shot back into reality without any answers. The frustration of that, coupled with his growing boredom, infuriated Chris so he stood up and started to pace the room. Back and forth, back and forth, glancing constantly at the entrance to Hunter's mind until, suddenly, something in the far distance moving caught his eye.

Running back over the wall and cupping his face against the glass, Chris squinted to get a better view and saw a small figure emerge from Hunter's Reception.

Ernest.

Chris watched as the figure in the distance ran down the grassy knoll and then disappeared behind the cover of the buildings on the street. Chris's eyes darted along the route he knew Ernest must be taking until he saw Ernest appear at exactly the same spot where he himself had stood earlier. Ernest looked ahead and began to run.

Chris rushed down the stairs, taking two at a time, and ducked quickly into the first aisle. Through the glass wall at the front, Chris could see Ernest cautiously climbing the steps, trying to get a view of the inside. Chris held his breath and inched forward until he came to the end of the row.

"Chris?"

Chris took a deep breath and then stepped out from the aisle.

"Where is she?"

Ernest didn't answer. Instead, the two boys stared at each other, each uncertain if the other was about to do anything unexpected until, finally, Chris walked out on the open floor and approached Ernest. When he was within a few feet of him, he stopped.

"I said, where's my mother?"

Chris could see, by the glint in Ernest's eyes, that he was enjoying having the upper hand.

"She's alive, and if you want her to stay that way, you need to listen to me."

A wave of anger rose up inside of Chris, but he forced himself to ignore it. "Fine. What do you want?"

"First, if you give the thumbs-up to the goons guarding you to tell them that I'm here, you can forget about seeing your mother again."

Chris nodded.

"Every day," continued Ernest, "when you were in your house, looking for me in your wardrobe, I was watching. Every single time you stepped out of your school's front door, I was watching. I was watching when you left in the car this morning, and I was watching—"

"I get it," said Chris, irritated, "you were watching me. So if you've been following me all these months, why didn't you get to me before?"

Ernest smiled. "Because I could see how much you were suffering. And that's the whole point of revenge, isn't it?"

"And my mum? What's she got to do with it?"

"She's the reason you're going to do exactly what I want."

Chris thought about this for a moment. "What makes you think I care? You don't know anything about her."

"I know a lot more than you think. I watched you at home, remember? It takes a lot more than what she's done to you to stop loving your own mother. I should know."

Chris saw a brief flicker of sadness cross Ernest's face before being quickly replaced by a cold, hard look.

"I want you to come to my house tonight. Alone."

"Why?" said Chris. "Why not do whatever you want to do here?"

Ernest shrugged his shoulders. "Too many people. Too many things to go wrong."

"So you want me to come to your house so that you can kill me?"

Ernest gave a small nod.

"It's not the best offer I've had," said Chris.

"You want your mother back safe. I want you to die. We both have something to fight for."

"And what makes you think that you'll win? We both know my Ability is stronger than yours."

"Maybe. What I do know for sure is that tonight, whatever happens, someone is going to die. If it's your mum, you'll suffer. If it's you, you'll, well, be dead. And if it's me, at least I died trying to keep my promise to my brother. Two out of three is good enough odds for me."

"You've thought about this a lot," said Chris.

Ernest nodded. "Not much to distract me these days—not since my brother was murdered."

Chris sighed. "I didn't mean to kill your brother—I've told you before it was a horrible accident. I was just trying to stop him from hurting anyone else."

Ernest stared at him for a moment, his face hardening with anger.

"I made a promise at my brother's grave," said Ernest, his voice like ice, "and I don't break my promises." He held up a piece of paper with a set of coordinates written on it in black ink.

"Your house?" asked Chris, committing the location to memory.

"If you turn up with anybody—anyone at all—your mother will be dead before you can get to the front door."

Chris nodded.

"Midnight," said Ernest, putting the note back into his pocket. Then, before Chris had a chance to say anything else, he turned and ran out the door.

Chris followed him out without running. There was no point, he thought. There was no way he was going to find him in the crowds. He was walking along Language Lane, wondering if there was anything he could do to prepare for their meeting later when, suddenly, he felt himself flying forward with a sudden whoosh.

Chris blinked and saw that he was back in the room. Ahead of him, completely unaware of what had just happened in his own head, Hunter was walking away from the table, waving at the screaming girls, many of whom appeared to be crying. Chris wasn't sure why.

"You see him?" asked John, suddenly noticing that Chris's blank stare had disappeared.

Chris knew what he had to say.

"No," he said, "he never showed up."

"What are we going to do now?" asked Ron, looking exasperated as he watched Hunter disappear through the side door. "Shall we follow him?"

Chris shook his head. "There's no point. He's not coming."

He noticed Ron and John give each other a funny look

and realized that he wasn't acting with the concern they would have expected. He wished, once more, that he were a better actor.

"I hope Mum's okay." It was the best he could do.

John looked down at Chris, and his face softened. "It's all right, son. The boy will show up. Something must have happened, but he'll get in touch—maybe even today—and we can get this whole thing worked out."

Chris nodded and kept his head down to hide his face, remembering how Ron had once told him that he could spot a liar from fifty feet away.

"Come on, let's get you back to the car," said John, leading Chris out from under the escalator.

· CHAPTER TWENTY-FOUR ·

Although it hadn't been intentional—there had just been so much on his mind—Chris's silence since discovering his mother's disappearance meant that he didn't have to do much to avoid raising suspicions. As everybody fussed around him, and Maura tried to fill him full of food— the best medicine, she said—Daisy, who seemed to have an unsettling way of noticing when something was amiss, watched him from a distance. If she had her suspicions that he was lying, however, she said nothing.

"You want to choose the film tonight?" asked Rex.

Chris shook his head. Out of the corner of his eye, he saw Lexi push Rex back in his direction.

"Um, what about a game of pool?"

Chris shook his head again. "No, thanks," he said.

Rex raised both his hands in exasperation, and Chris, seeing this, lost his temper.

"What do you want from me?" asked Chris. Everybody looked at him in shock—it was the first time they'd heard his voice in days. "Isn't it obvious that I don't want to join in?"

"Come on," said Philip quietly to the others, "I think he just wants to be left alone. We'll talk later, Chris."

"*What's the point?* None of you ever believed anything I told you about that boy. Maybe if you had, this wouldn't be happening." Chris hadn't really thought about this until now, but as soon as he said it, he knew it made sense.

"That's not fair," said Lexi.

"It's true," said Chris.

"Chris—please. We're your friends," said Sebastian.

"No, Sebastian. Maybe you don't understand the word 'friend,'" said Chris, his whole body shaking. "Friends support each other. Friends believe in their friends. Do you understand what I'm saying? *I have no friends.*"

Chris stormed past everybody as they stood open-mouthed and watched him leave the room. Chris slammed the door behind him and went to hide in his bedroom. Two hours left, he thought as he climbed up onto his bunk bed. Two hours and he would be gone. Now he just needed to put away any thoughts about what had just happened and concentrate on the only thing that mattered—his plan for that night.

There was a knock on the door. Before Chris had a chance to tell her to go away, Daisy had opened it and stepped inside.

"You saw him, didn't you?" she asked.

Chris sighed and closed his eyes. She was the only person who had ever believed anything he'd said. For a moment, he considered telling her, but then he remembered what Ernest had said: Come alone. If Daisy knew the danger he was about to place himself in, there was no way she would let him leave Myers Holt by himself.

"There's nothing to tell," he said finally. "I've already told you what happened."

There was a brief moment of silence between them.

"Fine," she said at last, "don't tell me, then."

She walked away, and Chris put his head in his hands. Sometimes, he thought, having friends only made things harder. It wasn't something he would have to worry about anymore.

The day had been a busy one, and by eleven o'clock, the whole of Myers Holt had shut down for the night. Chris pulled the covers back and climbed down from his bed, fully clothed, keeping as quiet as possible so as not to wake Philip from his sleep. The light from the moon of their artificial sky cast a dim, silver glow over the room— enough for Chris to be able to see where he was going— and he tiptoed over to the dressing area. The door of the bathroom was open, and the wall of jellyfish, pulsating softly in the purple light, swirled about gently as Chris reached into his sock drawer and fumbled about until he found the piece of paper he had hidden there earlier. He padded back over to his bed, reached up, and placed the note with the coordinates on it under his pillow before making his way quickly over to the door.

He found the entrance foyer empty and the lights off leading down to Ron and John's quarters. Chris looked over at the far wall, let his eyes lose focus, and watched as his mind suddenly transported him to the room on the other side.

The lights were off, but the room was lit by the gray glow coming from the bank of screens that displayed the empty rooms and corridors of Myers Holt and the street outside. Through an open door on the other side, Chris could see Ron and John asleep in their bunk beds—John at the bottom, a large framed photograph of Fifi, his poodle, on the bedside table, and Ron, who appeared to be cuddling a teddy bear, on the top.

Chris turned his attention back to the security panel, over to the elevator alarm. His eyes moved to the back of the black box and then focused on the power cord. It began to strain, then it suddenly popped out and fell to the table with a small *plonk*. He glanced over at the security cameras and decided not to bother tampering with them. Whatever happened, he was almost certainly going to be found out—all that mattered was that he had enough time to get out of the school.

This is it, thought Chris, blinking until he was back looking around the entrance foyer. He walked over to the open doors of the elevator, stepped inside, and pressed his thumb to the kettle's switch.

The good thing about living in central London was that the city was almost as busy in the nighttime as it was during the day. Tonight was no different, and before Chris had even reached the bottom of the steps of his school, he saw the bright orange light of an empty taxi turning onto the square. Chris rushed down and put his hand out to call it.

"Where are you going?" asked the taxi driver in a gruff voice.

Chris gave him Ernest's address.

The driver shook his head. "Forget about it—I'm not going that far." Before Chris had a chance to say anything, the driver pressed a button and the window began to roll up.

Chris quickly looked past the glass and stared at the driver.

You want to take this fare. . . . You want to take this fare. . . . You want to take this fare.

The driver rolled his window back down.

"Where did you say you were going?" he asked. Chris gave him the address.

"Good—I fancy a bit of a drive. Jump in."

Chris opened the door and climbed inside. The driver switched on his indicator and pulled out slowly as Chris looked up at the front door of Myers Holt and wondered if he would ever see it again.

"You sure you want me to leave you here?" asked the driver as they pulled up outside the closed wrought-iron gates set back off the unlit country road. The driver leaned forward to try to work out where the house was. "Must be behind that forest. It's going to be a long walk—why don't I drive you up to the door?"

"Here's fine," said Chris, thanking the driver as he jumped out. He had already suggested to the driver that he had been paid. He had done this before and had not only felt terrible for it but had also had to write to the drivers and apologize, paying his fare back with money that Sir Bentley had made him earn doing chores around the school. Tonight, however, he had no time for guilt. He checked the number plate as it drove off, resolved to make amends at another time, and walked up to the gates, which creaked before slowly beginning to open. Chris took a deep breath and walked through them, into the still black night ahead.

Chris hadn't thought of taking a flashlight with him, but his eyes adjusted quickly to the darkness, and he made his way along the overgrown path until, a few slow minutes later, the thick canopy of trees above him disappeared, revealing Darkwhisper Manor ahead in the distance.

The first thing Chris noticed about the building was its sheer size, so huge and magnificent that Chris was sure it must have been the home of royalty at some point in its history. Unlike any palace he had ever seen, however, this building was flat roofed and rectangular, with two vast stone columns that flanked the entrance and rows of tall windows placed perfectly symmetrically on either side of them.

The second thing he noticed was that the roof appeared to be on fire. As he approached, however, he saw that the flat roof was in fact lit up by flaming stone torches that rose up from the stone balcony running along its perimeter, each torch set only a few feet from the next. Ernest was waiting for him.

Chris broke into a run across the wide, uncut lawn, passing between two empty fountains before he reached the foot of the stone steps that led up to the entrance. He stopped and, heart beating wildly, began to walk slowly up the stairs toward the closed wooden doors.

Chris knew that Ernest would be watching him, but the sound of Ernest's voice suddenly appearing in his head as he pulled down the door's iron handle nevertheless made him jump.

"Follow the lanterns."

Chris didn't say anything, not certain what that meant. Instead, he opened the door and stepped inside.

As soon as Chris walked into the vast entrance foyer, he understood. All the lights in the room had been turned off, but the whole place was aglow with the flickering light coming from identical glass box lanterns placed along both sides of the grand staircase, a path of fire leading up to the first floor, across the landing, and up another set of stairs, then disappeared from view. Chris walked across the marble floor, and as he did so he looked around at his surroundings in awe: He had never seen anything like it. In front of him, the red-carpeted staircase with gold railings ran down to two enormous stone plinths, on top of which were a pair of identical wolf statues that looked as if they had been frozen in midattack—their fangs bared, their claws out. Chris turned to his left and stared up at a tapestry bigger than the front of his own house depicting a violent battle scene, and then over to the row of paintings on the other side, all of them of other battles and each one more gruesome and bloody than the one before.

No wonder this family was so messed up, thought Chris, passing a pair of stuffed vultures on his way over to the bottom of the stairs.

Chris was halfway up the first flight of steps when he noticed the shiny object glistening in the flickering light above him. Curious, he quickened his pace up the stairs, only to find that it was a discarded empty packet of cheese-and-onion crisps. He also noticed as he kicked it out of the way how dirty the carpet was, and for the first time, Chris realized that Ernest must be living here on his own.

Chris continued to follow the pathway of glowing lanterns, which led him across the first-floor landing, up another smaller set of stairs, and along a corridor lined with oil paintings of severe-looking aristocrats that seemed to be watching him in disapproval. The lanterns continued up a spiral staircase, and Chris wondered how long it must have taken for Ernest to light them all as he followed them up, round and round, until, finally, he reached a small wooden door.

The cool summer wind hit Chris as soon as he stepped out onto the roof—a flat gray terrace that spanned the entire length of the building below and was surrounded by a stone balcony, on top of which were the enormous flames rising from stone urns that Chris had spotted upon his arrival.

Chris, however, barely took notice of any of this, for as soon as he stepped out the door he saw Ernest. Ernest, however, appeared not to have seen him. He was standing only a few feet away from Chris, wearing a pair of jeans and a dark blue T-shirt, but his arms were by his side, and his attention was focused at a point somewhere ahead in the distance. Chris turned his head to follow the direction of where he was looking, and his heart stopped.

On the other side of the gray expanse, standing on the wide stone rim of the balcony, her hands bound and her hair wild in the wind, was his mother.

"CHRIS!"

Chris saw the look of terror on his mother's face, and he forgot all about Ernest standing beside him. He was about to break into a run when Ernest spoke.

"One more step and I throw your mother off."

Chris snapped his head round and saw that Ernest was still facing his mother, the familiar blank stare on his face. And then a thought occurred to him.

"You can't do anything to her that will guarantee her death. Your Ability won't let you."

"I'm not looking at her," said Ernest calmly. "I'm looking at the balcony she's standing on. One false move and it shatters, and even your Ability isn't strong enough to stop me when I'm already focused."

Chris took a deep breath. "What do you want me to do?" he asked, keeping his eyes on his terrified mother.

For a moment, there was silence, and then, without losing his focus, Ernest answered him.

"I want you to jump."

Chris felt his heart beat faster and panic rise up in him. "I'll die."

"Exactly. You've got ten seconds to jump, and your mum lives. Don't do it, and you both die. Ten . . ."

Chris's mind rushed through every bit of training that he had had as he tried to come up with a solution.

"Nine . . ."

The building was flat fronted, so there was nowhere other than the ground to land on.

"Eight . . ."

His mind couldn't view itself as an object, which meant he couldn't use his Ability to stop himself from falling.

"Seven . . . Six . . . Five . . ."

He could try to use his Ability on Ernest, but because he was already focused on the stone, it was unlikely Chris would be fast enough to stop him.

"Four . . ."

He didn't have enough time to get across the terrace to stop his mum's fall.

"Three . . ."

Or to get back down to ground level.

"Two . . ."

He started to walk across to the stone balcony.

"One . . ."

There was only one thing: If he could just distract Ernest for a moment, he might be able to use his Ability to make his mother fall forward.

"Okay! I'll do it: Look!"

"NO! CHRIS!" his mother screamed.

Chris began to climb up onto the stone balcony slowly, but Ernest didn't turn his head.

"Too late, Chris."

Chris snapped his head round in panic and tried to focus his mind on his mother, but Ernest had meant what he'd said: It was too late. The gray stone beneath his mother's feet suddenly exploded into a vast fountain of grey splinters. Chris's mother screamed as the ground beneath her disappeared, and her eyes widened as she realized what was happening. Then, just like that, she was gone.

"MUM!" Chris jumped down and ran faster than he had ever run. "MUM!"

"She's gone, Chris," called Ernest.

Chris knew that Ernest was right, but he didn't stop running, hot tears suddenly streaming down his cheeks, not thinking about anything but the look on his mother's face, until he reached the wide gap of the broken balcony. Knowing that Ernest would repeat what he had just done if he so much as touched the balcony, Chris threw himself down, barely registering how wet it was in spite of the dry weather, and looked out over the edge, terrified at what he was about to see.

As soon as Chris looked down, he saw the body of his mother lying facedown far below him. For a moment, Chris lay on the floor, frozen in horror. A hot surge of anger and grief welled up inside him.

"And now it's your turn."

Chris snapped his head round, blinking to get rid of the tears forming, and saw Ernest standing by the open doorway leading back onto the stairwell. He raised his hand to show Chris that he was holding a large red container. Chris couldn't immediately work out what it was, but then Ernest leaned down and picked up a lantern. Chris looked down at the dark wet patch he was lying on, and suddenly he knew exactly what was about to happen. He jumped up and began to run, but before he had taken even three steps, Ernest raised the lantern and threw it to the ground in front of him.

Chris watched in horror as the dark patch of ground in front of Ernest that he had already guessed was gasoline exploded into life and flames began to shoot across the ground, winding their way back and forth across the terrace, creating a vast, snaking wall of fire.

"Good-bye, Christopher Lane."

Chris looked up to see Ernest pouring the last of the contents of the canister in his hand at the foot of the doorway. Ernest looked up, and for a brief moment, the two boys locked eyes. Then Ernest turned, and Chris saw him take a step down just before the lanterns at the foot of the doorway exploded, engulfing in fire Chris's only chance of escaping.

Chris's eyes went down to his feet, and he saw he was standing in a dark puddle of gasoline. Panicked, and seeing that the flames were quickly approaching, he ran over to a small dry patch. Looking in the direction of the approaching fire, he let his eyes lose focus.

For a moment, the line of flames briefly faltered, but try as he might, Chris's Ability was no match for their sheer power, and they fought back, rising even higher into the air before rushing once more toward him. Chris looked at the giant wave of fire as it rose up above him, and he staggered back, his mind desperately trying to push it away when, all of a sudden, just as he was giving up hope, the flames suddenly parted. Chris looked up.

His eyes widened and, for a moment, his heart stopped.

There, standing in the doorway under an arch of flames, stood his friends. Daisy, Philip, and Lexi. And they were all staring intently at him as they pushed the flames away— their minds working together.

"What . . . ? What are you doing here?" he asked.

"WE CAN'T HOLD IT MUCH LONGER," shouted Lexi. "RUN!"

Chris didn't have time to think. He rushed forward through the narrow path that had been carved out for him as the intense heat and flames closed in on either side. He was nearly at the door when he heard the sound of Rex's voice coming from the staircase.

"He got away! He's coming!"

Chris could see the panic on Lexi, Daisy, and Philip's faces as he sprinted forward, but they kept their eyes on the flames, determined to keep the path open long enough for Chris to get through. And then, just as Chris was about to pass the final wall of fire, his friends were suddenly pushed forward with a force so violent that they all fell to the ground, and from the doorway emerged Ernest.

The fire suddenly roared back into life, and Chris lifted his arms to cover his face as the flames began to reach in toward him. He took a deep breath and was focusing every last bit of energy he had on creating a gap to get through when he heard a dull creaking sound below his feet.

Chris looked down and saw the cracks in the concrete, and when he looked back up, he saw that the flames had parted and Ernest was staring at the floor. Chris didn't stop to think: He let his eyes lose focus, and before Ernest had a chance to react, he was thrown upward into the air and landed at the foot of the stone balcony. His head slammed down on the concrete with a loud thud, and then he was still.

"Quick!" said Daisy, appearing at his side, "the roof is about to cave in."

Sure enough, Chris turned and saw the crack in the floor that Ernest had created. He took one last look at the body of Ernest lying on the ground, the flames whipping around him in a frenzy, and he broke into a run.

Rex and Sebastian were standing at the bottom of the small stone stairwell as Chris, Lexi, Daisy, and Philip rushed down. Deeply focused, they were holding back the fire that had already taken hold of the surrounding wooden paneling until Chris and the others reached the bottom step, and then the six of them all turned and ran off, the sound of the glass lanterns shattering behind them.

"YOUR MUM IS OKAY!" shouted Sebastian.

"WHAT?" shouted Chris, thinking he must have misheard. He had seen her body lying on the ground.

"DAISY SAW HER FALLING. SHE SLOWED HER DOWN BEFORE SHE HIT THE GROUND. SHE'S FINE."

Chris turned to Daisy as they ran through the corridor. "Is that true?"

Daisy nodded.

A wave of relief and gratitude suddenly soared through Chris, and he stopped, tears running down his face.

"Thank you," he said.

"You can get us presents later. Just stop blubbering and let's get out of here," called Rex. "We can't stop now."

Chris could hear the creaking of the floors above, but he couldn't move. All he could think about was his anger at having nearly lost his mother and how much it had hurt, and how it had felt to think that he had lost all his friends. He had thought he was completely alone. And then he thought about how Ernest must have felt losing his only brother, and everything about the way that he had acted suddenly made sense. At that very moment, any anger that Chris had felt toward Ernest completely vanished. Chris looked up at the others, who were all staring back at him impatiently, and realized what he had to do.

"I'm going back."

"WHAT?"

"I'M GOING BACK TO GET HIM!" said Chris, already running back down the corridor toward the orange glow of the approaching fire.

"CHRIS! STOP! NOOOO!"

Chris turned to face his friends, who were all looking up, their eyes wide with fear. His eyes followed theirs up to the ceiling, and he saw the chandelier above them shaking violently. They all threw themselves backward as the ceiling suddenly collapsed in front of them with a huge crash. The lanterns that had been lining the corridor shattered, and Chris watched as the flames took hold of everything around them until he could no longer see anything ahead of him but fire. There was no going back.

Chris rushed up to the small staircase, its walls ablaze, and ran up the stone steps. He stepped out into the air and looked over to where Ernest was lying.

The flames were almost on top of him.

"ERNEST!"

Ernest remained motionless. Chris looked down at the fire directly in front of him and began to push it back, one section at a time. Every time the flames would part, he would step forward and then the flames would close in behind him. He repeated it, taking one step slowly forward at a time until, at last, he reached Ernest.

"Ernest! Wake up!"

Chris leaned down and shook Ernest's body until, finally, Ernest opened his eyes. For a moment, Ernest didn't seem to know where he was. He looked at Chris blankly, and then his eyes widened and he lifted his head to see the wall of fire behind them. He looked back at Chris.

"You came back for me?"

"We have to get out of here—the whole building is about to collapse."

Chris stood and pulled Ernest up.

"I don't understand," said Ernest.

"I killed your brother, and I'm so sorry, Ernest. I really am. I never meant it to happen, but I know why you blame me and I understand. You can hate me as much as you want, but I can't let you die too."

Chris grabbed Ernest's sleeve and tried to pull him forward, but Ernest was rooted to the spot. Chris turned to him, and it was only then that he realized Ernest was crying.

"Come on," said Chris, gently. "We've got to go."

"You came back for me," he repeated, his voice breaking. "I killed your mother, and you came back for me."

Chris looked at the cracks running from the hole where

part of the roof had already fallen through, and then at the flames circling closer. He grabbed Ernest by the shoulders.

"My mum didn't die. She's fine—the others stopped her with their Ability."

Ernest looked up at Chris in disbelief. "Really?"

Chris nodded, and Ernest broke down, his shoulders shaking with heaving sobs.

Suddenly, the floor beneath Chris's feet moved. Chris looked down in horror as he saw a crack appear, and then . . .

CRASH!

Chris and Ernest, jolted back into reality, looked up at the doorway and saw that the area of concrete roof in front of it had fallen through to the floor below and that the fire, which had taken hold of the floor below suddenly gushed up into the air like a huge orange fountain as the rest of the floor slowly began to crack open.

The two boys looked down at the widening gap by their feet and then up at each other. They had only seconds left before they fell to a certain death. Without any time to think, both boys jumped up onto the stone balcony and watched as the ground opened up where they had just been standing, stone crashing down into the flames below. They stood up, balanced on the stone ledge, and faced each other.

"Do you trust me?" asked Chris.

Ernest nodded. "Do you trust me?" he asked back.

Chris nodded. He knew that they were both thinking the same thing.

Without another word, the two boys let their eyes glaze over, and facing each other, they jumped off the roof of Darkwhisper Manor, both falling gently as they slowed each other down with their Ability.

Chris landed on the soft grass with a dull and painless thud, never taking his eyes off Ernest until he, too, fell to the ground gently.

"We made it!" said Chris. Ernest looked back, and his face, suddenly soft and free of all anger, broke into a smile. They looked up at the building behind them, flames flying out of the broken windows, and then they heard a shout.

"RUN!"

Chris looked up, and the last thing he saw as he and Ernest turned to flee was John running toward him across the lawn. Then he heard a huge explosion and felt himself being thrown up in the air.

"Chris. Chris! Please wake up."

Chris moaned. Every part of his body ached, and his head throbbed with pain.

"Chris, darling. Please, wake up."

Chris was sure he could hear his mother's voice, but it sounded different, like it used to sound when he was a little boy. He wondered if he was dead, but, if he was he wasn't sure why he was feeling so much pain.

Slowly, Chris opened his eyes.

"Chris?"

Chris stared up at his mother and saw that she was crying. He lifted his head slowly as she placed her arms under him as support. Behind her, Chris saw Daisy, tears also streaming down her face and Lexi comforting her.

"Don't move," said his mother. "An ambulance is on its way."

"Is he . . . is Ernest okay?"

Chris tried to sit up so that he could look around, but a pain shot through his leg and he sat back down.

"I'm fine," said a voice. Chris turned his head and saw Ernest standing next to him, unhurt. "Thank you. You saved my life."

Chris looked up at Ernest and smiled. "It's the least I could do," he said. Then, as his friends fussed around him, he lay back in his mother's arms and let her stroke his hair as they waited for the ambulance to arrive.

CHAPTER TWENTY-FIVE

"You may not feel like it right now, but you are a very lucky young man," said the nurse, writing something down on the chart. "You could have been killed, by the sound of it."

Chris nodded and smiled. He looked down at the plaster cast around his ankle. "How long before it comes off?"

"The fracture's not too bad. We'll see how you go, but we can probably take it off in a month or so."

Chris reached up to his forehead.

"Don't touch it," said the nurse, telling him off gently. "We don't want that cut to get infected. I'll get a bandage now to cover it up." She smiled, closed the chart, and walked out of the room.

Chris was about to lie back on his bed when Sir Bentley appeared in the doorway.

"Can I come in?"

Chris nodded.

"How are you feeling?" asked Sir Bentley, walking up to Chris's bed.

"Okay. They gave me some painkillers, so it doesn't really hurt anymore."

"Well, good. I'm glad to hear it. That was quite a stunt you pulled last night."

"I know, I'm sorry," said Chris.

Sir Bentley shook his head. "No, I'm the one who should be apologizing. If we'd listened to what you were trying to tell us, this whole thing might have been avoided."

"I don't think so," said Chris. "Ernest was pretty determined. How is he?"

"He's fine. Just a few bruises."

"Where is he now?"

"He's in Myers Holt. We took him there last night after we made absolutely certain that he was telling us the truth when he said that he wasn't going to hurt anybody."

"Was he?"

"Yes. He agreed that the others could look inside his mind and check. According to them, he was a very different boy before his brother died. It sounds like his focus on revenge was the only way he knew how to deal with his grief. After what happened last night, it seems that all the anger has gone. In fact, he doesn't hold any resentment toward you at all—quite the opposite. How about you— how do you feel about him?"

Chris thought about everything that had happened. "I think we're a lot alike—I even think we could be friends.

I know why he did what he did, and I don't blame him. I think, if it had been me, I would have felt the same."

"Are you sure?"

Chris nodded. "Yes," he said, and he meant it.

Sir Bentley reached out and placed his hand on Chris's shoulder. "You are a special boy, Christopher. I've known it since the moment I met you. The way you have dealt with this all, that you can forgive him, well, it's a lesson for all of us."

Chris felt himself turn red. "What's going to happen to him now?" he asked, changing the subject.

"Well, I had a rather interesting call this morning from someone you may remember—your favorite author and ex–Myers Holt pupil Clarissa Teller."

"Really?" asked Chris.

"She's offered to look after Ernest."

Chris looked confused. "Why?"

"Well, I don't know if you remember, but Dulcia, Ernest's mother, was best friends with Clarissa when they were at Myers Holt. Clarissa always blamed herself for the death of Dulcia, or Anna, which is what we all knew her as then. Of course, we didn't know that she wasn't actually dead. We've all struggled over the years with what happened to Anna and the other pupil, Danny, but of all of us, it affected Clarissa the most. She never really came to terms with it—I think that's why she never had children of her own, and I'm sure that's why she puts all the money she earns into helping children in need. She's offered to look after Ernest as her way of repaying Anna for what happened that night. She's flying in this afternoon to meet him. I'm sure that—"

"Can I come in?"

Chris and Sir Bentley both turned to see Chris's mother in the doorway, smiling.

"Ah, Mrs. Lane. Of course, I'll leave you to it. Chris, we look forward to seeing you back at school."

"Thanks, Sir Bentley," said Chris as his mother walked in and sat down in the armchair by his bed.

"I got you the juice you wanted," she said, "and some grapes and crisps, in case you get hungry. I got you a magazine, too." She pulled it out of the bag and placed it on the bed. "I wasn't sure what you're into—I hope it's okay."

Chris looked over at the front cover and saw the cartoon fire engine that he had loved when he was five years old. He smiled. "It's great, Mum. Thank you."

"Oh, good," she said, looking relieved. "Is your head still hurting?"

"No, it's fine. They gave me some more painkillers."

"Good, good."

There was a brief moment of silence until, finally, his mother looked up into Chris's eyes.

"I'm so sorry, darling."

"You don't have to keep saying that, Mum," said Chris gently.

"But I am," she said with tears in her eyes. "I don't know how I let my life get like this. Ever since your dad died, all I did was think about what I had lost instead of thinking about how lucky I was for what I still had. All this time I've had this wonderful son, and I never stopped to appreciate that until I nearly lost you. All your friends and teachers were telling me all these wonderful things about you last night—how honest and kind you are—and I felt so incredibly proud and thankful that I have a chance to make it up to you . . . if you'll forgive me."

Chris felt a lump in his throat. "Of course I do, Mum." Then he placed his hand on his mother's and took a deep breath. "I can help you, Mum."

"What do you mean?" she asked.

"I don't know how much they told you about my Ability, but one of the things I can do is take away memories. I can make you forget everything that hurts—if you want that."

Chris's mother looked at him for a brief moment and then shook her head. "I don't want that."

"But it would make you happy again."

Chris's mother gave his hand a tight squeeze. "I am happy. I'm happy that I have another chance to be a good mother to you, and I need those memories to remind me how lucky I am to have that. I promise you that everything is going to change from now on."

"Okay," said Chris. "If you're sure."

"I'm sure," she said, leaning up to give him a kiss on the cheek.

Chris smiled, then lay back on his pillow and closed his eyes.

Chris returned to Myers Holt a week later to a hero's welcome. There were only two days left until the end of term, however, and everything that had happened was soon forgotten under the mountain of things they had to do—something that Chris and the others were grateful for, as nobody wanted to dwell on the fact that they would soon be saying good-bye to Myers Holt.

Aside from packing their belongings, they had other responsibilities. The commissioner had amassed a vast number of cases for them to solve, eager to put their powers to good use before they left. Miss Sonata had managed to get them to cram in two more exams, and Maura, who kept bursting into tears every time she saw them, had enlisted their help to clean the facility in preparation for the summer shutdown.

And then there was the matter of Ms. Lamb.

"Come on," said Philip as they toasted marshmallows over the open fire in the Map Room. "We've got to come up with something."

Everybody put their heads down in thought, but despite coming up with countless ideas since Rex had first suggested playing a prank on Ms. Lamb, they still hadn't managed to come up with a single one that they had all been able to agree on.

"Itching powder in her boots?"

Chris wrinkled his nose in disgust. "I'm not going anywhere near her feet."

"I could pen a venomous poem in her honor," said Sebastian. He shrugged his shoulders as everybody rolled their eyes.

"Shave her head when she's asleep?" suggested Rex.

"Rex! That's awful!" said Daisy, her first contribution to the discussion.

"Fine, then," said Rex, glaring at Daisy, "what do you suggest?"

"Well . . . ," said Daisy in a quiet voice, "I was thinking . . . that . . . well . . ."

"Spit it out," said Rex.

Daisy took a deep breath. "I was thinking that maybe we could do something nice for her."

Everybody looked at Daisy for a moment in total silence. And then, in unison, they all burst out laughing.

"No, really!" protested Daisy, her face turning red as she watched them all collapse in giggles around her. "I'm serious!"

Although Chris found the idea as ridiculous as everybody else, he could see that Daisy was beginning to get upset and did his best to pull himself together. He sat up and motioned for everybody to be quiet. "Hey—come on, let's just listen to Daisy for a second."

Daisy gave Chris a grateful smile as the laughter began to die down.

"I know she's not been very nice—"

"Well, that's the understatement of the year," interrupted Philip.

"But we all know that's because she's unhappy. Remember how Chris found out that she was most scared of being lonely? And then she had her heart broken by that man. She's got no friends, she lives by herself, and not even anybody at her work likes her. . . ."

The smiles on everybody's faces were slowly disappearing.

"And that doesn't include all the things we did to her this year. Attacked her with a dog"—Chris gave an embarrassed half smile and shrugged—"followed her on a date, listened in on her private conversations, watched her in her own house—"

"All right, all right!" said Lexi. "You've got a point. What were you thinking?"

"We'd need a bit of money. . . ."

"I'm not buying her chocolates," said Rex, his lip curled at the thought.

"No, not chocolates," said Daisy. "I was thinking of something else. . . ."

The next evening, whilst the pupils of Myers Holt sat on the steps outside their school and used their Ability, Ms. Lamb sat in her small apartment eating a microwaved meal for one, completely unaware that she was being watched.

"One for me," said Ms. Lamb, lifting her fork to her mouth.

"And one for you." She cut up a piece of chicken and, using the same fork, fed it to Medusa the cat.

Ms. Lamb skewered another piece of chicken and lifted it to her mouth.

"Another one for . . ."

Back at Myers Holt, Rex turned to the others. "This is disgusting. It's not going to work. Nobody's coming."

"Shh!" said Daisy, her mind still focused on Ms. Lamb's apartment. "It's only just turned seven."

"I don't know, Daisy. I think Rex might be right," said Lexi.

"Somebody's got to show up," said Daisy, though she was beginning to sound less sure of herself.

They all went quiet again as they watched Ms. Lamb

continue to share her meal with her cat until it was all gone. Ms. Lamb stood up, began to clear the table, and was just about to take the plate to the kitchen when . . .

Ding dong!

Ms. Lamb dropped the plate back onto the table and flicked her head round to the door, her eyes narrowed. She didn't move.

Ding dong!

"Who could that be?" said Ms. Lamb. Medusa yawned and stretched out on the sofa as Ms. Lamb walked over to the entry phone.

"Yes?" she asked brusquely.

"Hello?"

"Yes?" asked Ms. Lamb again, irritated.

"It's seven o'clock," said the voice.

"For goodness' sake—I did not order a speaking clock," replied Ms. Lamb, and with that, she hung the phone up and turned to walk away.

Ding dong!

Ms. Lamb gave a loud *humph* and picked up the phone once more.

"You have the wrong door!"

"My name is Dr. Michael Singh. I'm here about the advert," said the man's voice, talking quickly.

Ms. Lamb frowned. "What advert?"

"The *Times*, this morning. The address on here is . . ."

As the man read out her address, Ms. Lamb's frown deepened, and her eyes narrowed with suspicion. "What do you want?"

"You don't know?"

"I think that's abundantly clear."

"Come downstairs. I will explain."

Ms. Lamb considered this for a moment. "Put the advert through the letterbox," she said, then hung up the phone. She grabbed the keys from the side table and opened the door.

"I'll be back in a moment," she said to Medusa as she turned on the light in the narrow stairwell and stomped down the three flights to the front door.

There, sticking out from the letterbox as instructed, was a torn-out piece of newspaper. Ms. Lamb snatched it and held it up to the light.

Chris and the others held their breath as Ms. Lamb began to read.

SUITORS NEEDED

Lonely middle-aged woman looking for love. Must like cats, opera, being called pet names, and women who wear heavy makeup. Do not apply if you do not like loud colors, being told what to do, or have any children. Knowledge of classical literature and languages essential. Being hard of hearing an advantage. If interested, come to 3 Albany Street, Notting Hill at 7:00 p.m. Be punctual.

Chris watched as Ms. Lamb's face turned white, then red, then purple. Her eyes widened, and her whole body started to shake.

"I . . . am . . . going to kill them," she hissed.

"Uh-oh," said Lexi. "Maybe we shouldn't have let Rex come up with so much of that."

"I told you it wasn't nice enough," said Daisy.

"What do you mean?" exclaimed Rex. "This is brilliant! She's furious. Daisy, you're an evil gen . . ."

Rex stopped talking as Ms. Lamb, still holding the scrap of paper in her hand, threw open the front door.

There, standing in front of her, was a short, chubby man in a tuxedo holding a red rose.

"I suppose you think this is funny?" screamed Ms. Lamb.

The man, Dr. Singh, however, said nothing. Instead, he stared at Ms. Lamb, his eyes scanning her face slowly, his own face without expression. And then he smiled.

Ms. Lamb's mouth turned downward and Chris noticed that she was clenching her fists.

"This must all be very amusing for you," said Ms. Lamb.

"That's not why I'm smiling . . . ," said Dr. Singh calmly.

"I want you to leave right—" Ms. Lamb stopped mid-sentence and her eyes narrowed. "Why are you smiling then?"

"Because"—Dr. Singh held out the rose—"you are more beautiful than I could ever have imagined."

Chris felt his whole body tense as he waited for Ms. Lamb to punch him. Perhaps anticipating the same thing, Dr. Singh took the piece of newspaper from Ms. Lamb and quickly began to read.

"Middle aged. I suggest that this means you have experience of life—a very good thing. Cats. I have one—Athena."

"Oh," whispered Ms. Lamb.

"Heavy makeup suggests you like to take care of your appearance"—he glanced up at Ms. Lamb—"which is evidently very true. I have no children, my favorite color is orange, and I like a woman who knows her own mind. Would you like me to repeat all of that in German, French, or Latin?"

Ms. Lamb gave a small giggle but then shook herself and looked serious again. This time, however, Chris could see that her frown was not quite as firm.

"And the opera?" she said.

"Pardon?" he asked.

"Do you like the opera?" repeated Ms. Lamb, a little louder.

Dr. Singh's eyes twinkled as he pulled out an envelope from his inside jacket pocket.

"Perhaps this will answer your question," he said, handing it to her.

Ms. Lamb, her mouth tensed as if trying to suppress a smile, took the envelope, opened it, and pulled out two tickets.

"It starts at eight," said Dr. Singh.

For a moment, there was total silence, and then, finally, Ms. Lamb spoke.

"I suppose I'd better get my coat."

"Yay!" said Daisy and Lexi at the same time. Chris and the others weren't quite as gushing, but Chris had to admit it did feel like they had done the right thing. Only Rex, who was pouting with his arms folded tight across his chest, seemed to disagree.

"It was funnier when she was going to punch him."

Daisy put her arm around his shoulders. "There, there. She nearly did. And she was very angry."

Rex nodded his head slowly. "I suppose she was," he said.

. . .

The next morning, the light mood of the night before had disappeared, replaced with the sinking realization that they were about to say good-bye to Myers Holt. It wasn't helped by Maura bawling her eyes out as she showered them all with hugs and kisses over the biggest breakfast banquet that any of them had ever seen. Then, after enjoying a morning of swimming in the Dome, they had sat down to eat once more, this time with all the staff of Myers Holt, including Ron and John, and the commissioner.

The next person to arrive was Ms. Lamb. All the pupils held their breath as she walked straight over to her chair. It was only when she sat down that she looked up at them all and a small smile passed her lips. Chris looked down and grinned. He was about to turn to say something to Daisy when the commissioner arrived to surprise them all with a medal for their outstanding contribution to policing before offering them, as an extra thanks, the exclusive use of his luxury seaside villa over the summer holidays.

It wasn't the only surprise of the lunch. Sir Bentley announced his retirement, explaining that the work of Myers Holt would continue in September with a new batch of pupils to be headed up by Ms. Lamb, who looked less displeased with this news than Chris would have imagined. Ron and John also announced that they would be leaving, Ron to set up a survival-training center in the New Forest and John to open up a pampering salon for dogs.

Meanwhile Ernest, who had quickly settled into his new life on the island with Clarissa, had also flown in to join them. It was the first time that Chris had seen him since the night at Darkwhisper Manor, but they had talked many times on the phone over the course of the week, and perhaps because they had gone through so much together, or maybe because he seemed to be a genuinely nice person, Chris felt like he was greeting an old friend when Ernest had arrived. In fact, it had been his and Philip's suggestion that Ernest should join them at their boarding school in September, and they had all cheered when Miss Sonata confirmed at lunch that the place had been arranged.

And so it was that Chris's incredible year at Myers Holt came to an end. Chris said his good-byes to his teachers and hugged his friends.

"I'm seeing you in two weeks," said Daisy, smiling, though tears were running down her face as she pulled away from Chris.

Chris smiled back. "I know, but I just wanted to say thank you for being such a good friend."

"You're welcome," she said, and then she leaned over and gave Chris a kiss.

"And by the power vested in me, I now pronounce you man and wife. *Ta da dada da dada da dum de da . . . de dum!*"

"REX!" shouted Chris and Daisy, both turning bright red as the others all burst out laughing.

"Chris?"

Chris, still giggling, turned around to see John standing a foot above anybody else in his black suit, his arms folded. Of all the people Chris was going to miss, he was probably going to miss John the most.

"Now, none of that—it was hard enough saying

good-bye to the others," said John as Chris bit his bottom lip and walked over to him. He handed Chris a card.

Chris swallowed hard and smiled. "Paws Truly . . . It's good."

"My number's on there too. Call anytime."

"I will." Chris paused. There was so much he wanted to say. "John . . . I just . . ."

John put his enormous arms around him and drew him forward in a tight hug, then stood up just as Ron appeared at their side.

"Pleasure working with you, Chris," said Ron. He offered his hand, and Chris shook it firmly.

"Thanks, Ron," said Chris as Ron led John away.

"What's the matter with your eyes?" Chris heard Ron ask John.

"Nothing," said John gruffly, "just a bit of dirt in them."

"Right. Of course. For a second there, I thought you were crying," said Ron, shaking his head.

Chris smiled, and then he walked back over to his friends to join them for a final good-bye to Myers Holt.

CHAPTER TWENTY-SIX

Friday, October 31

Chris hung up his red cape on the back of his bedroom door and placed the bucket of sweets on his bed. It was Halloween, and nearly the end of the first midterm break from his new school. It had been Rex's idea for them all to dress as superheroes, though Chris was the only person left to turn thirteen and therefore the only true, if only for one more day, superhero amongst them. It had been a good night, and he would have been tempted to join them for the sleepover at Philip's house if he had not had something much more important to do at home. And anyway, he thought as he waved good-bye to them all, he would be seeing them the following day for his birthday party—the first birthday party he had ever had.

In fact, he had seen plenty of them all since they had

left Myers Holt. They had spent the summer at the commissioner's villa, swimming in the pool and competing against each other to make the most elaborate sandcastles on the beach (which Philip had won easily with his carefully engineered replica of the Antarctic Ball ice palace). Initially, despite them knowing that Ernest had changed, it had been strange for all of them to have a new member join the group, particularly one who had not so long ago tried to kill another member. However, of all of them, it was Ernest who found it the hardest and he tried desperately to make it up to the others by insisting on carrying everything, getting up early to make everybody breakfast, and jumping on any opportunity to help out. The more he did it, the more sorry they all felt for him until, finally, after much convincing and the whole group threatening to throw him into the pool if he didn't stop running around after them, Ernest began to relax. It was only then that Chris and the other Myers Holt pupils really got to know him, finding him to be quiet, sweet, and sensitive but yet, perhaps from years of practice of taking it from his brother, quite capable of handling Rex's teasing. He fit in well, and the others were all in agreement when, on the last day of their seaside holiday, they had officially named Ernest the seventh member of their Myers Holt team.

Only two weeks later, Chris, Philip, and Ernest had arrived at their new school, where they had all enjoyed watching the shock on their teachers' faces as they revealed their extraordinary academic abilities. In the short time the three boys had been there, in fact, they had made such an impression that they had already been invited onto the senior math team, where they had led their school to an outstanding victory in the nationwide Math Olympiad. Chris had returned home to his mother for his week-long midterm break full of smiles, stories to tell, and an armful of trophies to put on his once-bare shelf.

Chris looked at the clock. It was ten past nine in the evening. His mother had told him that he had been born at three in the morning, which meant that he had just under six hours before his Ability disappeared. It was strange, Chris thought as he entered the bathroom and locked the door behind him, how much it had once scared him to think that his Ability was only temporary. But, although he was in the habit of using it for the most mundane of tasks without giving it, literally, a second thought, he felt so content with the rest of his life that he was sure it wouldn't take long for him to readjust to normal life. It helped also that his friends had already lost theirs, and though they seemed to find it frustrating every once in a while, they all appeared quite happy without it. On their advice, Chris had spent the last few weeks making sure he read through every book he could get his hands on. He now spoke twelve languages fluently, had memorized every single line of Shakespeare's works, could solve the most complicated of mathematical equations, and so much more. With one final exception, Chris was ready to say good-bye to his Ability.

Chris turned to the bathroom mirror and looked at himself. Suddenly, he felt quite nervous. He hadn't seen his father in nearly eight years, and he just hoped that somewhere deep in his mind he still held the memories of him. He took a deep breath and let his eyes glaze over.

At first, Chris wasn't sure if it was working. He hadn't spoken about his plan to enter his own mind with anybody, and he had certainly never seen anything about it in any one of the few books on the Ability at Myers Holt, so he had no idea whether it was even possible. He focused his eyes harder at his reflection, then waited and waited until, finally, a familiar white light began to appear.

Chris smiled. *It's working,* he thought with excitement as the light grew in intensity and then suddenly disappeared, revealing a vast room with a single image floating at its center—a picture of Chris's reflection in the mirror. Chris couldn't believe it—he was inside his own mind! He looked around at the room, slightly disappointed that it didn't look any different from any other Reception he had entered, and then walked across to the wooden door on the other side and turned the handle.

Chris had never given any thought to how, exactly, his Ability would disappear. Had he done so, he would have guessed that it was like a light switch being turned off at the exact moment that he turned thirteen. As soon as he stepped out into his mind, however, he realized that it was a far more complicated process than that, a process that— judging by the fact that all the buildings in his mind were already partially submerged in concrete—was already well under way.

Chris stood still, rooted to the spot, as he watched the wet concrete creep slowly upward. Then, thinking that he might already be too late, he put one foot out in front of him. His foot sank straight down. Chris leaned back to wrench it free and then stepped back into the doorway. He looked across the moat of concrete, at the Family building in front of him, which was already submerged to the line of the second-floor windowsills, and he kicked himself for not having tried this sooner.

I'm so close, he thought as he tried once more, without success, to step out onto the road. He looked down at his sodden foot and took a deep breath. Not knowing what else to try, he stared down at the concrete directly in front of him and willed it to move.

Chris watched as the floor slowly began to bubble, gently at first and then faster until the patch of wet concrete between him and the top of the Family building was bursting with bubbles. Then, all of a sudden, the whole of the section in front of him exploded into a cloud of fine gray sand that flew up and evaporated into the air. Chris looked down at the narrow path that he had created between the two towering walls of concrete and saw that the door of the tall red brick house was now reachable. He had begun to run down the hill toward the Family building when, with horror, he saw that the wet concrete on either side of him was caving in. He had no option but to turn back and run to the safety of his own mind's exit.

"Argh," he shouted in frustration as the wet concrete pushed itself back together and the pathway disappeared.

He looked back down and tried again, and once more, the concrete bubbled and exploded, then pushed itself back together. Chris kept trying, again and again, but no matter how hard he tried, he couldn't get the concrete to stay apart long enough to let him through. Finally, with his head hung down in defeat, Chris gave up. He looked out at the rapidly disappearing city of his mind and was about to turn back when something caught his eye and he stopped. He leaned forward and squinted as he took a hard look at the Family building. There was no doubt about it: The level of the concrete was lower. It had been at the height of the second-floor windowsill when he had entered his mind—he was sure of it—and now it was at least four inches lower. There was a long way to go, he thought as he let his eyes lose focus once more, but he had nearly six hours left and the determination to keep going right up to the end.

With renewed energy, Chris stood in the doorway as he blasted the wet concrete into almost invisible particles over and over again with grim determination. Somewhere in the back of his mind, he heard his mother wish him good night, but he never lost his focus and kept going, watching the level of the concrete slowly get lower and lower until, after what seemed like hours, the cobbled stones of his mind finally revealed themselves.

Chris took a deep breath and looked around, surveying his work. The whole of his mind's city was now completely clear of the concrete, and its buildings, extending far beyond those of any mind he had ever visited, revealed their sheer size. Chris's head pounded with exhaustion as he ran down the slope and straight through the doorway, eager to do what he had set out to do before the concrete returned to start closing his mind off again.

Chris already knew, from the many times that he had tried in vain to access them by normal means, that any memories of his dad had to be stored up on the third floor. He climbed the spiral staircase as quickly as he could and rushed over to the wooden filing cabinets, uncertain as to how long he had before he found himself trapped. As it turned out, having only ever known a handful of relatives, finding the file on his father was not difficult. Chris opened the drawer marked D and pulled out that large file. Then, with his heart thumping loudly, Chris opened it and watched the files fly up into a hovering line as the rest of the room disappeared into darkness. Chris walked up to the end and touched the last memory, then watched as his living room suddenly appeared before him.

"Chris, come here."

Chris heard the sound of his own, five-year-old voice. "I'm playing trains, Daddy."

All Chris could see was his train set as he heard footsteps approaching.

"You can play in a moment. I want to talk to you."

Chris watched as his younger self turned round and looked up at his father, dressed in his army uniform. His father was smiling, but Chris could see that it was a sad smile.

"I'm going away now. I'm going to be gone for a while."

"Where are you going?"

"I'm going to work—remember we talked about it?"

"You're going to be a soldier?"

"That's right," said his father, smiling. Chris saw the tears in his father's eyes, and he felt a lump come to his throat. "Are you going to look after your mummy for me?"

"Yes, Daddy."

"Good, because you're the man of the house now until I come back."

"Okay, Daddy. I'll look after Mummy. I promise."

"Good. Now give me a big hug—the biggest hug you've ever given me."

Chris saw his father open his arms as he rushed into them, and for a while, there they stayed, holding each other tight as the young Chris began to cry.

"I love you, son," said his dad, finally letting go of him and standing up. "I'll see you soon."

Chris heard the sound of his own crying as he watched his father walk over to his mother, red-eyed by the door, and gave her a hug. Then he kissed her, picked up his bag, looked back at his wife and son, and, finally, disappeared.

Chris sniffed and wiped the tears from his eyes and walked over to the next memory in the line where he was playing in the garden with his father. That one finished, and he went on to the next until, finally, after what must have been at least an hour, he reached the last one and watched his father laughing as he threw him up in the air. It was a good memory to end on. Sad and exhausted but happy for all the good memories, Chris finally closed up the file, comforted at the thought that these memories were now fresh and he would be able to access them in his mind even after his Ability was gone. He climbed back down the stairs, ran across the ground floor, and then out of the Family building. When he stepped outside, he realized there was still no sign of the concrete that had been filling the streets earlier. He had done a good job clearing it, he thought, but he knew he had been very lucky; the cement could have returned at any time to close off his mind, and he could easily have found himself trapped.

Casting aside the thoughts of what might have happened, and eager to get out before the concrete returned, Chris broke into a run up the hill, stopping only when he reached the door. He took one look back behind him, then turned the handle of the door and walked out of his own mind.

Chris woke up in his bedroom on the morning of his thirteenth birthday with a smile on his face. He had slept well, dreaming happy dreams of him and his father, and he walked down the stairs, excited at the thought of his first-ever birthday party later that day. He walked into the living room and looked around, still surprised by how much had changed in the last few months. The curtains were open, the television was off, and the surfaces on the table were cleared. And he had done none of this himself.

CRASH!

Chris jumped when he heard his mother's voice.

"Oh, drats!"

Chris turned and hurried down to the kitchen to find his mother leaning over the cluttered counter, her hair, matted with flour, hanging over her face.

"Is everything okay?"

Chris's mum turned, and on seeing him, her face broke into a smile. She stepped over to him, put her arms around him, and started to sing, "'Happy birthday to you, happy birthday to you . . .'"

"Okay, okay, Mum," said Chris, smiling as he pulled himself away. He looked over at the floor and saw the upturned bowl there. "What happened?"

Chris's mother sighed. "I had a surprise for you, but it

didn't go very well. I'm not much good at all of this—I'm so sorry." Then she took him by the hand and pulled him over to the dining room table.

Chris looked at the collapsed cake at the center of the table and smiled. Watery purple icing had been poured over it, and what he guessed was the number thirteen—though the three looked more like an eight—had been iced on top in white.

"It's a disaster," said his mum, "we can go out and buy one from the shop."

Chris laughed. "I love it. Thanks, Mum."

"Really? Well, good—great! In that case, I'll make some, cupcakes too—I'm on a roll. I've just got to go to the shop and pick up some more eggs. Do you want anything?"

Chris shook his head as he sat down at the table.

"Okay, back in a moment. I made you a cup of tea," she said as she walked out of the room.

"Thanks," said Chris. Without thinking, he let his eyes glaze over as he focused on the mug sitting on the counter on the other side of the room, and began willing it to come toward him.

It was only when the mug was halfway across the room, floating in the air, that Chris realized what was happening. His mind lost focus, and Chris watched, shocked, as the mug wobbled and then fell crashing down to the floor.

Smash!

Chris heard his mother's footsteps running back to the kitchen.

"What happened?"

Chris looked down at the spilled tea and the broken mug, and he looked up at his mother.

"Is today really my birthday?" he asked in a quiet voice.

"Of course it is," she said. "I'm afraid you get your clumsiness from me," she said laughing, as she stooped down to pick up the pieces and wipe up the tea.

"Are you absolutely sure it's my birthday today?"

Chris's mum looked up at him, confused. "Chris—I think I know when your birthday is. I did give birth to you, after all—that's not something you forget in a hurry."

"But it was definitely the first of November—you're sure about that?"

"What do you mean? Of course it was. You arrived at three in the morning on the first of November. You dad and I were at a Halloween party when I went into labor. I was dressed as a ghost, a sheet was the only thing that would fit over my enormous bump. Why do you ask?" She put the pieces of the mug into the bin and rinsed out the cloth in the sink.

"It's nothing," said Chris. "Just checking."

"You are funny," said his mother, smiling. "I'll be back in a moment."

Chris didn't say anything as his mum picked up her keys and walked out of the kitchen again. He waited until he heard the front door shut, and then he stood up.

He turned in the direction of the living room and closed his eyes. Immediately, the living room appeared in his mind—the curtains open, the television off, just as he had seen it only a few minutes earlier. He let his mind wander over to the bookshelf and focused on each book in turn, watching as, one at a time, they hovered through the air, until every single one of them had landed gently on the coffee table in the center of the room. Chris opened his eyes and broke into a run—across the kitchen, up the small flight of stairs, down the corridor, and through the living room door. He stopped dead in his tracks and then looked slowly up at the tower of books, his heart pounding furiously. Every single thing that he had ever learned about the Ability ran through his mind, but there was not one good reason that he could think of to explain what had just happened.

And then the memory of the previous night came back to him. Chris thought about the wet concrete rising up in the city of his own mind. He thought about how long he had spent clearing it from the streets and of his surprise at finding that the streets were still clear when he had left. Perhaps the concrete hadn't returned because he had already gotten rid of it all.

Chris thought about what this all meant, and the more he did so, the more he realized what it was that he had done. Not quite able to believe it, he looked over at the line of balloons hanging from the curtain rod and closed his eyes. No sooner had he done so than the balloons began to pop, one by one. Chris opened his eyes and stared at the line of dangling ribbons and the scattered remains of the thirteen balloons on the floor. He gasped.